The World Withou

The World Without Arkhalla

Published in the United States by ARH ComiX Inc.

ARH ComiX Inc. 8312 E. Colter Bay Dr. Nampa, ID 83687

www.arhcomix.com

Cover Art design by Eamon O'Donoghue

Printed in the United States of America

First Edition

Abraham Kawa

The World Without Arkhalla

From a story by **Arahom Radjah**

Dedicated to Araceli Ramos, my mother,
for making this happen!

_Arahom Radjah

CONTENTS

PART THREE:
A WORLD TO DIE IN

The World Without Arkhalla

INTRODUCTION

So. Welcome back.

The middle part of a trilogy is a kind-of-great, kind-of-terrifying experience. It's when you and I both realize this is a bigger story, a world spread across three wraparound covers on the shelf, with twice more of the characters and the excitement – hopefully – that we discovered together in Book One. It's also when we realize there is at least one more book to go and twice more chances to screw it up. For all our sakes, I aspire to gravitate more towards the first option. Raise a goblet of the red stuff and wish us luck, friends.

I've said this before, and our finished Book Two seems an ideal place to reiterate it. Writing Arkhalla's trilogy often feels like working on an old Hollywood movie epic. I'm just the writer on this one, with all that entails. But the producer, Arkhalla's own Selznick, Zanuck, Spiegel, you name your favorite, that's Arahom Radjah. His is the vision, the grand narrative, and the saga's driving force, while your humble scribe is the one tasked with turning that vision to what you hold between these covers. Arkhalla's story is not just written, but developed, crafted, produced in a collaborative process, not unlike the one that gets a movie in your local theater. And like Arkhalla herself, who began as a statue and was then given life, almost Galatea-like, through a comic book series and then a prose novel trilogy, our collaborative process has above all been one of adaptation.

Arahom wanted his statue of a seductive, irresistible Queen of Vampires turned into a grand and epic tale of how this ancient, cruel bloodsucking queen is betrayed by her own kin and hounded to her death, only to rise again in the present day and wreak havoc on those selfsame vampires who had destroyed her. His original vision was of successive comic book series relating this tale, and yours truly was the scribe hired to craft the first 7-issue series, which would narrate the story of the queen's fall and set up her resurrection. Wanting to ground the premise in a more relatable setting rather than a generic quasi-Hyborian fantasy age, I chose to set it in Sumer circa 3000 BC, and rounded out the cast of characters with Shamath, Bel, Narama, and the rest of the Council of Twelve. In bringing these ideas to life, I was fortunate to have the great talent of artist Manos Lagouvardos in my corner. Manos' excellent eye for period, detail, and moments of character gave our cast that magnificent scope and great range brought to the movies by ace cinematographers and award-caliber actors, and his contribution is both treasured in my heart and what made Queen of Vampires so loved by those who read it.

My initial plan was to use Shamath and the fascination he exacts on our newly named queen, Arkhalla, to bring out her forgotten humanity, but resulting in a relationship that was abusive and which led them both down a dark path, Shamath to becoming Arkhalla's nemesis, and Arkhalla to begin an uneasy path to redemption centuries down the line, in the present day. But Shamath's inclusion ended up changing the entire story. Midway through the crafting of the comic book's script, Arahom grew fascinated by the prospect of turning his tale into one of love and tragedy, of star-crossed lovers plagued by the impossibility of their romance. So gone was their enmity and the coda leading to the present, replaced by the more self-contained version readers of the comics series are familiar with.

As Arahom's vision shifted and grew to expand the story into a Sumer-set trilogy of novels and beyond, changes continued to occur past the completion and release of the comics. Arkhalla was made more complex and positive a character whose myriad facets slowly eclipsed her previous cruelty; Narama grew from a driven Huntress of Men to an abused, traumatized antagonist; and the story's scope was moved from fantasy and horror in an antiquarian setting to an epic dark fantasy romance. Out of them, change by change, Arahom's vision begins to take shape. To place it within our moviemaking metaphor: I have a nigh-unlimited budget in the ideas that will expand Arkhalla's world; the finished books are our editing room, and Arahom has final cut.

My feeling about Arkhalla and Arahom is a little like something Shamath has said: we are in this together. I have great respect for Arahom's drive and passion and the fact that he has let me into his sandbox and encouraged and accepted most of the wild ideas and characters and scenes I threw his way. On my own, I doubt I would have set out to write a full-fledged fantasy vampire epic, much less finished two books of a trilogy in roughly as many years, and with such an expansive cast of characters. I have Arahom to thank for that. Crafting the tale from his outlines and notes is at once bewildering and inspiring, and a great schooling in how to tell a story within – and beyond – its set parameters.

I have come to feel a lot of these characters as my own, not just in the sense of having created them, but in seeing them grow. They and their world seem to have taken a life of their own on a continuing canvas that grows out of mine and Arahom's and Manos' sketches of them – or perhaps they grow despite us, out of their own strengths and weaknesses, and we merely chronicle their progress. It feels like that sometimes. In the book you're holding in your hands, Arkhalla's world, both in the literal sense and in the sense of the people her long life touched, seems to have grown beyond her, and yet this tapestry of vistas and characters, though bereft of her, still grows out of her memory even in absentia. This world and story, as Arahom puts it, is now left without her, but at the same time still so much about her. Arkhalla still casts her long shadow over the lives of those that loved or hated her, or sometimes did both, and even gone, she changes them forever. Not bad for a dead queen.

So welcome back, friends. This is the next chapter in our saga, and whether it grows into something more than just a tale we've crafted, it is for you, the readers, our own gods of literature and pop culture, to determine. We aim to please and entertain and make your visit a thrilling one. Ur awaits us there at the end of its forever sunset. Join us and hold on. It's a hell of a ride.

Abraham Kawa

PROLOGUE

The Queen is dead!

The cry rang out through the realm of Ur, over the towers and the hovels, the deserts and towns, bringing with it the end of an era. It was tinged with disbelief at the sheer impossibility of it; with joy as it echoed down the thousands that feared the Undying Queen. And in those who knew better, it grew deafening with doom, for they knew the gods could only laugh in anticipation of what was to become of a world without Arkhalla.

It seemed almost as soon as the cry rang out through the fallen Queen's ziggurat that the doors of the Sacrosanct burst open. Lilit the seer and Fazuz the slaver, two of the Council of Twelve that had betrayed Arkhalla, were at the head of the cabal of Undying nobles who stormed inside the once inviolate halls that housed the Queen's most valued stock. Guards already lined the entrances and walls, making sure none stood in Lilit's way. She pranced about the splendid hall, taking no note of the silk and gilded opulence, but slavering instead at the sight of the crowd of human youths before her. Arkhalla had been keeping them all to herself, the bitch, all these long years. All these boys and girls as beautiful as the most flawless of statues, healthiest among the captives from her wars, the tributes from her allies, the toll taken from her subjects. *She* had savored and drank and gorged the treasure in those youthful veins night after night, for countless years, her power granting her an endless supply of humanity to sate herself.

But no more, thought Lilit the seer, *no more*.

"Look at them," she hissed. "Look at how perfect they all are."

The youths cowered before her like muskrats surveyed by a snake. Talmas, the high priest, peered from behind the ring of Undying guards. The fat cleric had been the one charged with keeping the Sacrosanct. He had betrayed Arkhalla like the rest of the Council, but that did not stop him from sweating now. With

Arkhalla gone, there was no certainty, no rule. No one could know what would happen to them – or to the power and posts they held under her. All Talmas could be sure of was violence and death, and he saw both of them in Lilit's dark eyes now.

"Such can only be the life of the gods above," Lilit went on. She licked her lips, a bitch in heat. "So many of them, so perfect. This must be heaven."

Talmas felt what was coming. He made a weak effort to hold on to his office. "They don't belong to you... They—"

"No!" she screamed at him. "They belong to a *dead* queen!"

It was as unto a signal for the massacre to start. Lilit's guards began grabbing the boys and girls and hurled them onto the wave of hungry Undying that rushed to embrace them as the sea rushes to shore. Lilit, Fazuz and the rest fell on them with wild cries of lust. Smooth-skinned, youthful limbs were clutched, bruised, torn out of their sockets; virgin lips were ravished and commandeered; rich veins were torn open and feasted on.

The humans screamed as they died. It only made the Undying tear into them with heightened fury. There was rape, murder, disfigurement for nothing but their own sake. Arkhalla was dead. Atrocity was crowned.

Talmas watched, repulsed. This was beyond horror. This was waste, destruction. There was no purpose, to him, to anything, not anymore. The realm was falling apart, it could not hold. The Fountain of *her* Youth had finally run dry.

Canthanna, the old slave who cared for the wretched, butchered stock, rushed to him.

"Lord priest," she said, the tears in her eyes begging him to do something. "My lord..."

Lilit saw the old woman. Her long, talon-like hand reached out and grabbed her by the throat.

Canthanna gasped for air. Lilit raised her high above her head with but a jot of effort.

"Disapproval, is it?" she spat. "Defiance from an old wretch like you?"

The old woman tried to speak. She couldn't. The pupils of her eyes were mere orbs in a white space of panic.

"Do you think she was better than us?" Lilit's squeeze tightened with each word. "Do you think she deserved to gorge herself in *this* glory while we are left with scraps?"

No answer came. Talmas could tell that the old woman was no longer breathing.

Humans were fragile like that.

Lilit tossed the lifeless corpse to the side. She pointed to the youths still living. "Hoist them up," she roared at the guards. "I shall bathe in their blood!"

Just like *her*, she thought. What *She* had is ours now; mine. *Mine*.

The guards obeyed. The wretches were stripped, hoisted and hung upside down. Long-hilted scythes were prepped.

It was as it should be, Lilit thought; as befitted a realm built on bloodshed.

Talmas rushed from the grand hall, livid, just as Lilit, Fazuz and their followers began to squeal with delight at the torrent of blood washing down their filthy naked flesh.

Sin poured from the fine jewel-encrusted carafe into two golden cups. The carafe had been claimed from the bitch's chambers; her best. The blood was that of her favored handmaiden, while the cups that received it were heirlooms from long ago, from the heyday of Sin's family. What was once hers was now his. It was as it should be.

Sin turned and handed one of the cups to Idu. The young Undying was looking at his hands, mesmerized, then gawked at the tapestries on the chamber's wall. Sin had turned him mere days ago. He was still getting used to the vibrancy of his senses.

Freedom warmed Sin's insides even more than the handmaiden's blood. Idu had been his lover and confidant for such a long time now. But under the bitch's rule, no Undying was allowed to turn a human without her granting it first. She had known his feelings for Idu and had expressly denied him what he craved.

Well, no more.

"Two hundred years of planning," he said with a smile. "For a moment there, I thought it would not work."

Idu sipped the blood, wincing. The bitter tang was an acquired taste for all the newborn at first.

"You still have to deal with Bel, you know that," he said.

Sin chuckled. "That lovesick fool! His adoration for Arkhalla was all that kept her alive for so long!" He paused, letting the delight of it course through him. Oh, the bitch was dead at last. "I had almost given up hope," he went on. "And then the Gods Below sent us that wretch."

Delight turned to triumph. Sin absolutely shivered with it. He hugged himself, basking in its cool embrace.

"How perfect that was! An immortal whore queen falling for her human slave. I knew it at once, when she balked at killing him. The bitch had held her feelings down for so long they upped and drowned her."

Idu looked at him. The admiration in the youth's eyes went to Sin's head like sweet wine. He drank the blood still in the cup, threw it aside, and fell onto the divan next to his lover.

"It was everything I needed to stir that stupid fool into betraying her. Bel fell for it almost with no effort." He run his fingers through Idu's hair, then caressed the smooth, beardless face.

"Perfect," he said. "It was just perfect."

"What about the humans' revolt?" purred Idu.

"I'll let Bel deal with that first and then I'll take care of him. Ur will belong to its rightful rulers once more, dear boy. As it should have been when our sect destroyed Anshara."

"Gods below bless us," Idu chimed. "We are finally rid of his cursed bloodline."

Sin kissed his ruby lips, accepting their silent invitation.

"Ur was almost mine once, my dear," he said, coming up for breath, ready to dive into that pool of pleasure again in but a moment. "Now it shall be ours."

Criers shouted it from towers. It rang out in the squares and streets, over the din of weapons drawn and the screams of the dying.

The Queen is dead, the cry rang out.

What was done could not be undone.

Bel felt a hole where his heart was. There was an invisible hand on his throat, tightening with each breath he drew.

He led his men through the carnage. Riots had broken out everywhere, from the gates all the way to the ziggurat. Soldiers hacked left and right, breaking up one group of humans just as another formed in some bystreet to come at them from a different direction. It was worse than the mess he'd left before going after Arkhalla.

The cry rang out. It couldn't be undone. There was no going back, not for the rioting wretches, not for the Undying trying to cow them.

He turned to Narama. The Huntress rode silently next to him. She wasn't about to speak. Her wounds still hadn't healed on the road back from Dilmun, nor had her jaw settled back in place yet. It would take a while for her to be as she once was, in more ways than one. But her eyes told him she did not like what she saw even more than him.

A guard captain ran up to them through smoke and fire. He saluted, desperate for orders.

"It's like this all over the city," the man said, belaboring the obvious.

"What about the groups on the hills?" asked Bel.

"Getting worse, sire; more and more of these rioters flee to them. There are reports of outposts raided. Weapons and supplies stolen, even with double details manning every outpost."

Bel turned once more to Narama, lowering his voice. "Sin kept saying it was me who let this get out of hand. I don't see him faring much better."

Riot squads and outposts wouldn't be enough. Bel had to deal with this. He had to show Sin how he'd deal with this.

The guard captain waited for him to speak.

"No one goes in or out the gates," Bel said. "No wretches on the streets, on pain of death. Put thralls on patrol and guard duty in the daytime, do you hear? Thralls only. No conscripts are to be left unsupervised." He paused. "And someone send for the captains of the army. Forget manning the outposts. We'll take the fight to the hills."

He saw Narama nod, agreeing.

"No use pretending this is still something brewing," he went on. "We are at war. Let's start winning it."

The guard captain turned and left like he was on fire.

Bel drew a deep breath. If only he felt as hard and sure as his words. The hole was still in his chest. It wouldn't fill.

What was done could not be undone.

TEN YEARS LATER

CHAPTER 1

PORTENTS OF DOOM

The sun hung low in a scarlet sky, with endless fields of wheat stretching beneath it.

Shamath walked back to the farm, pulling his ox behind him, the large beast burdened with bales of wheat strapped to its back. It'd been another day's work, hard and earned. The sweat felt good on his brow. A breeze cooled the ache on his back. He remembered how harder the days out in the fields used to be back when he was a boy of eighteen. But ten years and the work had carved a strong frame out of that unshaped body. A man's beard underlined his face, short and trimmed and a good fit with the mane of hair that crowned his head. Everything on him, hair, beard, skin, was tanned golden and brown. The color of the fields he worked had seeped through every pore and inch of him.

His feet followed the familiar path and his eyes locked onto the smoke rising from the stack of the farmhouse. There was only one sight Shamath treasured more than this, and as he approached, that very sight came into view, rushing out the door. The apron she had on to cook their meal was in her hands. She left it on the porch and ran to him.

The sun wasn't going down, not anymore. It was in her smile, beaming. The world slowed, savoring each motion of her limber form, each light-as-air step as she met him in the front yard. Shamath opened his arms and she leaped into them, a diver giving herself to the sea's embrace. He tightened his arms around her, drunk for a moment with her softness, her scent, then lifted and spun her in a circle around him, both of them laughing. Shamath lowered her gently and they kissed, a long, lingering kiss as filled with butterflies inside of them as that first kiss long ago. Leaves rustled on the trees, accompanying the evensong of birds, the soft caress of their lips, the flutter of butterfly wings.

He spoke her name, soft as a prayer. "Arkhalla."

She smiled, his face in her hands as she looked into his eyes.

"Is this the life you dreamed for us?" Her voice was a choir of spirits, not of this earth. "Is this the life you want to live with me?"

Shamath touched her cheek and felt it hot. It was not the sun, or the running. A fever, he thought, worried.

The heat burned his hand. Her face was red, blistering.

"Is this it, Shamath?" she asked as her flesh caught fire.

She was on fire, burning like a torch. Shamath looked panicked about him. The house, the yard, the fields were on fire. He couldn't hold on to her anymore. The fire burned him; he let go.

They were not at the farm at all. They were back in Dilmun, and she was burning on the stake.

Shamath screamed her name. The memory came back to him now, burning him worse than the flames. It was just as before. She burned and he could do nothing but scream her name, again and again, choking with the smoke and the stench of roasting flesh.

It was just as before – except now Dilmun was burning as well, the square, the houses, the high towers of the oligarchs, everything was going up in flames. Shamath turned and there were Undying from Ur everywhere, soldiers, burning, biting, maiming, killing. The people of Dilmun died by the hundreds, screaming, each dying scream blending with the smoke into Shamath's throat and choking him until he had to let them all out again, hundreds of screams tearing out of his throat as he died with them.

Somewhere in the blood and fire, Shamath saw the fair-haired girl again, the one who had spoken to him years ago by the ashes of the pyre, running for her life, hordes of Undying behind her.

He saw Bel, the demon, laughing and crying tears of blood as he tore through the city's people with axe and sickle-sword.

Arkhalla was burning at the stake. He rushed at her, through the flames, but now Narama stood in his way. The Huntress drove him back with her sword, and even as she did he charged again. A sword was in his hand, armor on his frame.

Not this time, his mind screamed. I won't fail you this time, he cried out at the burning woman.

Yet even as he fought Narama – not in Dilmun anymore, he saw, recognizing the burning ruins of Ur about them, they were in Ur, and everything was on fire, the great ziggurat burning – Shamath knew that all was lost.

He saw Arkhalla and the stake collapse into the ground which opened up to swallow them. It turned into a maw, a demon's maw opening wide into the lands below, and she fell in it, burning, fading into darkness, screaming his name.

"...Shamath!" she screamed, dying again. "...Shamath!"

Shamath sat up in drenched wet sheets, an anguished cry tearing out of his throat.

Slow moments passed, filled with panicked heartbeats.

The dream, he thought, sick with the fear it always left him with. The dream again. Her, dying, again.

The nightmare had never left him these ten years since her death. It had stayed with him, a friend, a tormentor, never letting him forget her even in sleep. The same, every time. The fields of wheat, her running to him, her burning all over again while he watched helplessly.

Except it wasn't quite the same this time, was it?

Shamath got up, his sweating back shivering with the morning chill. He wrapped himself in a blanket made from mountain goat skin and lit the hearth. As he opened the window, sunlight crept in, bringing the dawn into the cabin. Blue shadows and purple hills greeted the sun, the memory of endless wheat and farmhouse fading from his addled mind, leaving behind only the horror that came after.

He dreamt of Dilmun, too, this time, in flames, that and Ur, burning. And there was Bel and Narama and -- that fair-haired girl from so long ago. And right there at the end, the demonic maw, engulfing her. It troubled him greatly.

He dressed, his eyes fixed out the window. The world was as he had left it the day before: the cabin on the hill, the small patch of land he farmed with bare necessities. And Arkhalla's grave, there to bask in the sunrise. Shamath walked out to the small, grassy mound of earth and sat next to it.

"I saw it again," he started, the grass cool beneath his hand as he touched it.

He waited, letting her soothe the storm within him, his heartbeat growing slower. Being with her calmed him. But the pain never went away.

His arm hurt. His fingers felt the spot, still scarred, branded with memory. Of his time as a slave. Of her. He remembered her touching his arm all those years ago, when he stared into a mirrored abyss and she had pulled him back from the brink. He remembered the first time she had touched him with love. Her brand was still on him, always.

He told her what he saw.

"It is a sign, isn't it?" he asked after he recounted the last horrific image, the maw, opening. "They say the dead send men omens in their dreams." He paused. "It felt like such a dream, my love. Was it that?"

He waited, as though he listened for an answer. There was none.

Was it an omen? And had it come from her? Or was it something darker from the lands below?

For years now, he had seen the dream as nothing more than that. It was his soul, aching from the loss of her, only that and nothing more. He had hoped against hope that Arkhalla was at peace, the peace of nothingness that was dying, and that in death, when his death came someday, they'd be together. But this twisted new addition to his dream reminded him of what he feared and had tried so hard to forget. He remembered the room in the bowels of the ziggurat, her fear as she looked down that dark mirror.

It was that fear of hers that now mirrored itself in his. A fear that perchance, even in death, she'd be theirs. That even then, her soul would be forfeit to the gods below.

Were those fears of hers true? Was her soul in some torment, torn to pieces by those dark lords of pain? Was she crying out to him, sending him some urgent message through the nightmare?

If this was a message from beyond, everything in it mattered. Ur, and Narama, Bel... Dilmun.

A sick feeling crept inside him. A foreboding, dark with smoke and fire.

"I'll go, my love. If that is what you want, I'll go." He would find out the meaning of this dream, no matter how much he feared it.

For he feared for *her* even more.

There are kinds and kinds of death and only one who has lived an unnaturally long life may claim to have witnessed them all. In some deaths, the soul perishes along with its flesh, as it should be. In others, the soul goes on existing, its acts in life rewarded with a blissful rest or torment in the lands below. And yet in others, the body lives on while the spirit is lost. Those in fear of the Undying often described them as such soulless beings, though it is true that the words applied just as well to living men and women, those who have lost the pleasure in living, their flesh still in vigor, their souls dead and gone. And while any and all death is a solitary affair – as the gods will it – there are also times it happens to many, to cities and nations massacred, to whole populaces extinguished from this earth.

Narama had seen an abundance of men die in her day, most of them at her hand. She had seen souls killed together with the flesh that bound them; she had viewed men sacrificed, their souls forfeit to the gods, as well as men dying certain that their virtue would be worthy of an afterlife in the halls of heaven that priests promised. She had known men who were dead inside, living and Undying alike. She had seen cities sacked and burned. Yet as she surveyed her domain, she felt a different kind of death present, in the air, in the city, in herself.

A chill wind struck her face, its force reminding her of the days she still felt the cold of winter in her flesh. On every side of her as she stood on the city's walls stretched blight and desolation, the oasis and that once embraced Carcosa replaced with an overgrowth of dried-up grass, the lake of Hali turned into a poisoned swamp. The structures that rose above it were thin and ravaged, like hermit monks who stumbled in the sandstorm looking for enlightenment denied to them forever. It was always cold and windy in Carcosa. And when it did not rain, no sun came out. There was something false in a daylight cast by metal-grey clouds – a sham promise, a hint of doom, a curse. It was as though the once bright city had felt each death, each atrocity and violence committed by the Undying who had claimed it, as though each of these were a wound through which Carcosa's brightness bled away. No bird sang, no beast roamed, and no insect hummed.

The wind screamed in decayed, hole-filled buildings. Not one of these stood upright or erect anymore. They leaned, they loomed, they lay half-in and half-out of the sand that slowly engulfed them. Their edges were worn round, their faces eaten away as though by a disease. Inside, groups of wretches lived and died, hugged around half-dying fires while the streets were empty except for the soundless patrols of Undying that haunted them.

It was near to ten full years that Narama had left Ur to rule over Carcosa. She shone her blazing torch on her domain, letting it trail long black smoke about her. Most of what she saw was her work. The once bright city was hell on earth, and she was its devil. A pleased smile creased Narama's face at the thought of how different it'd all be under the dead bitch queen. *She*'d rule through fear and bloodshed. Narama's law was dread and desperation. There were no feasts of blood, no grandstanding executions, no flailing demonstrations of power. She'd taken all hope from the wretches in her realm even before they were born; and they had seen it crushed long before the Undying came to take them silently in the night. This was Narama's work and hers alone. The bitch could never have achieved it. Carcosa stood, a burial ground of living men, a city of life-in-death. And she was the living death who kept it so.

The Huntress of Men had herself changed. She still carried her bow and arrow and neither year nor wound had left its mark on her unblemished skin. But anyone who had seen her last a decade prior, hurt, humbled and defeated by Arkhalla, would marvel at her looks now. The life she had bled from Carcosa, the death that she accumulated in her spirit, they had combined to make her into a beauty as terrible as the storm at night. There was lightning in her eyes; there was fire in her movement; she was graceful and relentless and unyielding. Where Arkhalla, the bitch, was a fine statue come to life, she was a lean and perfect sword poured and beaten into a woman's shape.

She looked up at a sky that could not decide itself day or night, at the pale moon rising between the clouds and the sun setting opposite it, so faded and cloud-covered it did not even itch her skin, and she felt strong and sure. Along the swamp, where the cloud waves broke, the shadows thickened. Stars rose, dark as pitch, shedding their black light on dim Carcosa. Narama's soul sang a deep and terrible song to greet the coming night.

She turned and headed back inside her keep, her robes of black, gold-threaded samite rustling in the wind like autumn leaves. Guards stood still as granite effigies as she passed.

Two messages waited for her in her chambers when she got there. She saw the clay tablets laid next to each other onto her bedside table. The first one made her heart skip a beat and she put it to one side, to read afterwards. The second one made her perfect brow furrow with concern.

It was a message from Ur; from Sin.

"My dear lady," the message began, *"I trust you are well, though no word comes from far Carcosa."*

Narama smiled at this. As was his wont, Sin started with a lie wrapped in civility. He knew exactly how she was, for his and Kuthan's spies were burrowed deep in Carcosa like angleworms, no matter how hard or often she had to dig them out and hang them on meat hooks.

"I write in brief, for the cause is urgent. I doubt not that you rule Carcosa unchallenged and without dissent, but such is not the case in the domains of Ur – would that it were! The wretched rebellion has spread all along the banks of the gulf. Allied, subservient and neutral states alike have rallied to the humans'

cause, seeing how ineffectual we have been at putting an end to the rebels' war after a full decade. The oligarchs of Dilmun were the latest to join the rabble. Bel campaigns there as I write with brigades entire, but I fear it shall be too little and too late.

"I will not hide that I am concerned with Bel's actions, my lady. He is greatly changed since you were here and I fear whatever influence you had in reasoning with him is gone with you. Even Arkhalla, may rot beset even the memory of her bones, occasionally heeded counsel. Our blood brother, I fear, has no response to crises and affairs of state but violence most extreme. He has angered and divided the council, while his errors of strategy have not only perpetuated this war but encourage more of the mobbing wretches to rise against us. I fear for the realm, Narama. I fear that Bel's inadequacy will be the death of us all and drown the desert in our blood. You know him well enough to understand we cannot sit back and allow him to drag us to either civil war or total doom. We must come to his aid.

"Tonight I set out for the East. The Akkadian king, Nimrod, shares my concern and has agreed to see me. Of you, my lady, I but ask that you be on your guard and at the ready. If I know Bel, he will turn to you for support in his campaign. I entreat you to join him in Dilmun, but that done, to watch him carefully, watch him for signs of fatigue, of stress, of lack of balance. If he is unstable, if he becomes – woe the day – unfit for his command, we need your level head and steady hand more than ever.

"I trust in you, my lady. Keep me apprised, as will I.

"Your blood brother,

"Sin."

Narama put the clay tablet gently down onto the table and sat on the bed. She had made an effort to distance herself from Ur and its wretches' rebellion – and Bel. He was a changed man after the bitch's death, crueler in his ways, harder on himself. Narama, like Sin and everyone who knew him well, had no doubt in her mind as to the reason for the turmoil in Bel's heart, though she refused to believe that time, the time an Undying has so much of, would not heal the wound of Arkhalla's death or Bel's blaming himself that it had come to pass as it had. But Bel took to crushing the rebellion with the same desperation a drowning man grabs onto a plank from his sinking ship. It was the only thing there to keep him alive, the sole salvation from the guilt that engulfed him. The rebels were the one enemy he could shift the blame to. He took no joy in anything else, no notice of anyone else. Narama became aware of that quickly enough and painfully so. She had dared dream, now that the bitch was no more, dream that perhaps Bel would see her as she saw him. It was after the first year, as Bel kept dashing from skirmish to ill-judged skirmish with the rebel forces, that her hope was dashed. It became clear that this was no war that was going to end soon. Certainly not one to be won by sending more troops and reinforcements out there to be slaughtered in desert ambushes and suicide missions by the daring groups of humans that vanished back into the hills and caves afterwards. As all that became blindingly clear to everyone but Bel, Narama knew he'd go on and on, chasing a redemption that would not come, until he died. And the one thing Narama would not do for Bel was watch him die. So when the council needed someone to secure the furthest provinces of Ur out in Carcosa, Narama volunteered, determined to stay there and not look back. She thought she had managed that, too.

Now Sin's letter had brought it all back.

She felt sick. Huge chunks of memory churned in her insides. But not even if the world ended in fire right then and there and the gods below rose up from the depths to devour everyone left alive would she be stopped from reading the second tablet.

It was a very brief message, though not at all simple in its brevity.

"Narama, I'm in Dilmun, fighting. I have need of you. Come."

She shuddered, then grabbed the small bronze mallet from her bedside and struck the gong that summoned her manservant. Even before the human came, she threw off her robes and began to dress herself for war. Just as she was about to storm out of her chamber and call on her lieutenants, the brief message echoed in her mind in Bel's voice. She vomited the blood from her night's feeding into a goblet she grabbed from her bedside without breaking stride.

CHAPTER 2

AN AUDIENCE WITH THE KING

Sin hated being impressed. The emotion, like so many that the councilor kept a tight lid on, was a sign that he had either misjudged or was ill-prepared for a particular situation, which in turn could be a fatal weakness. In fact, he prided himself on always being prepared and an excellent judge of *any* situation, which made it sting all the more when he could not contain his awe at the sight of the city of Akkad.

Carcosa at its brightest could not hold a candle to the sheer majesty of Akkad. The fortifications of the city were threefold, consisting of a massive wall that encircled it, a second wall within the enclosure that served as an additional line of defense, and a yet third one that protected its impressive two-hundred-foot tall ziggurat. As Sin's chariot drove from the great gates of the first wall towards the inner city, he could not but notice the marked difference between the cities of mighty human kings, so adamant on defense and security, and Ur, whose single yet impenetrable wall spoke most adequately of the fear its erstwhile queen had struck into the hearts of men. Ur had never been invaded, while Carcosa, with its high wall, had fallen in a single night. Sin was in no doubt that Arkhalla would have been able to bring down Akkad, too, though it would have taken much, much longer. But though Bel was far from her equal and more like a shadow of himself, the threefold walls of Akkad spoke just as well of the dread that Arkhalla's legacy could instill so many years since her demise. That was something Sin counted on, in fact. He hoped his calculations would not be proven wrong in that respect.

A flurry of slaves and attendants appeared to help him off his chariot and onto a stylish litter lifted by no less than four men. A silent signal was given and the men started up the ziggurat steps as smoothly as though they were carrying a feather. Soldiers lined the whole length of the assent, standing at attention by the braziers that lit up the night, and once more Sin could not help being impressed. The Akkadians were tall, brawny men of a complexion that was pleasingly duskier than that of the men of Ur. Their features were chiseled, their lips full and fleshy. Toned bodies glistened with oil, wrapped in white and blue loincloths and little else, while the men's faces were adorned with elaborately trimmed beards and fine heads of hair visible under their pointed helmets. Sin doubted King Nimrod's hospitality would extend to granting his guest one of these fine specimens to feast on, but the sight of Akkad's youth on display did whet his appetite even though he had fed just before he set out of his camp.

The smooth assent was stunningly fast and in no time at all Sin found himself helped off the litter and escorted inside the ziggurat and towards the throne room. Everywhere, the walls shone with lapis lazuli and displayed tapestries of rare artistry, depicting war scenes and lion hunts led by Nimrod himself or his warlike daughter Aisyah. More attendants lined the way as he passed. The women among them were, admittedly, great beauties, with bronze-skinned features complimented by hair worn long and down their backs and richly colored gauze organza and gold leaf dresses that were both form-fitting and embroidered with black and white rectangles that heightened the clinging effect of the fabric on their well-toned limbs. Torches were clustered together on the ceilings, mounted on fixtures encrusted with precious stones. A bevy of lute players and dancers spread open like the petals of a flower to let him pass. It was clear Nimrod was out to impress Sin and was sparing no expense to do so.

At last, Sin was led to the foot of the throne and in the presence of Nimrod. The king sat and regarded him with calm sagacity that belied his quick mind and lightning reflexes. A living lion cub was snuggling in his arms, quiet as a kitten as it let him run his fingers through its soft fur. For the third time in an hour, Sin found himself impressed. Close to his middle age, Nimrod was still as formidable a warrior as in his prime. His great bow, with which it was rumored he could shoot an arrow in the heart of heaven itself and draw blood from the gods above, was resting at the side of his throne as a reminder to Sin that this man was no one to be trifled with. For those of his guests that were more conventionally impressed, Nimrod had seen to it that he cut a figure of high magnificence. Already a tall man, he was made even more imposing by a richly crafted crown that was part-helmet and gave him an added head of height, heavy blue robes decorated with golden spirals and a purple toga with red trimmings, a ceremonial six-foot staff instead of a scepter and a jewel-encrusted knife sheathed at his side and, last but not least, a long black beard so elaborately braided it must have occupied a half-dozen handmaidens on the task alone.

The only presence that came close to eclipsing the king – and Sin would wager that she would have done just that had she held herself in any other manner but the respectful, quiet stance she assumed at the side of her father and liege – was the princess Aisyah. Precious few ornaments adorned her, for she needed them not. A slim diadem of gold complimented long and straight dark hair that outdid it in luster. Twin armlets of finely-wrought gold snaked down her arms, shaped into serpents, but all they did was draw the eye to the lissomness of the princess' limbs. As for her samite-threaded gown, it paled before the form it clung to, as nimble as a dancer's yet as taut and bronzed as a desert warrior's – a balance tipped to one side by the sight of the sickle-sword strapped to her waist. Her eyebrows were bows stretched and poised to perfection, ready to release a killing look or, if Aisyah was in a forgiving mood, to inspire devotion to the death. Her eyes were both large and pleasingly drawn out, with something of the jungle cat in both their shape and the amber of their hue, while in her features Sin could see the sharpness of the nomad tribe her father hailed from clash and parley with a silk-like softness that evoked some far, Eastern ancestry on the part of her mother.

Sin took as deep a bow as dignity could warrant before he launched in a long greeting filled with epithets ranging from "celestial majesty" to "most powerful and sage potentate", but cut his tirade short when he saw Nimrod raise his hand impatiently.

"Let us not stand on ceremony," the king said. "Not at the cost of action. You have dared show your face in my city, Undying Lord; the first of your kind to do so in eons. That was bold of you."

"And you, dread King, have shown me how your city is ready to receive an army of my kind, though not in welcome." Sin responded. "I would say this earns the name of action on your part just as much."

The puissant visage allowed itself a smile. "Well spoken," Nimrod said. "But then I expect nothing less of Lord Sin of Ur." He leaned forward, peering. "You were a canny politician in life, councilor. The chronicles of Akkad are replete with tales of your diplomacy back in the days when your King Anshara and my forefather Daar split the world between them. That quality may well have persisted even in *undeath*."

He stressed the final word as though it was the name of the vilest disease. Sin let the insult slide. Diplomacy was paramount, indeed.

"I'd like to think I was more than just an ambassador to your noble ancestor, sire," he said. "I was often with him when he dictated to his scribes and no word was used more in his account of our time together than *friendship*."

"You were a friend to Akkad, aye," Nimrod granted. "Both you and your family, for generations. That is the only reason you were allowed through our gates with your head on your shoulders."

His voice rose as he went on, not quite in anger, but a controlled, seething variant of it. "But your family, my lord Sin, is no more. And you, its last scion, are a corpse walking the earth for hundreds of men's years. How can the bitch Arkhalla's spawn be a friend of mine?"

Sin let a moment's pause linger before he essayed an answer. "I am cursed with life eternal, true. I am Undying, though through no machination of my own. I kill to survive, like all beings on this earth, and shall not try to justify that. But I still am the man I was, my dread king. And it was that man that threw down the bitch Arkhalla from her throne and sent her to her doom."

Sin saw the spark in Nimrod's eyes and fanned it. "She was an enemy of her own people," he went on. "A monster drunk with power and bound by neither parley, treaty or law except for the savage desires of her heart. No price was too steep for ending her existence."

At this, the fair princess stepped forth. "We need no reminder of Arkhalla's cruelty, Undying." Her voice was iron dipped in honey. "Or flattery from her kind."

Nimrod raised his hand and Aisyah bowed, returning to her place.

"The Akkadians remember Arkhalla all too well, Lord Sin," he said. His voice was quiet; too much so. "Did not our own King Daar present her with a sacrifice so great that he is still considered the greatest man who ever ruled these lands? And did not your own Queen's cruelty turn that sacrifice into something so unspeakable that Akkad has never forgiven it?"

Sin tried to deflect the question. "My dread king, I was there –"

"Do not interrupt me." The fire in Nimrod's eyes would not be argued with. He pointed to his daughter, who glanced back at him with concern. "To lose a child is the direst curse gods can visit onto a man," he said. "To have the man sacrifice his child himself is infinitely worse. Daar was well aware of this when Arkhalla's ambassador – you, my lord Sin, *you* – came to him with her demands for a tribute to seal the treaty between Akkad and Ur. She demanded no less than one of Daar's four daughters to be offered to her, and that the offer was to be made on the occasion of her eighteenth birthday. Otherwise, the treaty would be null and Arkhalla would unleash her army of monsters on a full-scale war against us."

Sin could almost feel the anger kept in check by the king's sense of decorum. It would not be proper for such strong emotion to be shown to any guest, let alone a cursed Undying.

"The chronicles are very specific about your role in this, my lord Sin," Nimrod went on. "How you argued with Daar to make him accept the appalling terms, as the alternative would mean the annihilation of Akkad and his people. How you reminded your friend that this sacrifice was exactly what had been demanded of Anshara when the priests of Ur had him sacrifice Arkhalla herself to your gods below. You were there, my lord, as you say. Enlighten us on how you made that rather thorny argument."

Sin swallowed hard but tried not to show it.

"I..." He began, but his throat was still sore. He coughed to clear it. "I told him it had to be a test. That... that for Arkhalla to make him perpetrate the same atrocity committed against her was clearly a way to manipulate him, either into a war or into betraying his own flesh in the most unforgivable fashion."

"And how did you suggest that he handle this dilemma?"

"By... not getting out of it. By calling on Arkhalla's bluff and sending his daughters to her birthday feast as offerings so that my Queen could choose her sacrifice."

Sin stopped there.

"And?" came Nimrod's question, as he knew it would.

"And that he ought to do it with pride and defiance. That his daughters should appear willing and ready for one of them to be slain for the good of their people, not forced into it at sword point like Arkhalla and her father were. I... convinced him that the sight would thaw the coldness of the Undying Queen's heart. That backed into a corner thus, she would at least mitigate her cruelty."
"That she would let the four girls live? Just like that?"

"No." Sin bit his lip. "Neither Daar nor I were that naive, my liege. We... I... thought that she would indeed choose one of the four princesses and, instead of outright killing her, turn her. The girl would be made into an Undying, which, I argued, was still life of a sort instead of the nothingness of death. She would still *be*. And it... it might even strengthen the alliance between Akkad and Ur."

"And what *did* happen?" the Princess Aisyah cut in.

"Princess, you know too well. Need we dwell –"

The sickle-sword was in Aisyah's fair hand before even Sin's Undying sight could fathom it.

"I want to hear you say it, Lord Sin. I want you to admit the shame Ur bears at last, before my father, his council and his entire court."

The sword was inches from Sin's throat. Her hand was as balanced as her voice. No emotion was betrayed.

"My people," she went on, "have been burning that she-demon in effigy for two hundred years, on her birthday, long before the Lord God saw that she met that same fate. And she has merited each and every burning. Admit what she did, or you will not merely hold your peace, but rest in it."

Sin sighed. He lowered his eyes. The princess lowered her sickle-sword.

"The princesses came to Ur in pomp and circumstance, as we had planned," he said, his voice wistful. "They stood before Arkhalla on her birthday and declared their purpose and intent, in both respect and defiance. They danced for her and their dancing was the peak of the entire month of celebrations, for none who live had seen such art in dancing before and none shall see it since. And then... then Arkhalla smiled and summoned them to her chamber." He shrugged. "The gods were merciful in that I was not privy to what happened there. The scene was witnessed only by the girls and Arkhalla and one other."

"Who?" demanded Nimrod, who had kept silent until then.

Sin hesitated just a little. "The high Lord Bel, her general and consort. It was he... who told me what came next. So that I would write Daar and tell him what happened." He paused again. "I had not the courage to face him myself. I never did so again, as long as he lived."

"And what did Bel tell you?"

Sin nodded. "The four girls lay prostrate at Arkhalla's feet for her to make her choice. They were still sweating, heaving from the effort of their dancing. She... was overtaken with desire. At her bidding, they looked up, deep into her eyes. She entranced them, like a serpent. My king, I beg of you –"

"No. Speak."

"She... lay with them, all four, in front of Bel. I know not what he did and did not ask. But when her lust was spent, Arkhalla took a dagger to their throats. Right before Bel's eyes. And then she invited him to feed on them together."

At that, Sin fell silent. He knew more of the gory details of the deed, of course. Bel had obliged him with a most detailed description, drunk with Akkadian virgin blood as well as Arkhalla's lust and fury. But Sin knew better than to regale Daar or his descendants with all that. He had already said more than enough to fuel their eternal hatred of the bitch *and* seed a just as deep-seated antipathy towards Bel, thus advancing the cause of his visit.

"That witch was truly sired by demons," Nimrod said, his aspect pale and haggard. "She was everything our Lord God stands against. Humanity could not suffer her to live."

Sin suppressed the satisfaction that filled his chest to burst. He had Nimrod right where he wanted him and didn't even have to lie to do it. The Akkadian was an overly devout man, inordinately faithful to the One God he worshipped. That he regarded Arkhalla as an affront to his beliefs and principles as well as the murderess of members of his house was most convenient to Sin's suit.

"That, my king, is precisely why I have journeyed here to your realm," he said. "Arkhalla may be dead, but Bel now rules Ur in her stead, which bodes most ill for human and Undying alike."

Neither Nimrod nor the princess offered a retort. Sin had their attention. He was allowed to proceed.

"For ten years now, ever since Arkhalla burned in far Dilmun, the council of Ur has faced rebellion from the humans and dissent among its own ranks. Our war is one of attrition: no one decisive battle fought to tip the scales and end it all but, instead, a constant plague of raids, attacks and skirmishes that doesn't seem to end. It is costly in gold and lives alike. And not only does it mire the realm into stasis and decay, but over time it has spread to all the neighboring lands, so much so that no realm between the great rivers Idigna and Buranuna is free of strife."

He stopped, expecting Nimrod's reaction.

"That is some fine oration, Lord Sin," the king said. "But why should I care for the Undying's war except to join the human side if Bel is foolish enough to let it spread to my borders?"

It was just what Sin had hoped he'd say. "Of course you shouldn't, dread King," he answered. "Not as long as the Undying fight a united front against the rebels. But that is no longer the case."

"Explain, Sin. And no orations, please."

"The council of Ur has no idea of either what to do or how to deal with this revolt, sire. There have been too many factions over the years, almost one to each member. So Bel has slowly taken the lead and now rules under military law. But he produces no result and that puts him in a precarious place. He is irrational, afraid of us conspiring against him."

"And you are not?" The princess' smile was almost playful.

Sin was not intimidated.

"Would *you* not, your highness? It is Arkhalla's reign all over again, all oppression and fear. Bel has even taken it on himself to sit on Arkhalla's throne, which none of us had done in years. We had left the damned thing alone as though the dragon heads adorning it were real enough to strangle us. I tell you Bel is in their coils now, in the grip of power. He sits there above us all and orders us like subjects."

"I take it you do not approve," Nimrod interjected.

"Of course I bloody don't approve!" Sin allowed his voice to rise just enough for an effect of righteous indignation. "I have been Bel's friend for more than two centuries. But in those centuries, Undying and human alike suffered under Arkhalla. They had to endure her blood feasts and purges. Her casual cruelty. I may sustain myself on blood as she did, but in all other respects, we couldn't be less alike. I have always been a councilor; I have always stood for the rule of law and the treaties of diplomacy. My record, taken by your ancestor, speaks of this."

It was time to drive his point home. "So yes, my liege and your highness, I have been conspiring against Bel. Half the council is. And yes, I have turned them against Bel and I am sad to have done it. It was my hope that I would be able to achieve a peaceful solution. That we would have been able to split the realm amicably between our factions. But one cannot come to a consensus with madmen. A war for Ur *will* take place. It is inevitable. But the terror of Arkhalla is not. And it is for one reason above all, to spare the world another reign of terror, that I come to ask for your help."

Ever the consummate orator, Sin took a breath before his final words. "I am wary of queens wallowing in the blood of their subjects with no regard for anything. And I am wary of men who would be kings after her example."

At this, he stopped and waited. Nimrod took pains to show how he pondered and thought on his answer. Anyone but Sin might believe he had not already settled on one. But the manner he phrased it at this moment would determine him either a leader of men or a fool.

"You presume, Lord Sin," the king began, inflecting *presume* with a hint of scorn, "that I want the same thing you want. That I wish – how did you put it? – to spare the world of another leech king like *her*. And that I wish this above all other things. So much so that I'd be willing to do anything. Even join one such as you."

A wise man knows best when to keep silent. Sin did not speak.

"This audience is over," said Nimrod. "You will wait in the hall. Someone will come for you. If you are still alive when next we meet, we shall talk further. If not, I shall be talking to your head."

"He was not scared, father," Aisyah said once Sin was shown out.

She was the only one who spoke. Her thought was on the minds of all the Akkadian nobles and councilors of war present, though none would dare voice it. They knew their liege would only address them if he deemed it worth his while. The decision was his and his alone. Nimrod and Aisyah might as well be all alone in the grand hall.

"I doubt one such as he ever is," the king retorted. "He knows his case is convincing, otherwise he would not have come here. But it would not do to grant him his suit without deliberation. And to threaten him means I save face."

"Then you will accept his suit?"

Nimrod stared at her. "Tell me what you would do."

Aisyah bowed. "My lord, it is not my place –"

"Oh, but it will be, Aisyah. One day I shall pass from this life and you will rule in my stead." He paused. "You, child. Not some unworthy lout that would marry you. Marry if you will, but the kingdom goes to my daughter, who's worth every grain of sand in it."

"You honor me with your trust, sire."

"Which you prove to be well-founded every day. Do so now, daughter. Tell me."

Aisyah's chest heaved ever so slightly. It was the sole sign of hesitance she'd show.

"My lord," she said, "you raised me to hate the Undying. Such is the passion breathed into every heir of Akkad since the days of Daar."

"Indeed."

"You had me trained in the arts of death. My teachers schooled me in the secrets of the Magi and the ways and weaknesses of the Undying. In every way there is to kill them. In every recourse to survive them. All this you did to a single end and to this end only."

Nimrod, seeing his daughter's reasoning, smiled. "Arkhalla's death."

"And when the witch-queen died, yet not by Akkadian hand, what did you do, my dread lord? Did you cease my training? Did you instruct me in another course for my existence? Nay, you had me trained twice as hard. Arkhalla was dead, but not by Akkadian hands. There were still Undying walking the earth, and Ur yet stood. So anything could happen, including that someone even worse than Arkhalla reign in Ur. And now that possibility comes true."

Nimrod's smile widened. "You are right, daughter. Your life, your reason to be. Everything I raised you for. It begins now."

Aisyah looked her sire in the eye. "Therefore it is a moot point even to ask what our course should be. We must join in the war against the leech Lord Bel. Your true question, my father, is whether we kill the leech that waits in the antechamber now, or when he has further served our cause."

CHAPTER 3

ASHES

Long riders crossed the desert, a storm of shades that chased each other every time the moon peaked from behind the clouds obscuring the plain. No sound came from the four hundred men that cast them, nor from the black-clad woman at their lead. No sound was heard from their stallions' hooves. They rode in eerie silence, gliding across the desert plain like the clouds that covered it, as charged with menace as a stroke of lightning that steals across the sky before the sound of thunder.

Narama rode on, followed by four hundred men on just as many horses, bearing death and leaving behind them trails of dust. She had hand-picked them from among her very best, their number small enough to grant a speedier journey yet great enough to turn the tide in any battle. Another warlord would have needed more, but with four hundred Undying behind her Narama knew she could shake the world.

The trek to Dilmun had taken half the time it would have taken the best army. They had been riding all night and every night, ten-minute bursts of full-out speed followed by one-hour marches at an even pace to keep their steeds fit and going. The days they spent in the mountain range caves or in shelters dug into the sand. It was fast progress and it was efficient. The men were tough and able to go for nights on end without feeding. There were no slaves or conscripts or provisions brought along, nothing to slow them down or to distract them. Narama was the first to follow her command and the men adhered to it without the slightest thought.

She was their leader in every way, ready to subject herself to the same punishment and hardship she commanded from them, just as she was more than capable to mete out death and to ensure survival. The route she had laid out took them through villages and oases frequented by caravans just often enough so they wouldn't starve. Yet even then they fell onto the wretches like a swarm plague, never stopping, and left nothing but drained corpses behind them in mere seconds.

But in the last couple of nights, as they cleared the beachfront and rode across the final stretch of plain towards Dilmun, the men had slackened their exacting pace. Getting closer to the war had slowed their progress down and made them sick with apprehension. Narama sensed it too – that unseen violence that charged the air and burdened the spirit and comes with the approach towards a battlefield – and yet there was something different about it this time, some twisted and revolting thing she couldn't name. Like the dust they breathed, it was always there, always around them.

At first, she put it down to herself. She knew the violence of war, how terrible it was. Though she had never flinched from meting death, she had not fought a war these ten years. And because she was honest with herself, she knew she was too far conditioned and trained for it to ever let it go, not completely. Maybe she had reconditioned herself not to give in to the urge. If so, then this was her soul, what dregs were left of it, tugging at her as she neared another field of death and atrocity.

But that did not explain the quiet earth they rode across, nor why no vultures roamed the sky.

The next she knew something was awfully amiss was when they began to see men. They were in bands of two or three and huddled dozens and solitary figures trekking across the landscape, but all of them were coming from the opposite direction, from

Dilmun, and invariably ran when they caught sight of Narama and her men. She didn't even have to send riders after them to verify what instinct and her Undying sight could tell her. These men were deserters, human conscripts from Bel's army, a slow trickle of them that, man by man, grew into a massive wave. They were running because they knew they'd be killed on capture.

She knew then that some terrible thing had happened. It hadn't been defeat, no. Bel had not lost the battle, he wasn't lying on the field burning in the sun. Narama would have felt it if that happened, though she would not admit so outright. Moreover, had Bel been defeated at Dilmun, there would be no deserters trudging their way back across the plain. The conscripts that survived would have surrendered to the humans and joined with them. A lot of wretches had been known to do that; the human armies swelled with them. Or, had they been too afraid to switch sides, they would have tried to join Narama rather than run away. Something else had happened. If it was not defeat, it was victory.

But why desert a winning army?

Narama realized she was afraid to know.

She signaled her men to press forward. It'd be another full night's march to the gates of Dilmun. Soon, she'd find out.

The hours passed. The moon peaked, then began its downward arch, a bright glowing arrow shot by the huntress in the sky as she stalked the constellations. In a while, it'd be dawn. They'd have to dig for shelter.

She was about to give her captain the command to set up camp when she saw the dust column. It was so faint at first, so far into the distance and the dark, that even one with Undying sight might think it a trick of the moonlight or, at worst, a whirlwind caused by swirling sand.

Narama knew it was neither.

She raised her hand and four hundred men stopped as one behind her.

"Riders," she said, her voice dry.

Her men fell in formation, weapons ready. They waited. Now they could all see the dust trailing behind the riders as they edged closer along the horizon. There were men following close, rows and rows of them.

No deserters, these. No huddled, frightened men walking in small groups. This was a full division, perhaps twenty thousand strong, perhaps more, cavalry and infantry combined. Narama surmised that Bel had set out with close to forty thousand men. That was the largest army Ur could muster for a campaign, conscripts and Undying together. With casualties and deserters factored in, this would seem close enough for an army coming back in victory – though a very, very costly one at that.

Something had happened.

Narama felt fear clutching at her heart – a hollow dread not bred by danger or an instinct for survival but by dejection and awe. She felt small and insignificant before something vast and terrible. It was the terror bred in mankind when first they realize the immensity of the universe or the inevitability of death. For years countless to her by now, she had considered neither of these, which was why the advent of this holy terror shocked her so.

She could see the men coming across the desert now; scouts first, lean and haggard, their shoulders hunched, their mien that of men who had seen too much and lived. Riders came next, sluggish ghosts on horseback, not quite there as they trudged along, their movements like those of drunken men. Narama could scarce recognize Bel's elite corps of Undying in this cortege. They more resembled revelers at one of Arkhalla's orgies, fat and bloated with blood, the effect clashing with the skeletal appearance of their mounts.

The conscripts stumbled forth, most of them unable to keep in line or maintain a steady pace. It was not exhaustion that had caused this pitiful lack of coordination. There was madness in the twitching of their limbs. Something had unhinged reason from these men's minds. Something that had outdone even the worst of Arkhalla's atrocities.

The division came closer. Narama saw death haunting the men's eyes, a specter that roamed the empty house where once their soul had lived. But it was when she saw Bel riding forth from among the disarrayed cortege of men – Bel, who she had both yearned and dreaded seeing again after so many years apart; Bel, who she never dreamt could let an army fall apart as much as the rough and sorry mass that crawled towards her now – it was then that Narama was genuinely shocked.

She saw a haggard shell of a man. His armor had turned the color of rotten copper, caked with dried-up blood from head to toe. The sickle-sword sheathed to his waist was broken, while the shield fastened to his horse's side was cracked and blackened with soot. His steed was the pale horse of death itself, green and yellow with sickness and what looked like spleen, as though he had made it stomp into a mound of entrails, its eyes completely black and glistening.

Bel rode close enough for her to see his face now. There were black circles around eyes set so deep within his emaciated skull they seemed more like the empty sockets of a dead man. He was paler than a corpse, his lips parched and bleeding, his head lolling to and fro to the rhythm of the movement of his horse rather than by his own volition. A dead man tied to his horse, that was what he looked like most.

The division came to a stop, all except him. He rode towards her, closer and closer, and Narama had to fight the urge to tug at the reins and draw back from him. His eyes were looking straight at her now, hollow, sparkless, lost halfway between madness and regret, so much so Narama could swear he didn't recognize her.

The death horse came to a stop inches from hers. She held tight onto the reins, feeling her steed stir uneasily beneath her as she looked back into the lifeless eyes.

"Bel," she whispered, shocked at the tremor she heard in her voice. It was terror. And anger at seeing him reduced to this. And holy awe at what had brought him low thus.

The man who was death did not answer. Death does not answer to women or men, neither does he respond to entreaty or anger or awe or pity. He simply is.

"Bel… what did you do?"

Dilmun was no more.

Shamath knew it before he saw the giant pillar of smoke rising from where the city's gates once stood. He had felt it miles before, when he was crossing the burnt fields with their ashen crops of wheat and all of a sudden images and sensations from his dream rushed onto him like harbingers of doom. His mind's eye widened at the sight of atrocity. His senses reeled from the smell of killing and the touch of fire and the keening of the tortured.

He threw up then, the remnants of the bread and olives he had nibbled on with little appetite a few short hours ago cleaned out from his stomach. It was a small mercy that when he eventually rode into Dilmun there was nothing in him to churn out. But he did not know that. Not yet.

He rode on, a cold hand gripping his heart.

The sky above the city looming in the distance was neither blue nor grey nor, as Shamath had half-feared after his nightmare, red with clouds pregnant with blood. It was a blank expansive nothingness, as though something had burned it white-hot till there was naught left to burn.

Shamath rode on.

Beyond the ashen fields and to his left he remembered the gulf that led into the ports of Dilmun, but there was nothing along the horizon now except a blackness that almost seemed to heave with the breath of unseen waves. Intrigued, Shamath nudged his horse closer to what he had remembered as a coastline. Only when he got close enough did he realize what the blackness was. The sea of his memory was still there, bloody and choked with corpses that covered it completely, their hacked torsos and limbs stretching as far as his eye could see.

Shamath rode on.

To the right of the fields of soot were the remnants of the farms that used to line the outskirts of the city, so similar to the one he had spent his youth in or the one he had dreamed to share with his dead, lost love. Clean, simple farmhouses built on sweat and toil, where the laughter of children gave their parents strength to go on day after back-breaking day, the mouth-watering smell of stew was there to welcome the men back from work at eventide, the linen and freshly washed tunics and loincloths on the clothesline stretched all-white as they caught the light of the sun in the morning. None of that was left untouched as Shamath rode past. The brunt of the assault wave that descended on the city had ridden through here first. Houses were charred husks letting out pitiful wails as the wind passed through half-crumbled walls. The only smell in the air was that of death, brutal and pungent with suffering. And on the clotheslines, beside the blackened, burned sheets, hung the skins of the children that no longer laughed and of the parents that had died screaming with them. There was no telling what their slayers had done with their bodies, no hint other than suspicions too terrible even to consider.

Shamath rode on.

The gates of Dilmun still stood, built not of the melted iron and burnt wood that once formed the foundation of their structure, but with staked, charred bodies heaped and lined together to form an edifice twice as high as the gates were when these people lived. Instead of the city's crest sculpted in low relief above it now stretched an array of human skulls. It was the clearest sign to those that came to abandon all hope that anything still lived in this accursed place.

Shamath, hopeless, rode on.

Tendrils of smoke still twined their way out of the burnt buildings. Like black trees growing from fields seeded with fire and blood, they rose mighty, their shade stretching for miles, covering the city entire in despair. No breeze would put out the flames still burning under the ashen streets; no rain would put them out. There was too much pain fanning them.

Shamath rode on.

There were streets strewn with human limbs from end to end. Hands and feet on one thoroughfare, heads on another, breasts and cocks on a third. Ash piles stacked high as pyres at the end of every second street pointed to what fate had befallen the bodies of all those poor souls. Shamath shut his eyes as they stung and burned with tears and soot. He tried to cover his ears with his hands at every crunching step his horse took across this field of mutilations. It was senseless to a point beyond madness, it was violence taken past war, past execution, past torture and genocide. In his heart of hearts, he knew this was punishment. And he knew the devil who reigned in this place of torment.

Bel.

The pyres were the clue that made realization flash incandescent in Shamath's mind. He had recognized, to his dread, a touch of Arkhalla's hand in this atrocity, her cruelty taken to depths unfathomed even in the Lands Below. She was dead, but her right hand still gripped onto the world. *He* still lived, Bel, he who was her damned soul, the enforcer of her will, the Undying who had loved and hated her with an obsession Shamath had recognized even then, in the Undying Queen's court, because the fire that burned in Bel was so different yet also so alike to the passion that consumed the young slave. Bel burned with it, too, and the flames had consumed him at last. After all these years, then, *this* was punishment for the killing of his Queen, the Queen only he was allowed to love, only he was allowed to kill. He had waited all this time for this moment, the hatred of them, the folk that had burned her, and of himself, too, eating at what passed for his heart. And now that the moment had come, he had leapt into it the way a crazed suicide throws himself into the fire of a volcano.

Shamath rode on.

The smoke rising from the city's burnt corpse took on the shape of nightmare, as though it were the form of the dark Lord Asag the demon-king himself, and Shamath knew he was teetering on the brink of insanity. He could hear the laughter of the gods as they saw all that they had made. There were broken chariots enmeshed with dead body parts, structures of stone and metal twisted and turned to shapes unimaginable, wan and paper-thin faces stripped from skulls and draped over doors and windows and severed heads on pikes and carts staring blankly or screaming at him as he passed, like an audience at a litany or a funeral cortege. Except these were not mourners, but the mourned, lined up to gaze at their own funeral. For them Shamath could do naught but weep. And he cried till he thought his heart was a sponge squeezed of every single drop of water it had held, till it lay in his chest all dried up and dead.

And still he rode on, his heart dead, his mind amiss, through the carnage.

Those streets clear of body parts glistened with pools of half-dried blood; so much of it was spilled that the Undying had let it go to waste. The heat of the ashes burning underneath kept the pools from cooling, like a cauldron on coals; it was impossible, unnatural. Yet what about this bloodshed adhered to possibility or nature? Shamath shuddered as he saw himself reflected in the bubbling scarlet surface, his mind flashing back to Arkhalla's demon mirror.

The Ones Below would have their fill that day.

Bel had crammed the few short hours this took with a decade-full of pain, with the memory of eons of ritual sacrifice. He had outdone Arkhalla. What torture was ever devised by man he had inflicted on those people in a single day, till he had run out of variations on his hellish tune. But that hadn't stopped him. Once he realized there were more people than stakes, he stacked three and four heads on every pike. He piled up corpses and atrocities in new configurations, group sculptures of pain, gigantic monuments to his revenge, his cruelty. And once there were no more stakes or wood to craft them from, he had impaled living men and women to anything within his reach. Gates and fences and masonry and statues, all turned to impalement tools. He'd burned houses and carts and men and temples and then burned their ashes, till there was only a single structure left, composed of all the city that had went into building it. One temple to the goddess of atrocity that haunted him. Shamath pictured him through his bloody work, a mad destroyer with nothing in his burning eyes, a god below wearing only the skin of humanity. There was no redemption to the doom he brought or that which he suffered. Nothing but emptiness and massacre.

In between this exhibition of atrocities there were mounds of corpses filling the gaps from one horror to the next, each made of random bodies burnt and bodies hacked and others merely killed and thrown together with the others pell-mell. So many of the dead people around him were killed in mid-stride, trying to flee from the onslaught of dark riders, the terror frozen on their faces along with the promises of a life unfulfilled.

Shamath rode on. Wind shrieked through burnt out buildings like carrion birds, circling the dead all around.

There were survivors, except they were not. He saw three men piled on top each other, their heads pierced by a single stake, and as he looked the topmost of them flapped his mouth and uttered one final pain-filled curse. There was a woman with no eyes, her arms severed at the elbow, who wondered the streets wailing for her children while the last dregs bled from her stumps. He saw hanged men dangling from their entrails, their limbs twitching in death throes. A man crying by the bodies of his family, his hair gone bone-white, looked up at Shamath and keeled over, succumbing either to some unseen wound or to the enormity of his pain.

Shamath rode on through death and despair until he came to the square.

Here Arkhalla had died ten years ago and yet only last night in his dreams. Here Bel had piled up babes in arms, still suckling at their mother's teat, a giant mound of little bodies, and set them all afire. Shamath could still glimpse the odd twisted tiny limb peeking from the rubble enough to tell the awful tale. From the dead strewn about the pyre, their throats slashed, he surmised these were the children's parents, made to watch as the Undying stole their future before they snuffed their lives.

Exhausted by atrocity, Shamath dismounted, his head reeling. He went on his knees and stayed there, unable to even lift his head. He wasn't sure whether he'd be able to get back on his feet and flee from this accursed place, or whether he'd lay there till his strength abandoned him and he joined the hecatomb of the dead.

He stayed there a long time, in the silence of death, till he heard a scratching.

At first, he thought it a product of his fevered brain; or worse, the work of rats feasting on the banquet of dead flesh. It was only after he remembered he had seen no vermin in his progress through the hellish town, nor seen a bird of carrion or any living creature from miles before he came through the city gates, that he was truly frightened.

The sound was coming from a pile of corpses to his left. It was as though some small animal was scratching at a door. But for the deathly silence, it'd be too indistinct to hear. Even so, Shamath's heart was stilled with dread, his mind straining to make some other sense of it – that it was the wind, the rats, or wild hallucination, nothing more – any sense *but* that it might be something living under there. He was scarce sure he had heard it after all.

Then the mound shifted.

It was the slightest move; if he hadn't been looking, he wouldn't have noticed. He tried to tell himself he had imagined it, nothing more. Pebbles and stones shift on rocky hillsides and there is nothing living underneath, nothing trying to crawl out from under there.

Even as he stared wide-eyed at it, the mound shifted again, even less noticeably this time. It was some poor soul dying, Shamath told himself; one of those survivors he had glimpsed, breathing their last, nothing more.

His mind screamed at him to turn and get back on his horse. But he knew he couldn't leave it at that, whatever it was.

It was hellish work, digging through the dead. Some of them were all limp weight, others stiff with the rigor of hours past their demise. The act of lifting and shifting through them took all of a man's strength and more. A torn piece of tunic wrapped about the nose and mouth was all the protection one could muster against the dead-killing stench. Shamath's stomach crawled each time his fingers gripped sundered flesh or a lifeless limb touched his. But still he went on. Twice the mound heaved and almost crushed him; endless minutes passed.

He was about to give up when he brushed past a woman's hand and it reached out and grabbed him.

CHAPTER 4

LEFT BEHIND

The woman looked at him, shivering. Shamath wrapped her tighter in his blanket and pressed the wet rag to her forehead. Her fever had begun to subside sometime in the past hour, but she was still sick with hardship and exposure. He had dressed the cut on her head. That she had survived could almost make one believe in the kindness of the gods – until one thought of the countless that had not.

She had been one of the many caught by the first wave of Undying rushing through the city streets, she told him, half delirious. A glancing blow from a sickle-sword had caught her on her head. It was also what had saved her, he surmised. Senseless, the whole side of her face and neck drenched with gore, she was another dead body to be heaped onto the side of the street, before the tortures and the executions really started. By the time she regained consciousness, she found herself being slowly crushed by the dead thrown on top of her, barely able to breathe. Some of the bodies must have shielded her, the way some people survived whole buildings collapsing about them. It was one chance in an infinity that she'd live, and yet she lived. Had Shamath not helped her out from under the rubble of corpses, she would have perished.

The woman's eyes sparkled behind the fair strands of hair that fell across her face. She was crying.

"It's all right," Shamath said. "You are unharmed. You are going to live through this."

"Th-the people," she managed to stutter.

Shamath nodded without saying anything. She probably had family or loved ones out there. What could he say that wouldn't hurt her?

Her eyes grew wide with terror. "Blood," she whispered. "Blood."

"It's over now," Shamath tried to soothe her.

"They... came with... the dark," she went on. "So... many. Like h-hounds. On... scent. Like we were... game. Gods... the screams. The s-screams."

She was delirious again. "Shh," Shamath said. "Try not to talk. Don't strain yourself."

"The dark... man," she hissed, not hearing him. "The dark... in his eyes."

"What? What dark man?"

"He l-led them. Egged them... on. His voice... thunder."

She grabbed onto him, the strength of madness in her slender hand. "*For Arkhalla*. He... screamed it. I heard... him." Shamath's blood froze.

For Arkhalla.

Bel. It had to be.

The woman stared into his eyes. "You," she said, her voice clear now, focused. "You were there. Her pyre." She winced. "All those... years... ago. Arkhalla's young man." "Yes," he said. "I'm Shamath." She nodded. She remembered.

"You tried to comfort me," he said. "You told me to live."

Tears streamed down her cheeks, washing through the soot that smeared them.

Shamath had remembered her the minute he had laid eyes on her. The years had not marred the girlish features, only changed them. There was experience in her eyes, too much of it, and not the good kind. But under the blood and the soot and the faint lines on her forehead and going from her nose down around her mouth, he could still see the fair-haired girl he had last glimpsed in a nightmare.

Her eyes fluttered and shut, and like that, she was asleep. Shamath stayed with her, pressing his lips on her forehead to check her temperature from time to time. After a couple of hours passed and she opened her eyes again, her fever was gone. Shamath gave her some bread and water and she gulped them down like a hungry pup, which was another sign that she'd be on the mend in a couple of days.

"I'm Dumu," she said, her mouth full. She chuckled at how she sounded, swallowed, then said it again. "Sorry."

"It's all right."

The smile faded from her face, a flash of sunlight hidden again behind clouds of sorrow.

"Eleesha," she said. "My friend," she explained, turning to him. "We got separated in the stampede. She is still out there."

This time Shamath could not stay silent. "I saw nothing but dead people, all over the city."

"I know she is dead," Dumu said, surprising him. "She must be. But I must look for her."

Shamath nodded. He understood.

They went together through the carnage again, Dumu weak on her feet, Shamath letting her lean on him. She never screamed as she took on the horror. She only cried. Now and then, Shamath felt her shiver under the blanket.

She led him quietly to the last place she recalled seeing her friend, and from there they began searching, corner to corner, street after street, from one mound of unburied dead to another. Hours passed. Every nerve in his body struck numb by atrocity, Shamath went on without a word, stopping only to note the movement of the sun as it rose to its zenith and then began to draw a slow lowering arc. He'd let her go on as long as he could, but he did not want dusk to find them still in that accursed land. A bad feeling gnawed at his insides. After seeing his dream come true, he was not inclined to disregard it.

Her scream snapped him back to alert. Dumu had wandered down to the end of the street. He saw her standing opposite the burned, rubble-strewn front of the house in the corner and rushed to her side. She was frozen, shaking uncontrollably as she stared at the doorway. His lips had barely parted to ask her what was the matter when he saw.

There was little left of the doorway to the house. The entry stood open, a mouth into its dark, soot-blackened insides, parts of the front wall and the rafters crumbled into a pile of masonry that blocked it. The woman was lying in the rubble, one of her legs crushed under a wooden beam, pinned partway between the dark interior and the light of day. She was badly burnt. What was left of her hair was dark with odd streaks of white here and there. Her dress was torn down the front and hitched up to her waist, giving a hideous view of bruises, cuts and wounds. That shredded garment and the blood pooling between her legs told Shamath how the beasts that mangled her had not stopped there. She'd be a terrible sight if she were dead, but she was not.

Horror seized Shamath as he saw her limbs twitch; her eyes blinked, bloodshot. She was looking at Dumu and him. And as they looked back, the woman made to raise a trembling arm towards them and it began to break out in welts and burns where the sunlight hit it and she screamed.

Even among the blood and the bruising and the burns, Shamath could glimpse the bite marks on her neck and chest, each of them made by twin punctured wounds, their edges caked white and worn.

They had tortured and abused her thus, right there in the doorway, but that was not enough for them. They had not just bled her and set fire to the house afterwards. Perhaps they had her drink of their blood out of cruel sport and the thrill of forcing their vile essence down her throat. Or perhaps they knew what would happen to her if her corpse was not consumed in the flames, and had done it on that very purpose – just for the added thrill of knowing how she'd suffer now. For her corpse hadn't burned. She was slowly waking up now, coming back, turning. Already her eyeteeth were pulled back from the gums and looked sharp as a beast's. Except the sun was burning her and her wounds were so massive even the blood of the Undying coursing through her could not heal them fast enough.

The woman screamed again. Dumu jumped.

"Eleesha," she cried out pitifully.

Tears were streaming down her face, as they were down the woman's cheeks. The woman's were tinged scarlet. Shamath shivered with a sharp recall of Arkhalla, that time he had seen her cry tears of blood. He had tried to save her life, back then in the swamp, by giving his. In the end, it had been for nothing.

The woman called Eleesha moaned. New welts broke out onto her skin with every move she made. Shamath could not even fathom how much she suffered.

He felt Dumu's hand digging into his arm.

"Is there n-nothing we can do?"

Her voice was shrill, teetering on the brink of madness. Shamath did not look at her. His eyes were fixed on Eleesha's, shedding red, pleading.

He took a couple of steps back and felt Dumu's fingers loosen their grip. Shaken, struggling to stay on his feet, he turned, scanning the ruins about them. At last he caught a dull glint in the rubble and stumbled toward it. It was a sickle-sword, broken and stained by whoever dropped it during the massacre. Shamath picked it up, rose and walked back to the doorway.

"No," Dumu whispered as she saw the blade in his hand.

Shamath walked past her. "There must be some other way," he heard her say.

He said nothing. The blade was heavy in his hand as he raised it. He hadn't held one for so many years.

Eleesha looked at him. Her eyes closed, then opened again. She tried to speak.

Shamath nodded.

"I'm sorry," he said, and brought down the blade.

There was whispering aplenty among the men during the way back. The Undying were no strangers to massacre, so there was neither remorse nor accusation in their hushed talk around the campfires. Instead, there was questioning – of Bel's leadership, of his fitness for command, and worse of all, of the *reason why*, after they had already plowed through Dilmun's defenses, were they commanded to exterminate the populace in such a thorough fashion that it made the sacking of Carcosa no more than a skirmish. It was as Sin had predicted and Narama feared.

"No slaves taken, not even to feed us on the journey," was one of the most persistent complaints.

"Such a waste," the complainer's comrades would agree.

"And did you see him? Acting like his brain was tainted on some madman's blood?"

"Slaughter is one thing, mates. A senseless hack job like that, though..."

"Aye. We're Undying. We slay to feed. We put fear into the hearts of wretches. What is the use if there are no wretches to put the fear into?"

"Never mind how he acted," one of the sharper in their number would inevitably say. "Did you hear him? What he screamed?"

"Arkhalla's name."

"Aye, what about that?"

"I heard him, too. When he had us torch those infants up on the pyre. *For Arkhalla*, he cried, at the top of his voice, he did."

"For *her*? Was *this* for her?"

"I was there with him when we first came here and he saw the pyre they burned her in. I swear I saw tears in his eyes, scarlet as this here blood upon my blade."

"Has he gone mad?"

"Does *She* still command him from her grave?"

Narama would listen up to this point and then she'd slip among the shadows and out of ear reach, as she did now, the men around the campfire none the wiser to either her presence or her leaving. Wrapped in dark and worry, the Huntress of Men stalked through the camp and headed past the sentries to the dunes, where clouds gathered awhile now. It was going to be a storm to remember; she could smell it charging the air. None of the jackals that circled the camp at night were in sight. The wanderers of the desert had felt the coming thunder and scurried to the caves deep in the mountains.

She saw Bel out there, climbed onto the topmost dune, wind and sand lashing at him. Something in the way he stood there made him seem quite mad, as though he welcomed the torrent to come and the storm to grow into a hurricane maw and swallow him. Lightning slashed at the sky, letting her see his bloody eyes wide as he spread his hands, baring his chest to the full brunt of the winds. A thunderclap followed on the sky-fire's train, loud enough to cleave the tallest tree on its strength alone. Narama smelled sulfur in the air, poisoning her reason. The Great Below must be like this, she thought.

Another bolt illuminated Bel, his hair turned white for a moment by the flash. Narama saw his mouth open, the thunder drowning out his scream. She rushed to him.

"Come, Bel," she said, clutching his arm, as softly as she could. "Let us go back to your tent now. It is no night for man, nor for Undying."

He tore away from her grasp, ignoring her.

"What can storms do to me?" he growled. "What more than *She* has done, or I to her?"

He turned back to the wind. "Burn me, gods, I dare you!" he cried. "You cannot do worse than her memory!"

He laughed, as though he realized the madness that had seized him. The rain came with his laughter, a rage of whips beating mercilessly on the two of them.

"She left me! She abandoned me! And I --"

"Bel --" she tried to speak.

"Come, Arkhalla!" he screamed. "I am here! Come!"

He tore his tunic open, his hands clawing at his flesh as though it were laced with poison.

"Your love! Your slave!"

He raged on and on, wild incoherent cries mixed with vile oaths and mumbled pleas, and it was as though the storm answered him in kind. Not since she was a mortal woman did Narama recall such wrathful skies, nor as skin-crawling groans of thunder. The sky was weeping *with* Bel, *for* him. She felt his pain and fear in the whipping of the storm, so synchronous to her own heartbeat she thought she was losing her mind. No ordinary storm was this. Her people, long gone from this earth, used to call it the dark night of the soul. A warrior might lose himself on such a night, she recalled the elders saying, his sanity claimed by the storm's wrath, his own primordial terror of the darkness attuned to nature's rage and heightening it to the point of breaking him.

This, she knew, was what Bel was going through now.

"Come away, Bel," she cried out, struggling to hold on to her footing against the howling sandstorm. "Let us not linger here." Bel turned to her, his eyes afire.

"It is punishment," he howled. "Let it come, ye gods! On all your enemies! On that cowardly wretch that took her from me! On this head of mine, too, for my betraying her! Aaaaah!"

With that great cry he fell down on his knees and collapsed onto the sand. Narama tried to help him up but he thrashed about wildly, his body gripped in dreadful spasms. Blood started coming through his clenched teeth; Narama threw herself on him, thrusting her hand into his mouth to stop him from biting off his tongue. She cried out in pain as he bit deep into her, but she did not pull back. Her senses reeled from pain to shock and from the whip strokes of the storm to the fire his words had started within her. Bel had lost all sense and measure; there was no balance in his soul. Like a murderer unpunished for some secret crime, a sinner keeping all his guilt pent-up for years behind a brittle mask of righteousness, he was finally letting it all out, and it was shaking him to pieces.

He loved her, damn his eyes. Even after all this time, after what had happened, the fool of a man still loved *her*. And it had ruined him.

Narama fought back tears. *Lie down with him*, the cursed storm howled inside her head. *Let the sand bury you both. A grave is the only thing you'll ever share.*

No, she thought.

Lie down. Let go.

I won't.

With all her might, she pushed back at the despair. Bel was senseless, dead weight in her arms. The storm was an axe cleaving at her, taking her breath away. It'd take more than her strength to move him a bare inch.

She heaved, digging her heels into unsteady ground. The sand loosened even more; her leg sank. One false move and the desert might claim her like a swamp.

She heaved again, cursing.

Bel's body moved; a bare inch.

She managed to find purchase enough to get her leg out of the sand and tried once more.

Another inch.

Fighting sand and storm and the dark, she heaved, dragging the senseless man across the dunes. She knew not how long it took, or where she found the strength. She just did it.

At last she got to a sandpit near some rocks. It was a sun shelter, began but left unfinished. Narama dragged Bel's body inside its mouth and fell exhausted next to it. The wind raged wild above them, heaving sand into the pit, but she clung close to its wall with him in her arms and waited it out. It was a long time later that she heard his breath change pace in the dark.

"Narama," he spoke through parched lips.

"I'm here."

"Are you cold? I'm cold."

"Hold on to me," she said. "I'll warm you."

"My mind returns," he said. "I'm sorry."

Her heart skipped. Her breast was so close to his she feared he'd feel it.

"Sorry?" she said, steadying her voice. "Whatever for?"

"That you had to see this. I went mad, I --"

"Hush. It was blood fever, nothing more. The night and the storm did the rest."

He frowned. "Blood fever. Dilmun. I..." A pause. "Gods. I remember."

His fingers dug into her arm. She held him closer. "Hush, I say. It is past, Bel. It is past."

"Past?" Something like laughter escaped his lips. "I doubt it."

Narama doubted it too. But she couldn't tell him.

"The men. They saw me like that."

He was not asking. Neither could she lie. "Aye."

"I must be on my horse tomorrow. Show up before them. Sane. A leader."

He fought to get up, but had not the strength.

"I'll tend to you," she said. "I'll nurse you back."

"I must be on my horse tomorrow."

"You shall. Even if I have to lash you to it."

This time the laughter sounded more like mirth. "Ever the taskmaster. I missed that." Another pause. His hand found hers. "I missed you."

His voice cracked, and Narama knew she'd shield him from the rancor of the men, that she'd nurse him back like she promised. Even if he had lost himself in the dark night of his soul. Even if he was still in love with *her*. There was still too much of him inside Narama's heart not to try.

She pressed his hand.

"I never left," she said.

CHAPTER 5

PLOWSHARES INTO SWORDS

Dumu and Shamath laid Eleesha to her final rest in a small grave in what was left of the docklands of Dilmun. She had lived there all her life, Dumu told him as he arranged her friend's brittle body lengthwise in the pit of earth, her head placed as neatly as he could onto her shoulders. Her parents had sold her to the brothel master to feed their other children, like's Dumu's own family had. It was a fate all too common to poor girls in wealthy nations. The girls worked until they were too old to, or, if luck and beauty favored them, until they earned enough in tips to settle their debt. Eleesha and Dumu had found each other in that other pit of despair and abuse, and they had held each other up through the years, saving up pittances and crumbs until they purchased back their freedom. No employer would hire a former whore except for laundry work or other lowly tasks, but they both worked hard enough to rent a tiny but clean hovel. No honest man would take a former whore to wife, but neither of them cared much for honest men, for they had seen too many of them in the brothel, and as for the dishonest ones, the two of them were smart enough to stay clear of. They'd climbed out of the pit together, and together they had stayed, until this moment. Their hovel was gone now, and so was Eleesha. So Dumu said farewell and threw a lock of her hair in her friend's grave, for this last pit she could not help her out of.

There was a look of peace on Eleesha's wasted face. Gone were the sharpened teeth, along with her pain. She had suffered, but would no more.

Dumu nodded, and Shamath began to fill the grave and cover her. It was brief work, a part of him noted as he did it. He had spent too much time digging out the living and the dead that day, harrowing hours he'd take with him to his own grave. But there was something peaceful in laying this one woman to her rest, like planting a flower. It'd take years before plants grew across this blighted land, but they would in the end, like they did over Arkhalla's grave. Life had its circle and it'd go on. Shamath believed that. Even when faced with Dilmun's horror, he had to. It held him on to some semblance of hope.

They packed up and left soon after, the rest of that day spent silently as they rode away from the city. Dumu, seated in front of him on the saddle, was soon lulled to sleep by exhaustion, while Shamath let himself be carried off by thoughts. By the time he realized he'd left his horse to decide their course, the sun was plunging lower in the sky. A sandstorm was forming along the horizon, coming from deep in the desert and the way back to Ur. The safest refuge for them was the mountain caves, so Shamath nudged his mare in that direction.

In twilight, the mountains were jagged axes of stone, left buried in the desert by giant hunters long gone from the world. There was much akin to slumber in their quietude, unlike the dread silence Shamath and Dumu had left behind them. But as he spied the caves pocking the craggy stone faces, Shamath was once again seized by coiling unease. For the caves and crags were silent.

He woke up Dumu, motioned her to be quiet, and once they tied his horse to a rock, they set out for the largest-looking cave mouths that faced away from the coming storm. Dumu followed him, unsteady on her feet as the climb got steeper. He helped her along, their progress slow and cautious. Shamath was not sure what he feared in the silence, other than that it was no guarantee of emptiness. There were beasts in the mountains sheltered in the caves. But there might be other things, too.

Dusk wrapped itself about them like a cloak. The only thing darker was the cave mouth that beckoned as they approached. He saw no sign of light in the darkness within, no fire burni–

"Who goes there?"

The words cut through his thoughts like a blade. Shamath cursed himself for a fool. His edge was dulled from years of farming. He had neither seen nor sensed the sentry until they had almost walked right into him.

"I said: who goes there?"

The man was hidden from their view, in the dark. His words, spoken in the common tongue used along the Gulf, were the familiar challenge.

"Friend," said Shamath, his mind racing. He felt Dumu's hand tighten onto his arm.

The sentry laughed.

"Well spoken," he said. Then he cawed, a strange cry not unlike a night bird's. "And pretty stupid. You'd have to see me to know if I'm your foe or not."

Shamath was not intimidated. "But you can see me. And you are no Undying, but a man."

"How so?"

"No Undying would have bothered with banter. He would have killed us both on sight."

Another laugh. "Hear that, lads? We got us a right military genius come a-calling."

He came out of the cave mouth. More men appeared out from behind the rocks about them. Shamath was relieved to see they *were* men, but tried not to show it.

"The question stands, asked now in plain view," the first sentry said. "Who are you?"

"Mortals, like you," Shamath answered.

"That we see," said one of the other soldiers. They all wore armor, but of no standard army Shamath could recall. "And that you trek alone in this godforsaken place, with a woman dressed in tatters."

"A fine one, too," another one added with a nasty grin. "Tatters notwithstanding."

Their helms, breastplates and arms, on closer look, were mismatched, different from man to man. Shamath could recognize bits and pieces from the armors worn in Ur along with more from other cities along the Gulf. The men were as patchwork as their gear – rough-looking, haggard, and scarred by combat.

Shamath placed himself in front of Dumu.

"We bear nothing of value," he said.

"We see that, too," the first sentry retorted. "Though it must be said your woman *is* fine. What we asked, however, is who are you?"

"You have an odd accent," a grizzled soldier said. "Namurrian, maybe. Even Larakian."

"There's no more Larak," another scoffed. "Or Larakians."

"His pitch reminds me more of Ur."

"Your spymasters should have trained you better, thrall."

The men grunted at that. They tightened the circle around them, spoiling for Shamath to make a wrong move.

Shamath stayed still. If he wasn't careful, they'd cut him to pieces in seconds. And then they'd start on Dumu.

"Final answer, genius," the first sentry said. "Make it a good one."

Shamath opened his mouth, unsure of what to say.

"We come from Dilmun," Dumu cut in.

A basilisk staring them right in the face could not have frozen the sentries as fast as her words.

"There is no Dilmun either," one of the men whispered after a long silence.

"It's gone the way of Larak," the grizzled soldier said.

"That's where we come from nonetheless," Dumu retorted. "You can see we are not ghosts. Neither are we spies." She paused, her voice shaking. "But we came out of hell. We survived. This traveler found me buried in the wreckage. He helped me."

She steadied her voice. "And if you are men and not beasts like those that killed my people, you will not touch us."

There was a susurrus of chatter among the men. The first sentry held up his hand to stop them.

"Yssur will want to hear news of Dilmun," he said.

"*If* these two come from there," the grizzled man argued. "If they are not lying."

"It is Yssur's place to judge, old man. Not ours."

At that, the grizzled soldier fell silent. A look around the faces of his comrades revealed no one would press the matter further.

"All right, genius," the first sentry said, beckoning inside. "You and the lady come this way. Our commander will want to see you."

The inside of the cave was a long and twisted nest of forking paths and chambers, chosen, without doubt, because once deep within, these rock corridors would not allow a campfire to be seen from without. Whoever chose it was trained in army tactics and had not forgotten them. Shamath still felt foolish about not seeing through the sentry's ruse. There were men everywhere in this maze, huddled in small groups in niches and small cavities found into the bedrock. With sentries as well-placed as the ones he and Dumu had come across, they could hide out in these caves for days, perhaps even weeks. But hiding from who? And who were these patchwork men? He counted as many as fifty of them, all mortal, some of them dressed and armed in the same haphazard, piecemeal fashion, while others he gathered to be dressed in the colors of the army of the Gulf alliance. Much to his surprise, he glimpsed more than a few soldiers bearing the armor of Ur. A suspicion began to form in Shamath's mind, which grew to nigh a certainty when the sentry led them into a larger chamber filled with another sixty, perhaps seventy or so of these patchwork men. Their guide told them to wait by the entrance and strode in to speak in hushed whispers to a man standing by a campfire.

"Not quite an army," the man said as he took a few steps towards them. "Isn't that what you were thinking?"

He was a few years older than Shamath, with hair and beard cut in the military style he still remembered from his days in Ur. His speech, too, identified him as a man from those parts, though those were the only two consistent things about him. This was another raggedy soldier with armor made from pieces from a dozen armies and a myriad battles. Yet there was a warmth to his eyes behind the leathery, sunburned and scar-ridden face, along with something familiar that Shamath could not place.

"You are rebels," Shamath said.

The man looked at him quizzically for a moment.

"That we were, until a week ago," he said, darkening. "Now we're what's left." He gestured at the other patchwork men. "You'll find in these here caves the remnants of a full brigade. Along with men from the Gulf alliance and deserters from the Urian side. Two hundred-and-five strong in all."

"What happened to you?" Shamath asked, though he knew the answer.

"Bel," the man said. "We were the port cities' line of defense. He thrust into us like a cock into a seasoned whore. Four thousand men gone. And then so was he, bound for Dilmun." He paused. "All we did was whet his appetite."

At this he cocked his head towards the sentry, who stood still but at ease, awaiting orders. "He tells me you may be spies. Are you a spy?"

The question seemed to be directed at Shamath alone. Perhaps they believed Dumu, at least.

Shamath bared his throat for him to see. The man peered at the tanned, but otherwise unblemished skin. There was no mark of the Undying on him. The one Arkhalla left had faded at her death.

"You are no thrall, true," the man said, nodding. "But a spy you could still be. I've seen my share of Ur's infiltrators. Men have sold their own kind for gold." He peered straight into Shamath's eyes, as though to catch a lie reflected there. "Other things, too."

"We told your men the truth," Dumu said, her voice strained, a dam holding back a torrent of tears. "I come from Dilmun. And I survived only because this man came by and succored me, though he had no reason to and did it at great danger to his life and soul."

The man grunted and smiled without taking his stare off Shamath. Then he said something strange.

"Well, I guess we're all in this together."

Something sparked in the back of Shamath's mind. And the man's face now seemed even more familiar.

"Call me Yssur," he said, turning to Dumu. "I am the leader of these men."

He took her hand and shook it. "Any who have suffered the Undying's cruelty are welcome in our midst. And so," he was quick to add as an aside, "are those that offer succor to the suffering."

His eyes were on Shamath again. It made him feel uneasy.

"Come," said Yssur. "Warm yourselves by our fire."

There was warmth, indeed, as well as bread and water and some cold salted meats. On Yssur's signal, the men opened up and received them as companions sharing a fate and a journey. Their acceptance was a thing Shamath only now realized how sorely he had missed all those years out on the mountains. The warmth of humanity; the kindness to strangers; the waves of laughter rippling from mouth to mouth after a jest; all those trivial things that keep a man a man instead of a beast on hind legs. A man alive and not alone.

Sensing how the ashes of Dilmun still burned behind their eyes, Yssur and his companions asked them nothing of the massacre, neither did they regale them with their own tales of woe. Instead, they spun a story of skirmishes and dreams. The skirmishes were colorful and bold, painted in strokes spanning ten years of fighting. From bits and pieces in them, Shamath gathered that Yssur and some of the others were veterans of the war, from when it was nothing but a revolt in Ur, and once more he had the uneasy feeling that he knew this man though he could not place him. With it crept deeper into his heart an even colder feeling. What if there were men here that recognized him? Men who recalled that boy slave of the She-Demon, the one who had saved her from death at their hands? No one had shown such signs of recognition when Dumu and he had shared their names with the company. Shamath had looked at Yssur then, anxious for some twitch or nervous tick on the man's face, but the rebel had only responded with a ghost of a smile and a firm grip of his hand. Was he pretending? If so, why had he welcomed them as he did?

The dreams their hosts weaved together with their skirmishes touched him deeply. Among the daring raids, the flashes of bravado, the overwhelming odds these men beat time and again to find themselves about this campfire, there were brief brushstrokes of the homes and loved ones they were fighting for, even though there was no assurance they'd still be there if they won. Yssur himself was tearful as he outlined a vision of going back to Ur one day, with an army tried and true at his side. He told no prophecy of victory; he dwelled not on lines of pikes bearing the heads of Bel and the Undying Council. Instead, the image he painted was of a summer morn, of him and his men entering the fallen city and throwing open the door to every house to let out the friends and loved ones and strangers that were the humanity of Ur, out at last, free at last. And after they had all been lifted out of the dark, they'd up and leave, just like that, a long line of men, women and children, of soldiers who would have thrown down their arms, of livestock and carts packed with paltry belongings, all of them leaving Ur to march into the sunrise.

"It shall be then," he concluded, "that our lives will have been lived for something. When we shall owe no more to this world and shall be men. Not wretches and slaves, not thralls, not rebels. But men. And as a man, I shall meet a woman, and she will claim me hers, and we shall spend together what life the gods grant us." He paused, aware of the eerie silence his words had brought onto the company. "Such is my dream," he said, and went quiet.

There was not a dry eye among the crusty, battle-hewn men, and Dumu and Shamath too were wiping tears. Yssur had spoken to everyone's heart, for the same words were in every breast. Such is the dream of peace.

As soon as the group collected themselves, a new discussion was begun, this one of news from the other fronts of the war. There were too many accounts of Bel's power being challenged to be dismissed as wishful thinking. Besides all the desertions and the tales of his unfitness for command, told firsthand by those who had witnessed them, there was a rumor that all was not well in the court of Ur and that some members of the Undying Council were about to rise up against Bel. Indeed, just before they had joined the battle for Dilmun, more rumors had risen from the East, about the Akkadians being about to join the fight on the side of these dissenters.

"As soon as it is safe, we are getting out of these here caves," Yssur said. "Decimated we may be, but not beaten. Not in our spirit."

The others offered him ayes and grunts of approval.

"Somewhere," he went on, "in all this plague of battles that has infested every land betwixt the two great rivers, there will be one that we can pledge our blood to. We are two-hundred-and-five of us; that is some good we can do."

Shamath spoke before he even realized it. "Two-hundred-and-six," he said.

"Two-hundred-and-seven," came Dumu's voice from beside him.

The men looked at her. There was something in her eyes that would not brook jests about her manhood, so none of the soldiers made any.

Yssur, however, looked at him, frowning. "Because we are all in this together?"

Shamath stared back at the war-worn face. "There was a time I lived by those words," he said.

Yssur nodded. "They are as good as any to live by."

His smile was an enigma. Perhaps it was there; perhaps not.

Shamath realized he did not care if this man recognized him or not. He had to say what was already coming out of his mouth.

"I was never a soldier, but I fought, once. A long time ago. My cause was better than I was, but we still lost, and I became a slave."

He sighed. It was the next part that was the hardest. "I had a chance to fight again during the Rising. But I gave it up. I failed my comrades and myself. And even that thing I failed them for, that precious heart's desire that made me drop my sickle-sword, in the end I failed that as well."

Faces around the fire scrutinized his. No one raised his voice to mock or scoff at him. In some different way, his words spoke to their souls, as Yssur's had. To that part of their souls that was sick of it all and yearned for something gentler. Was there one of them who had not thought of dropping their blade at some point in these ten long years?

"I dropped my sickle-sword and I dreamt I'd pick up a plain sickle and be a farmer again, as I grew up to be. For years I thought was done with life and lived only in that dream. But the dream soured and twisted because of my failure. And when I sought out what it was that still haunted me, I found myself in Dilmun. In the hell that was Dilmun."

He paused and glanced at Dumu. Her eyes were stars reflected in a lake of tears. But she reached out, and she squeezed his hand. That was humanity.

"And in that hell, I knew," Shamath went on. "I knew sometimes there is no choice but to beat the sickle back into a blade, the plowshare back into a sword. I knew being human is a tale we tell each other, around campfires such as this. No more, no less. And those times that tale stops being told, then Dilmun happens, and Larak, and Carcosa. Because some men stopped telling it and stopped being human altogether. And because others, like me, stopped sharing it around the fire."

He squeezed Dumu's hand in turn. "I knew no one should be alone, drowning among the dead."

He turned to the others. "And as I see you about me, I want to be one with you. I have spent too long among the dead, too long alone. No man should. Every death that occurred while I did not take part, it is on my head, for it makes me less human. No man should be alone, and if you will have me, I will shed my blood at your side, the way I ought to have done years ago. It will be a small recompense, but it is my life; it is all that I have. As do you. But die as we will, we shall die together. And the tale will go on."

For long seconds, nobody spoke. Then someone did, to Yssur.

"So we recruit poets now, Cap'n? Because I'll be devilled if I know most of what this fellow meant, but I *feel* like I could take on a hundred Undying."

There was much laughter after that, and the mocking was gentle and done with love.

Humanity.

It was hours later that the fires and voices and laughter died down and the company settled down to sleep. Yssur had already set a spot for Dumu and Shamath, and as they made their beds on folded cloaks and rolled-up tunics, Shamath saw the lean commander walk up to him.

"Sickles into blades, plowshares into swords," he said with the faintest of smiles. "You always did have a way with words."

There was nothing random in his pause. Shamath looked up and saw that Yssur was studying his face for a reaction.

"You do not remember me, do you?" the commander asked him. He glanced about, then crouched down next to Shamath before he spoke again, under his breath.

"Your face seemed familiar from the first, even ten years on. And I still recall your name, Shamath of Larak."

"Who are you?"

"The first time we met, I was a conscript sergeant in Arkhalla's army and you were her body slave. It was around the time when Gilmesh, the Carcosan, was plotting revolution along with Bel. You told me something I never forgot."

We're all in this together.

The words came to Shamath's mind like an incantation, with a vision from the past brought with them, conjured from the pit of a life he thought lost. He saw Yssur then, as he was ten years ago. A young man, already aged by battle and hardship.

He looked at Yssur, waiting. The commander smiled.

"I know what happened in the ziggurat that night. I was outside, with the ones fighting in the streets. When Gilmesh and the others inside were captured, we fled into the hills and picked up the fight from there."

Shamath glanced at Dumu. She was on her makeshift bed with her back to them, hopefully asleep.

"Do with me as you will. She had no part in all that."

"I know she didn't." Yssur's smile had faded. "What do you think I ought to do with you?"

"What do you do to traitors?" It was Shamath's turn to smile. His was wry and bitter. "I failed the humans' cause. I suffered the She-Demon to live. I aided her escape. Bel killed the others because of me."

"Bel would have turned on us anyway."

Yssur was still speaking in hushed tones. Shamath had to wonder why he had not told the other rebels.

"That does not alter what I did," he insisted.

The commander scratched his beard. "No, it does not. Ten years ago, I would have had your head. For a moment there when I saw you, the thought did cross my mind again. But," he stressed, "time offers hindsight."

He fixed his eyes on Shamath. "Had you not rescued Arkhalla, the rebellion would have been over. Bel and Sin and those leeches would have made a pact with the rebels, gotten us to lay down our weapons and then slaughtered us all. The way I see it, you forced their hand. They had no time to plan our extinction. When Bel took Gilmesh's head and enforced martial law, he showed us all what fools we were to even hope for peace. It was a disaster. But enough of us lived. To fight another day. To keep the rebellion going, ten years on."

Yssur tapped his temple. "I did not know all that then, but I do now. Hindsight."

"And your comrades?"

"I would not count on *their* hindsight so much. Arkhalla's name still strikes terror by its very mention, so they'd probably kill you. But then, not many that survived that night lived through the war, and of those that did, not many would have met you face to face or remember your name. A lot of water has coursed through the great rivers, brother. And too much blood."

"But I... I helped her."

Yssur shrugged. "What does that matter? The bitch is dead now."

He put his hand out. "Now *Bel* is the enemy we share, you and me. We are still together in this. What you did all those years ago is liable to have saved my neck. If what you said back there was you asking for a second chance, who am I to say no?"

Shamath could not speak. The lump in his throat kept him from forming any words that were coherent. All he could do was clasp Yssur's hand.

The commander's grip was tight as iron. He smiled. "But fail our cause this time, and I will kill you with my bare hands." Shamath nodded. It was fair. It was more than he deserved. Yssur got up and turned to leave.

"You were talking about her, weren't you?" he said suddenly. "When you spoke about your heart's desire and how you failed it."

"Yes."

"Did you really love her?"

"Yes."

The commander seemed to think on this response. “You must explain that to me sometime. Should we both live and all.” And at that, he faded into the darkness of the cave.

CHAPTER 6

THE RED FLOWER

Bel looked at her and his eyes burned.

"Do not ask me to yield; I cannot."

"No, of course not," said Narama. "You are a warrior born. I would never ask you not to be yourself."

She tried to shift her eyes away from his and found it nigh impossible. It was good to see his gaze afire like that. Bringing him back to Ur and back from the abyss was the hardest thing she had done in all of her Undying life, but she had managed it. A little less than three score days had passed since that storm, when she had promised to get him back onto his feet, but now at last, after so many nights spent at his side after he woke screaming and so many times she had nursed him out of trances not unlike true death, even feeding him blood out of her own mouth when he would not so much as raise a finger to the choicest of young prey set out before him with their throats slit and bubbling, now at last he seemed himself once more. Strength had been restored to his limbs; his speech made sense and there was no trembling in his lips, only the sneer of cold command; and the passion rekindled in his eyes was so clear a sculptor could have caught it. Narama felt a surge of pride at the notion that she had brought him back, pride mixed with other stirrings. Even his stubbornness was something of the old Bel returned.

Perhaps, she hoped, he wasn't thinking of *her* so much anymore.

At last, he took his eyes away and moved towards the window, flexing cord-like sinews. The moon was full outside, bathing the chamber and his form under his tunic with its lustrous hue.

"So what *are* you asking? It is clear that Sin is plotting. This has gone much further than slurring my command. Should I not crush him and the humans in a swift twin stroke?"

"Alas, you cannot."

He snapped back. "What is that supposed to mean?"

Narama pursed her lips before she answered. "That Ur's army is in no shape to fight both foes in a two-front war and win. Not after ten years of fighting, Bel."

She did not say 'Because *you* are in no shape'. She wouldn't even if torturers burned her with hot coals.

"He's out there in the East building his own army. There are whispers that he's leaguing with the Akkadians, Narama! The Akkadians! Asag's blood, am I supposed to let that pass?"

"No. But you are supposed to plan."

Narama set down her cup and rose from the table. Princes would prostrate themselves and sign away their kingdoms to see her rise from their table. Her lithe silhouette, evident beneath her veil-thin dress in moonlight, moved softer than a jungle cat's. She had dressed casually to talk of these affairs of state because she wanted to create an atmosphere of ease and persuasion, for Bel was sorely in need to be persuaded to the line of action she'd propose. That said, she'd never dress like that for anyone other than Bel.

"Listen," she said as she came to stand next to him. "You need to stall for time while you gather a fresh army. The only way you may do that is to placate Sin. Set up a parley. Somewhere on neutral ground. Offer him a treaty."

Bel gnashed his teeth. "A treaty that I'll keep?"

"For now. So that you can exterminate him later."

He offered no retort to that. Narama knew Bel not to be one for slow and calculated strategy. The thought of it perplexed him. She decided to press her advantage.

"The parley alone may take months to set up. The talks are bound to take longer. During that time, you shall only have the rebel wretches to contend with. And you will present the appearance of negotiating for as long as you need to regroup your forces."

Bel paced the room. "Won't I be giving Sin time as well?"

"That is something you cannot avoid. But for better or worse, our resources are those of Ur and Carcosa. We know our strengths. He has new friends and alliances to fathom. Such things are fragile over time."

"His dallying with Nimrod."

Narama nodded, tracking him with her eyes as he strode up and down the chamber. "And his flirtations with the members of the Council."

Bel scoffed. "Only the weaklings. They are all he managed to have flocking to his side out in the East. Uthara and Lilit and Erun. The rest are still with us."

"Talmas and Anul are not exactly prime material." "Yes, but –"

"And Kuthan has already joined Sin's cause. He and Fazuz only pretend to support you. They are Sin's men through and through."

Bel stopped dead in his tracks, his eyes wide with surprise. "I will –"

"Do nothing of the kind," Narama cut him short. "Because I've had Hadu pretend to be allied to them. He is supposed to be Sin's third agent in the Council here. But in truth he reports all his faction's doings to me."

Bel seemed astounded.

Narama shrugged. "If our enemies cling close, we must have them even closer."

He smiled. "I am impressed."

"Thank you. You should be."

She tried to appear nonchalant, but a hint of color crept behind the dead pallor of her skin. To Bel's Undying sight, it must have been as manifest as a forest fire at night. But if it were, he made no show of it.

"My apologies, Narama," he said. "I keep regarding you the way you were ten years ago. The formidable Huntress of Men. I am still getting used to what you have become."

Narama could have sworn she saw the ghost of a blush behind *his* cheeks this time.

"Oh?" She tried to keep her voice steady. "And what have I become?"

He lowered his eyes. "A ruler of men. A sharp tactician. And far better than I deserve."

There can't have been more than five paces' distance between them, and in a second, there was none. She held his face in her hands before she even realized she was doing it. Her mouth attacked his. His lips surrendered, spreading to the thrust of her tongue.

For long seconds, their breaths were all the world.

"I am a ruined man," he whispered. Narama felt the burn of his tears on her cheek. "You waste your feelings on me."

"Shut up," she said softly. With a push, she pressed him against the wall and flung herself onto his body. Their lips fastened again, and they kissed thirstily, like birds beaking each other, their breaths harsh and acrid from the blood they had dined on. Bel put a clumsy hand about her waist. She moved it down onto the round firmness of her buttocks, the flimsy fabric between them and his grip fanning the lust of their embrace all the more.

She felt him shudder all over as she took him in her hand. He took the hint and thrust his free hand between her legs. His progress up her skirt met less resistance than an army marching through a field of daisies. Her loins had flowered long before he touched her.

"I have felt this way for you for lifetimes," she said, coming up for breath from his kiss. Her eye fell on the door of the chamber, left ajar, and she thought of the guards posted outside. "See that we are left to our devices," she whispered in his ear. "Our pleasures."

He looked at her, his eyes reading the earthy yen in hers. He moved to the door, whispered something to the men outside and then shut the door.

By the time he turned back to face her, her dress had slipped down to her feet. She stood facing him, nude as a spring morning.

He stood looking at her, aghast. She chuckled.

"You're embarrassing me," she said, and meant it. "Come here."

He rushed to her embrace and she tore his tunic off him. Her limbs vibrated as he touched her again, like before, and she lowered his head to her breasts to double her bliss. Sharp fangs toyed with her raised nipples and his tongue tasted a single drop, a red jewel of desire. She let out a tiny yelp of sweetest pain, rigid with convulsions.

Her eyes opened to the sight of his feasting on her beauty. She could feel his admiration filling her hand, his lust filling her being. It was desire she read in his eyes, and something else, something she yearned for even more. It was those eyes that told her she had flourished in those years away from him, like a flower in bloom, scarlet with passion like the single drop that reddened the pallor of her breast. She had come back different, stronger; his response was all the proof, all the confidence she needed. In his arms at last, she was content, like she never thought she'd be since that black day her life was taken from her.

Well, no more of that. No more holding down or holding back. There was only holding him.

He was in perfect sync with her. Feeling her need, he pushed her up against the wall. She clambered about his thighs, her legs and arms enwrapping him like tentacles as he lifted her with shocking ease. She moved up and down against him, prolonging the moment in a series of circuits of flesh brushing flesh, and tears of ecstasy ran down her face. At last she heard him moan, near the end of his tether, and lifted herself by that fraction of an inch that'd be enough.

The long moment over, she felt him strain and pushed herself onto him. Her nerve endings bursting with rapture, she bit him. He gasped, in rhythm to her thrust, in tandem with the rush of blood in her mouth. She raised herself up and down, his hands helping her motion, his chest heaving against hers, its hairs brushing the smoothness of her skin. The great flood was beginning to swell inside her, and as she slid along him faster he gave a bellow as he stiffened, trying to delay the moment.

She braced her back more firmly against the wall and pushed outwards, arching back as much as she could, bringing him almost against her forward edge. He pulled her to him again, all the way. She heard something then, a soft creak, or the tiniest shuffle, but there was no minding it. The flood was coming closer now, and would not be denied. One bubble of it burst through the dam she had blocked her ecstasy with, willing it to submit to her until she let it all out and it engulfed her whole. Narama could not keep it down any longer. Her lips parted, ready to release a great shuddering cry – and a hand that was no man's massaged her breast.

Her mind refused it. No, it wasn't there. It was a ghost, it was the bitch, in her mind, spoiling her fun. Two hands was all there was, Bel's, gripped tightly about her rump. She tried to focus, to get back on the current, the flood already washing away from her. But no, there the hand was again – She opened her eyes.

The woman was there, hugging Bel from behind. She had one hand thrust forward against Narama's breast, the other massaging his chest. She was kissing him, her tongue in his mouth.

She was not Arkhalla.

Bel felt her thrusts stop. He turned to her, opened his eyes, gaping at the horror in her face. The woman, too, stopped what she was doing.

Narama pushed herself from him and stood against the wall. She fought the urge to cover herself. The woman was still dressed. She was a human wretch, a slave girl by the outfit on her. She was young.

Bel knew he had done something wrong. That he looked at her like he was wondering *what* enraged her all the more.

"What is it?" he asked.

The girl knew. She stepped back, away from him, reading the naked hatred in Narama's eyes.

"What," she answered him, unable to get more than one word out at the time. "*Is. It*?" She struggled for breath, all too aware of her heaving breasts, her nakedness in full view of the girl. "What," she began again, marshalling all her strength to untie her tongue. "do you *think*. You are *doing*!"

His mouth moved a couple of times before he spoke. "I saw to... our pleasures."

"You think *this* brings me *pleasure*?!!"

He gasped. "Narama, calm down –"

"You *thought* another *woman* being with *us* while we are *fucking* would bring me *pleasure*? You thought *another* woman pleasuring *you* and *feeling me up* would bring me *pleasure*?"

By now, almost every second word she uttered was as pitched as a scream. Bel backed away from her, his terror palpable in the fast-shriveling manhood now limp between his legs. "Narama, please –"

"And what," she spat at him, *"what, pray, gave you such a notion?"*

She took a step forward, her nakedness a red blur in her mind. He took another step back. "I thought..."

The slave girl, eyes wide with horror, had almost reached the door.

"Yes?"

"I thought... it'd be good. Like it was..."

"Yes?"

"Back then... with Arkhalla."

The shriek that tore through the room wasn't human, just like it was neither a jackal's bay nor a lion's roar. That it came from Narama's lips was something she realized hours later.

The red blur now filling her eyes, she leapt forth, springing catlike clear across ten feet and onto the girl. The young slave screamed only once. She tried to lift up hands, to claw at Narama's face. Narama clawed hers to pieces. Fangs straining her mouth so much it hurt, she raised her head and bit down on the girl's neck fiercely, welcoming the pain, any pain. She shook the girl by the throat, her grip lion-strong, and didn't stop even when she felt the girl's heart give out and the flow of her blood slowing to one last desperate pump. And even that wasn't enough. With clawed hands and feet and a mouthful of fangs she tore into soft flesh.

Narama felt her body soulless, her self as detached from the grip of her flesh as in the moment of dying, only the body of a beast left behind, a beast that had stolen into her while she observed it with mild bemusement from afar. She was a beast, after all, who had only dreamed of being a woman, and now the dream was over, and the beast tore into the girl's flesh till it was neither soft nor flesh anymore.

She had no inkling of how much time had passed, seconds or eons. But she got up at last, slick with blood, her nakedness covered by it, oddly calm as she faced Bel.

"Narama..." he began, not knowing how to go on.

"Don't look at me," she said. She was not ashamed of his gaze like she had been of the girl's. She was insulted by it.

"I..."

"Don't you dare," she cut him. "I gave myself to you and you offend me like this."

"I wasn't... thinking."

"You didn't have to think. Doing was enough." He

opened his mouth, then shut it again.

"Did you think to even ask what I thought? Did you think to ask whether I'd want it?"

He raised his eyes.

"I told you I am ruined," he said. "*She* ruined me –"

"Don't you dare say her name again!"

The slap came so fast Bel didn't see it. The blow was sudden, so hard it snapped his head back.

A dull ache spread across his cheek. He tasted blood; his, and the girl's.

"Narama..." he said, massaging his face as he turned to face her.

But she was gone.

The room was draped in rich materials that covered every piece of furniture – silks, for the most part, of every color in the rainbow and some that weren't anywhere in nature. But the bed, like a temple virgin about to be offered to the gods, was draped in white. Narama stood at the open door, locked and bolted just moments before, now broken and hanging loosely from its hinges. She was still panting from the exertion of the slaughter of the girl, but there was little trace of that on her unblemished skin, whose pores had sapped the blood of her crime. Arkalla's blood baths had never appealed to her; she had never aped that habit, unlike Lilit and the others, thinking it filthy and disgusting. The very notion bothered her, especially in this setting.

Naked, she entered the bedchamber, her presence disturbing the fine coating of dust that time had weaved about it. Bel had had that entire wing of the ziggurat locked up and had allowed no one to venture there on pain of death. Narama had learned of this on coming back from Dilmun, and it had bothered her. She had wondered how many times Bel had been here, whether he had sat onto this bed all night, brooding about his lost love, or perhaps his lost hate, for Arkhalla's true place in his heart involved a lot of both. He had not done so all these weeks since their return; perhaps he never had. Yet now Narama knew it was not because he had locked up the past and forgotten it, but rather because he was too scared and pained to face it.

She paced the room with slow, cat-soft steps, removing the draperies. Unveiled, the bedchamber took her breath away. Everything was untouched, as intact as the last day Arkhalla had slept here. Dresses neatly folded on shelves and packed in trunks, and others dropped carelessly on the floor as though she had tried them on and left them there mere moments before; bright jewels that sparkled on display cases; even her crown, its sheen and luster undiminished by her absence, defiant in the face of her death. At first, the only marks of the passage of time, tainting the chamber like the mark of the Undying on their victims' throats, were the long-dried flowers on and beside the bed that once served as scented decorations and now resembled wreaths on a forgotten tomb. But after those first moments in which she saw these things, Narama noted how everything she saw that should be white had faded into a sickly yellow. Doubtless the ravages of time had affected all the colors, but all other hues had merely grown paler or more muted, and only the white had deteriorated thus, as though a strange sickness had affected only that color. The sheets on the bed, the finest of the transparent silks, were pale and motheaten, the ashes of silks, as though the virgin had never been offered to the gods but left in this musty chamber to shrink to a crone all skin and bone.

The chamber was Arkhalla's ghost, all right, or all that the notion meant to Narama as she surveyed it. A thing that was there, untouched and untouchable, almost alive, but rotting underneath its beauty, sucking the life out of all that touched it.

Her hate for the dead queen was so palpable she felt it like a vise about her heart. Each item was there to compound her revulsion. There were brushes and combs with black lustrous hairs still entangled on them, and dried-up bottles of lingering scent. A silk gown was laid out onto a padded stool with a pair of jewel encrusted sandals underneath, ready to wear. Narama felt unstuck in time, taken back to some random moment in Arkhalla's life and reduced to a selfless spectator of it. Any moment now, the ghost would rise and return to relive this frozen moment, taking soft steps about the room, picking what gown to wear, combing her hair with a comb bejeweled with tear-shaped diamonds. And through it all, it'd be Narama that would stand bodiless and invisible, watching this woman who, here, in this eternal moment, was more alive than her.

Tears came to Narama's eyes, red, their sparkle eclipsed by the treasure of jewels strewn about. What did her tears matter – or those shed by the thousands of victims who died to furnish this room? *She* and her world would remain. They, like tears, would fade.

She was dead. All those long years, she had been dead, buried under the tree on a branching road outside a city that was no more, naught but ashes and nothingness. But here she was vivid and alive, and Narama was nothing but a ghost.

With a shiver, she walked to the padded stool and picked up the silk dress, half-hoping it would crumble in her hands, reduced by time to so much worm silk. It did not. She felt the softness of the fabric running through her fingers, lighter than air yet as pleasing as a man's touch. The slave that had weaved it might as well have used a spider's gossamer. It was royal purple, expertly worked, and defying her to wear it. Narama put it against her face. It was cold, as cold as winter's tears. A faded, musty memory of *her* scent still lingered on it. Like lilies after rain. She studied it, its folds, its creases, telltale clues to how it fell on the queen's form, how it had embraced her living flesh. Her eyes wandered from the gown to the contours of her body. She was shorter than Arkhalla, more wiry and toned in her limbs, and her breasts were smaller, the size of fine wine goblets. But she could have worn this gown as well as any queen, and any man would be peeling it off her with his eyes, his hands itching to do the same, even unto a penalty of death. She was beautiful. She felt beautiful – or had felt so until a half-hour ago.

But she would never wear this gown as *She* would.

Red anger clouded her eyes once more. Clutching the gown in her fists, she tore it to shreds.

Her gowns. Her combs. Her jewels.

Her man.

She threw the stool onto the wall, smashing it to pieces. She smashed the chairs next, and the jewel cases, and she tore the sheets from the bed, baring it as though she was tearing the clothes off Arkhalla's flesh.

By now there was a film of scarlet before her eyes that covered all she saw. Every fine shade and hue spread about her, veils and garments beyond the colors of the rainbow, was nothing but another shade of red to her. She tore and rent through silks and samite and threw the lot down in a heap about the room as though they were naught but piles of dead leaves for kindling.

The statue of the king, her rival's father, spared the sacking of the ziggurat ten years before, she tore from its pedestal and smashed to pieces onto the floor.

Combs and perfumes, gold mirrors and ruby-encrusted pins, nothing escaped her wrath. She broke all that could be broken, smashed everything there was to smash, tore cloaks and curtains to shreds. She was meticulous in her obsession, leaving nothing intact, destroying it utterly, till all the contents of the chamber, from bedposts and stands to chestfuls of jewelry lay crushed together, a battered, torn, pulped carcass of the memory she hated. But still the mustiness of traces of scent plagued her senses, in tandem with the sick dull pain in her heart, the pain that throbbed with the knowledge of how she would have basked in all these things she had so viciously destroyed if only they had been her own. For a moment, she found herself pining for death, for the completeness she would feel even in non-existence had Bel preserved this shrine in memory of *her* instead of the one he truly and always loved.

Arkhalla was in everything in here. Narama felt her everywhere, even in the deepmost reaches of her own heart. She could almost hear Her footsteps behind her, the sound of Her laugh taunting her, the rustle of veils brushing against silken skin as She crept at the edge of her vision.

Narama had to obliterate everything, even the remnants of scent, or else Arkhalla was alive, always alive and watching her, haunting her. It all had to go, disappear, otherwise there'd be no respite other than Narama tearing out her heart with her hands, because it was there in her breast that Arkhalla still lived and mocked her.

She lifted the torch from its holder on the wall as though she was a moth drawn to its flame. With trembling movements, she carried it to the heap that covered the floor and set it alight. Flames caught on silk and musk and wood, caressing it all like a lover's hands. For one long awful moment Narama thought of laying herself down onto this bed of memories and abandoning herself to the fire's touch. Then there'd be truly nothing that remained; nothing to remind her of Arkhalla.

She fought the urge as the flames licked the walls of the room, rising higher. Her eyes watched objects of beauty burn to blackness. With every new thing the fire consumed, she found a little more of herself, a little further cause to live and not surrender. She was casting out the ghost, she realized, her breath less labored with each heaving of her chest.

Something gleamed among the rising flames, in a chest she had smashed onto the floor. It was burned right through, its lid overgrown in the blooming of her red flower. She would have known the gleaming thing anywhere. She had last seen it ten years before, that night in the throne room, but she recognized it as though that night was a mere breath ago.

Let it burn, too, she thought for a moment. Let all that reminded her die as *She* did.

But the very next moment, Narama was wading through flames, ignoring the blistering heat. Her scorched hands clutched the red-hot crown and she cried out as though she had walked into sunlight, but she held onto it, through the fire, till she had cleared the chamber. Only then did she drop the damned thing, but still she stared at it, ignoring the pain and the blisters on her palms and her arms and legs where the red flower had touched her.

The room burned behind her. She let it till there was nothing else in it to burn and the fire died down.

She had no inkling why she had saved this one thing from the flames, not at first. It was instinct, pure and unreasonable, and only when she tried to fathom it did she shape her act into something recognizable.

More than every other thing in the chamber, the crown for her was all that Arkhalla had been. Encircled in its goldwork were all the respect and admiration and envy and hurt the queen had inspired in her, along with Narama's own shame for how she had been wrought in Arkhalla's hands, worked into someone she hardly could recognize. This diadem was all that Arkhalla was, but also what it had made Narama into.

Nude, blistered and soot-stained, Narama still smiled as she knelt next to the red-hot diadem, her hands stretched to its glowing warmth as though it was a hearth promising comfort in the night.

She'd burned all that was Arkhalla's. All but a crown wrought like Narama had been wrought, claimed from the flames that engulfed the last of the Undying Queen like Narama herself yearned to be saved from the flames of her memories.

But the very fact she held this reminder in her hands meant she would always burn.

ALARUMS OF WAR

CHAPTER 7

THE FORGE OF TIME

The old man toiled at the anvil. Sweat beaded in a fleeting diadem across his brow and flowed profusely over his thin yet wiry limbs, its moisture offering small comfort from the heat. His fist went up and came down, clutched tight about his hammer, in a motion rich with the rhythm and grace that is the working man's. His wealth was nothing but day in and day out of work that slowly and surely broke his back, like it had broken his father's. His father had passed it on to him in slow, painful lessons that the old man had learned at his side, and he in turn had passed it to his son. No king could ever lust for the old man's riches, yet neither could said king boast their like in all his vasty treasure horde. For each man's life is treasure that is his alone, and the working man's toil is beyond the means of even the mightiest potentate.

It was a day like any other in the small village and in the old man's life. Time and the world flowed and poured and cooled into being about him as though forged on the anvil of the gods, but the old man and his village remained untouched by them. The village still stood even as battles raged on for years now in the plains beyond it, and cities that dwarfed it a thousand times had long since perished in flames and bloodshed. And the old man still lived, even as his son did not, for he, like so many of the young men of his village, had joined the fight so many years ago that the old man had lost all hope of ever holding him in his arms again. So he went on, making shoes for horses and ploughs for farmers and tools and sickles, but no swords, for the very last sword he had made was the one he had given his dead son. He went on existing, like the village went on standing. All that time had done was rob their lives of meaning. It was no little thing, indeed; but only kings in poems rave and rage against time's arrows like the proud, larger-than-life figures that they are, and only mighty cities burn forever, their death throes captured by epics that outlast them by millennia. Little men and small villages suffer their wounds in silence as time is forged relentlessly about them.

There was another war on; the old man had heard as much. Or perhaps it was the same war with forces and foes shaped anew on the anvil of the gods. There was talk of a rebel force raiding the lands between the gulf cities and Ur these past two years, moving back and forth across the entirety of the South, striking fast, then fleeing. The old man was not puzzled by their tactics. This, after all, had been the rebels' way ever since Arkhalla of Ur fell. But there was something different in the rumors about this rebel army. The word was never uttered out loud, as if in fear there'd be a jinx in the uttering of it, but to an old man who had been hearing tales of battles all his life, the inference in the hushed, excited tones of the travelers that told these new tales was clear.

Whatever these rebels were doing, they were winning.

A village that was more within the world would be abuzz by rumors such as these. Its young men would have risen to go and join this army of rebels that was beating the cursed Undying. But there were no young men in the village anymore; its people, like the old man, had let the world be forged around them. So they and the old man went on with their quiet lives, in silence, suffering, existing, thinking there'd be no more than that till the quiet end of their days.

Which, of course, is exactly the kind of thinking that brings the gods' hammer down on quiet men.

It was dusk. The old man could tell from the length of the shadows in his smithy. Soon, he'd stop his work, wash with water from the well, sup on the gruel he had made for himself and settle for the night. Dusk meant quiet, and rest, and peace. So when he put down his hammer and still heard the awful clanging of bronze on bronze, he knew the war had finally spilled into his village, and that he'd been a fool to think that this would never be.

Screaming joined the clash of weapons. There were men dying beyond his door. His neighbors had picked up the tools he had forged, the swords he and his father had forged years before and were now rusting in sheds, and they were fighting and dying with them in their hands.

It could have been anything. As little as a stray patrol of the Undying on the lookout for blood after days in the desert. As much as a full company of them, the village picked at random as a way station in the path of its advance. It mattered not a jot. The village was doomed in either case.

The old man waited, pursing his lips as the clang and the screams got closer to the smithy. The cries drilled through his ears, setting his teeth on edge. As it drew closer, the clash of bronze shifted to a wet, fleshy squelch that was all too similar to that of cattle meat on the butcher's block. Smoke and the acrid smell of slaughter teared up the old man's eyes. He clutched his hammer in one hand, his tongs in the other. Those were the tools he had wielded all his life. In that moment, so close to death, he prayed to no gods. What gods could he put his faith into when they had failed him? What had he to hold onto on the point of dying but the tools that fed and clothed him while he breathed?

Something smashed through the door of the smithy. Wood chunks and splinters flew onto the old man's face, and he shielded his eyes as he fell. Blinded, he saw not the twin lean, black shapes that flew in out of the blood-tinged smoke, swords in their taloned hands, cloaks flowing behind them like leathern wings, so fast it would have made no difference if he had seen them. All he had time to do was swing his hammer before it was knocked off his hand; even his scream was cut short by sharp-clawed fingers clasped onto his mouth. He was flat on his back, the monsters' hands on him, pinning him down, a bitter breath making his flesh crawl as one of them lunged onto his neck –

A gust of wind came, so sharp it cut through the Undying's growl. The old man thought of a sickle cutting through wheat. Clawed hands held him no more. He stayed there, still, his eyes shut, shaking to the sound of grunts and blades clashing. A cry as chilling as a cat's death wail almost made his heart stop. And fast on its heels, another whoosh of sickle-like wind… and then nothing.

The old man lay there forever. He realized he was afraid to open his eyes. Better to wait for death to come, or whatever it was that was there – for he could sense he was not alone.

Soft footfalls stalked towards him. The old man held his breath. A hand fell on his shoulder.

"Come, grandfather. Open your eyes."

The voice was quiet, human. So was the hand. The old man opened his eyes.

"Here," the young man said. "Let me help you up."

Stunned, the old man let himself be propped up to his feet. The young man's grip was soft, yet firm, his slim build a veneer hiding strong sinews.

The old man's hands made clutching motions, closing around empty air. He should have been holding something, but he wasn't.

"My tools," the old man said, without quite knowing why. His brain was all fuddled.

"Right here."

The newcomer picked the hammer and tongs off the floor where the old man had dropped them. He smiled. “I’d have thought you’d have more of a choice of weapons in a smithy, grandfather.”

He held out the tools. The old man didn’t take them. His eyes had followed the young man as he bent down, and were still fixed on the two bodies on the floor. Both of them were long-limbed, their pale skin in sharp contrast to their black armor, and both were headless. Their heads were near their feet, monstrous mouths still open showing fangs, pinprick-like eyes still wide with a final look of shocked horror.

A sickle-sword was sheathed in the young man’s belt, its blade still stained with demons’ blood.

“We couldn’t save your village,” he said sadly. “But we saved some people.”

He could not have been more than thirty or thereabouts, but what the old man could see of those parts of him left uncovered by his armor was battle-scarred here and there, while fresh cuts on his cheek and arms marked where the Undying’s blades had grazed him.

The tools were still in the young man’s hands. Seeing the old man did not move to reclaim them, the young man smiled again and placed them on the smithy’s workbench next to the anvil. Then he took the old man by the hand, and the old man let himself be guided out into the smoky ruins that were his village only an hour ago. There were other men there, all dressed in hodgepodge, shabby-looking armor like the young man was, some searching through burnt houses and helping survivors like him, while others guarded fifteen-or-something prisoners, all trussed up and on their knees in the village square. Two of them, the old man saw, bore a bat-shaped crest on their breastplates. But what most surprised him was seeing a young woman there among the soldiers that helped people out from the wreckage, armored herself, but with her helm doffed, revealing straw-bright hair cropped like a man's and framing a strikingly beautiful face.

Another rebel soldier, a little older than the one who had saved him and twice as battle-scarred, was coordinating the company of men, and the young man greeted him not with a salute, but with a handshake, his free hand clutching the other man's forearm as he would a brother's.

"The leaders?" he said, nodding towards the two captured leeches with the fancy breastplates.

"Aye. See their crests? Black Guard. Sired by the devil, Bel, himself."

"And the survivors?"

"Some twenty or thirty. Old men, women and children."

"The men are gone," the old man heard himself say. "The wars took them."

A day ago – perhaps even an hour ago – he might have said '*Your* wars', and spat out the words. But it seemed ungrateful at that moment, so he did not say it.

The young man darkened with sadness nonetheless. He studied the old man before he spoke.

"Who have you lost, grandfather?"

There was compassion in his voice, the real thing. He had lost people too, this young man.

"My boy," the old man said. His eyes watered. "I've lost my son."

The young man sighed. Then he did something very unsoldier-like.

He hugged him.

"I am sorry," he said, his voice broken.

It was these three simple words that caused the old man to do something that was very unlike his own crusty ways. He began to cry, with slow, gentle sobs, his face buried in the young man's chest.

Moments passed. The old man, his breast unburdened, drew back.

"Who are you?"

"Shamath of Larak," the young man replied.

"That is far from here."

"As far as your son, grandfather. My people are gone from this earth."

The old man nodded. "How was it you came here?"

"It was on our way." The young man called Shamath pointed to the other soldiers. "We have been fighting some two years now, crisscrossing the lands of Sumer, freeing who we can."

"Your way? Where to?"

"We're building an army. We're going to Ur."

The old man stared at him in disbelief.

Someone laughed. It was one of the two captives that had led the Undying; a long man with a hawk-nosed face.

"I won't live to see it," he rasped. "But it is good to know my slayers march to their death."

He spat blood. It landed inches from the young man's feet.

Shamath walked up to him, calm. "I agree with the first part," he said. "You won't live to see it."

"Kill me, then, wretch. But you shall die sooner or later. We are Undying. And Bel has tasked us to rule the world." Shamath stared at the Undying, silent.

"Kill him," the rebel commander said. "If only to spare us his prattle."

The old man watched the young warrior as he seemed to weigh his response. There was a battle going on inside him, and the old man could see it on Shamath's face as clear as though it took place on a wide field on a crisp spring morn. That compassion and humanity the old man had glimpsed in him were fighting with cold murder and necessity. To spare prisoners as dangerous as the Undying was unthinkable; to hold them captive a waste of men and resources this ragtag army clearly did not have. But the decision still troubled the warrior. The old man wondered what Shamath had seen these two years of fighting; how his mettle was tested and shaped on time's anvil.

"No," said Shamath at last. "Not till he gets it."

The old man saw the Undying warlord frown. Whatever he expected – a swift death, most likely – this was not it.

"You say we are marching to our deaths, leech," Shamath went on. "But how many of us are on that march? And what are we? Villagers and farmers? Sons of men? Women?"

At this, he glanced over at the light-haired girl, who smiled back at him.

"Your eyes deceive you, leech," he resumed. "We only seem these things. We are not villagers. You have burned down our villages. We are not farmers, for you took our farms and turned them into killing fields. We are not sons, for we have no fathers anymore. And we are neither women, nor men."

A grin creased his face. "Do you want me to tell you what we are?"

The prisoner said nothing. But the old man thought he saw something in his eyes. Something not unlike alarm.

"We are the ones you failed to kill. The ones that lived through anything you threw at them. We are many, and we are becoming more." A pause.

"We are what you fear."

At this, Shamath turned and started back towards the old man.

"Chain them all to a pole and leave them there under guard," he said to another soldier.

"Leave them? How long?" the soldier asked.

"Till the sun rises."

He looked at the rebel commander, who hesitated, then nodded.

The old man turned to the captives. They had heard. Their pale faces looked bleached with terror.

Shamath came up to him. The old man returned his look.

"Do you think me cruel, grandfather?"

The old man stayed silent for a moment. "No more than them."

That brought a fleeting smile to the young man's face. "It is cruel. Though I have seen worse. Far worse. Believe me, it is also necessary."

"To make them fear you."

"And win this war."

The old man looked at the soldiers, rummaging through the wreckage that was once houses, looking for poles fit for their grim task. He shrugged.

"It won't bring anything back," he said. "The village. My son. It won't bring them back."

Shamath pursed his lips. His face seemed gaunt, haunted.

"Tomorrow, grandfather," he said. "When the sun comes up. If I were you, I wouldn't watch it."

The old man didn't have a mind to do so. "I imagine it will be horrible."

"It is. I've seen it."

CHAPTER 8

VOICES IN THE WILDERNESS

Bel stepped out of his tent into the sultry dusk. He took a deep breath, his throat and nostrils feeling clogged with heat and dust. It had been a scorcher of a day even down in the sun shelters. Woe to the Undying caught in it, Bel thought. Their flesh would shrink and burn and peel right off their bones. It'd take the better part of the evening for even the chill of the desert to cut through this oppressive invisible curtain that seemed to cover the world.

Hadu and Kuthan greeted him with silent nods as he walked forth. Kuthan had insisted on being on site during the parley for security's sake, though Bel was certain it was because he wanted to make sure he'd lend a hand to any mischief Sin might have planned. Of course, what Kuthan did not know was that Hadu, whom Kuthan thought an ally, was there to make sure that a blade would sever Kuthan's head from his shoulders were any such mischief to actually happen. The intrigue of it felt almost as cool as a gentle wind.

At this thought, Narama walked out of her tent as though the heat did not touch her, resplendent in her armor.

"Narama," Bel greeted her, fighting his urge to smile. He knew she would not smile back.

"Let's go," she said and set out, not waiting for a response.

Bel caught up with her and they walked side by side out of the camp, with Kuthan and Hadu at their heels.

Brokering a treaty can often take longer than fighting a war. For two years now, envoys and ambassadors and couriers crossed thousands of miles from West to East and back again, wasting long hours and nights upon nights and month after month bargaining terms, disputing borders, challenging claims. Choosing the neutral ground alone for this parley had taken nigh to four months. Narama had overseen it all, as canny a tactician as Bel was on the field, but Bel had no tolerance for negotiating and had stayed away from the talks and conference chambers, which seemed to suit Narama fine, for she had little tolerance for him.

He stole a look at the finely drawn visage, an inner light combining with the haze of dusk to form a blue-gray aura about her features. Her lips were parted, reminding him how they had parted for him that distant night. In all the time since then, she had not spoken a single word to him that wasn't about the splitting of the kingdom, Sin's scheming, or this parley. She was his eye, his brain, the strongest arm a man could have. But she was not his heart, for he had wounded hers and she would not let him forget it.

"Remember," she said, not looking at him. "If he is ready to go to war, he will try to goad you, make you lose your temper. Resist that. He may be ready, but we are not."

"I know."

"If you agree to a treaty, even a few months more could give us the edge."

"We would have had the edge already if not for the rebels," he flared. "Damned cockroaches."

She glanced at him. "That face is exactly the one you cannot show him."

Bel made to speak, but thought better of it and nodded instead.

"It will be only you and him out there. Two leaders. Equals."

"Without the Akkadians backing him, he'd be no equal of mine."

"Except they *are* backing him. Nimrod is out there." She pointed at Sin's camp, a thin dark line of tents just before the horizon. "Remember that, too, if you get the urge to gut him."

He couldn't help smiling. "You know me too well."

She said nothing. The mirth died on Bel's lips. They walked on in silence, and after a while they reached the banner bearing the crest of Ur. Far ahead, Bel could see another banner, this one bearing the colors of Akkad, at roughly the same distance from Sin's and Nimrod's camp as this one was from theirs. Between the banners stretched five hundred yards of desert, in the exact middle of which stood a table and two folding chairs, set up at twilight in anticipation of the parley. A couple of tall standing torches were planted in the ground to light the scene.

It seemed a rather elaborate show, all to get two old friends to sit across from each other and talk.

Narama frowned onto the distance. "They are ready on their end." Her huntress' eyes were sharp as ever. She came to a stop under the banner. "This is as far as I go. From now on, you are on your own."

Bel hesitated. "Narama," he said.

She waited.

He wanted to say something to her. A lot of things. Sorry was only one of them. But sorry was only a word. The chasm between them was much deeper than words.

With a heave of his broad shoulders and a motion he tried to make seem sure and steady, he unfastened his sickle-sword and gave it to her. The terms of the parley were to come unarmed.

Narama took the sickle-sword with a nod. He nodded back, turned, and walked out into the desert and the coming night. From afar, he saw a mirage, a pale, ghostly reflection of him as it did the same.

He stopped. The pale ghost stopped. He took a couple of steps, and the ghost did the same.

A wolfish grin cut into Bel's face, sharp and bitter. He walked on, each step aped by the pale figure in the distance as they crossed the emptiness towards the two chairs and each other. When he got close enough, Sin raised his hand in a slight wave, so Bel raised his.

"Hello, old friend," said Sin with an easy smile as they reached the table.

"My lord Sin," said Bel formally.

"Always, my lord Bel, always," Sin replied, still smiling. "Shall we?"

They took their seats. The table was bare, with no refreshments – for blood would go bad too soon out in the desert and, as Sin's missive on the matter had put it, it would be decidedly rude to slaughter a live human while talking peace – and no tablets or writing instruments to sign the treaty with. As Bel, or rather Narama, had put it, all the two of them had to do was talk and shake hands on what they agreed. Lower men would put the thing in writing.

"You look well," said Sin. "Robust. Healthy."

Bel didn't bite. But then, he reminded himself, neither was this the baiting Narama had warned him against. Sin was having his fun, that was all.

"So do you. The air of Akkad becomes you."

"You are too kind."

Bel was in his black dress uniform – full armor would be frowned upon at a parley – while Sin was attired in white, in the Akkadian style. The finery suited him, true, but his hairless cheeks clashed with the fashions of Nimrod's court, which were rigorously attuned to long beards and curled locks.

"Is that Narama I spy back there?" Sin asked, pretending to glimpse into the distance behind Bel. "She is as well as you, I hope.
Will you give her my salutations?"

"Of course."

"I always thought the two of you made a striking couple. Much more on an equal basis than, say..."

He let his voice trail off, leaving his sentence incomplete. Bel forced a smile. The inside of his mouth tasted like vinegar.

"And Ur?" Sin enquired. "I hear some disturbing things about the wretch rebellion."

"Everything is under satisfactory control."

The councilor flashed a wide smile. "Satisfactory. Lovely word. How it rolls off the tongue, eh?"

Bel chafed at this banter, but tried not to show it. "We're dealing with the wretches just fine, old friend," he said.

"But of course." Sin paused to acknowledge the empty desert about them, or at least as much of it as the torchlight allowed. A moment of silence stretched between them.

"So here we are, across a table at last," he went on. "Face to face."

"It is good," Bel replied.

"What is?"

"That we can come to an agreement." Sin
laughed.

"An agreement? Is that what you think this is?"

Bel gritted his teeth. Here it was, like Narama had warned. The goading.

Play along. But stay firm.

"No," he said. "We're carving up an empire like a roast, Sin. We're splitting Ur's domains amongst our factions. Because we can't agree to share the throne. And because none of us wants a war." He grinned, a tiger sizing up prey. "*That*, old friend, is what this is."

Sin pretended to think of Bel's words. He was a great pretender.

"That would be nice, Bel. It would be – how would you put it? Satisfactory. Except, of course, I *want* a war."

Bel frowned. He did not expect such a direct approach.

"Then you'd best be ready to put an army where your mouth is," he said, acting nonchalantly.

"I am going to put two. Mine and Akkad's."

"That still makes about three-quarters of Ur's forces."

"But Ur's forces also have a war going on down South."

"The wretches are no challenge."

"But the wretches *and* Akkad *and* me ought to be."

Bel fought to hold his temper. "Ought to be?" he scoffed. "You want to take that chance?"

He was prepared for Sin saying something smart and throwaway. In fact, he was already mulling a quite insulting and vulgar reply to that. If Sin wanted a war, then by Asag he would give him one.

Instead, Sin settled back in his seat. "Let me try this again. You think all this is me and the rest of the council, don't you? That we're making a play for power. I mean, now that Arkhalla's dead and all. That is the carcass we are carving up, isn't that what you think?"

"All right, Sin, that's quite –"

"You think this is warlords and statesmen at each other's throats over a stretch of land, don't you? As it has been since time immemorial? Is that what you think?"

"Sin –"

"*Is* that what you think?"

Bel bit his lip, trying to quell his anger. "All right. I'll humor you. That's exactly what I think, you greedy piece of shit." Sin smiled as though he had heard a compliment.

"No, Bel. No. *This* is much more important than all that. *This* is your *life*."

Bel considered drawing his sickle-sword and carving up the bastard before he remembered he was unarmed. Even so, he still thought of grabbing Sin and tearing him limb from limb for a moment. But there was something in Sin's words that gave him pause.

"Fine," he hissed. "Tell me. Why is this my life?"

"Because it is also mine. Because this night is where our lives finally take on their true meaning. And because, old friend, I was never a friend to you, and you never knew how true this was until now."

Bel shook his head. "Sin, you always talked too much." He shrugged. "So you were a false friend. So we'll go to war. I get it." He made to get up.

"You get nothing." Sin's tone was so cold it froze him in midmotion. "Sit down."

He sat down again.

"You think Arkhalla made you, is that not so? Your Undying Queen? Your unrequited love?"

Bel frowned. "I know so, Sin. Like she made you. She was first. You know that."

"And who made her?"

"What are you driving at?"

"Who?"

Bel weighed his words. "The gods below."

"I could read as much on a tablet. The full story, Bel."

"They and their priests demanded her life from her father the king. Arkhalla was to be sacrificed. Her father reneged at the last moment and his own guard killed him. You *know* all that. I *told* you I was there. I tried to save them both and I failed, and the guards nearly killed me, too."

He could tell from the hunger in Sin's lean face that he had to keep going, to say all. It made him all flustered, ill-at-ease; he felt a cold trickle of sweat down his back.

"And Arkhalla – she..."

"Yes."

"She ran for her life, down into the sacrificial pit, and she gave her life to the gods. And they... they made her into what she was."

Sin steepled his hands in front of his mouth before he spoke. The pose of a master thinker.

"So one could say it was the priests that brought this on her just as the gods did." He smiled. "After all, they spoke for the gods. They made Asag's wishes known to the king."

"Yes."

"Unless, of course, they also spoke for someone else."

Bel shivered. "Someone... else?"

"Me, for instance."

Bel's hands clenched into fists. "You go too far."

"Oh, trust me, I already have. I did it."

The night and the desert were no longer there. Bel was drowning, in nothingness, falling from a dizzying height down, down, all the way to the great below.

He tried to fight the vertigo. "You did what?"

"I told the priests to demand Arkhalla's life, my dear fellow. I knew he'd either be forced to obey the gods' command, which would destroy him, or that he'd back away from it, which would bring his end."

Bel was dumbstruck. He thought he felt his mouth open and close, several times, but no sound that he heard came out of it.

"You see, the priests and I were in league," Sin went on. "Mine was the plan, of course. I was the mastermind behind Anshara's fall; I led the uprising against him." "You lie," Bel managed to whisper.

"Bel, this is the first time in all the years I've known you that I speak truth. No half-truths, no dissembling. All true."

He leaned forward, his face aglow with glee. "Forget the Magi, or those ridiculous occultists that tried to ape them, like Erun. Long before Anshara, my ancestors honored the old gods as gods ought to be honored – with lives. And we were rewarded with power in return. We were the rightful heirs of Kur before its fall, and when Anshara unearthed the mirror, we knew we would be so again. To stress my point once more, my dear fellow, I brought on the old king's death."

Bel, senses reeling, tried to get up, to reach out and grab Sin by the neck. All he managed was to nearly fall off his chair.

"Of course, my intention was for Arkhalla to die as well," Sin continued. "You, I'm afraid, were nothing but a collateral loss. A loyal dog killed while trying to save its master."

"You bastard."

"Oh, I am. By definition as well as in terms of character. You are not insulting me, old boy."

For all his efforts, the one word was all that came to Bel's mouth. "Bastard."

This time, Sin ignored him. "Yes, well; *now*, we all know how things did not turn out quite as I intended. The gods work in mysterious ways, indeed. So our young princess became an Undying queen, blessed with the dark mercy by Asag himself. This put me in dreadfully dire straits. I could do nothing but wait until Arkhalla bled me to death, like she did with so many of those that did not yield to her –"

"Or you could join her in undeath."

Sin beamed. "*Now* you're getting it. Precisely, Bel. Join her in undeath and bide my time, playing the councilor. A thrall among thralls. A thinker surrounded by fools."

He chuckled. "No offence, dear fellow. As far as blunt instruments go, you were infinitely more effective than the rest of those mindless clods. I had nothing but appreciation for your skills."

Bel said nothing. It took every ounce of strength he had in him to stop his lip from trembling. All he knew was that he had to hear the rest of it, no matter how much he didn't want to.

"Now, I know what you are thinking," Sin went on. "*What made me as effective as all that?* Well, bluntly put, your being such a fool for love."

The councilor's mouth stretched into a slit as thin and as sharp as a dagger. He was enjoying this.

"As you recall, I was biding time, waiting for the opportune moment. But with Arkhalla as entrenched in power as she had become, that moment turned to eons. You being stuck to her side was a further bothersome obstacle, I must admit. And then that dear, wonderful young man came along, and in him I saw the perfect chance."

"The Larakian boy."

Bel heard himself speak as if it was someone else, far away.

"Exactly. With Arkhalla in love with that wretch, you were putty in my hands. I could use the same fool's love that had protected her against her."

"You played me for a fool."

Sin chuckled. "You say that as if I were a friend who betrayed you. We were never friends. I never even liked you. But you allow yourself to be used so completely, Bel, and I do love you for that."

Bel bared his fangs. His claws dug deep into the wooden surface of the table. If someone offered him a sickle-sword in exchange for the entire realm of Ur, he'd take it.

"Temper, temper," Sin mocked him. "I do sympathize, but you have to see things for what they are. I have gotten most of the council to come over to my side; at least the ones worth the trouble bribing. And as the scion of a family as old and powerful as Anshara's, I have a more legitimate claim to the throne than an old soldier and an uppity lowlife slut. Everyone will say so, from Akkad and the other human nations to our own people. All I have to do is best your army."

"Good luck with that, you son of a bitch."

"You think you can stop me? You are a failure, Bel. You failed to protect the woman you loved; you betrayed your queen. You were Arkhalla's lapdog, true. Still, it was the best deal a nobody like you could ever have. But you wanted it all, and you got her killed. And now you'll end up with nothing."

Bel roared. He pushed himself to his feet, his claws reaching for Sin's flabby neck.

Pain shot through his hand and yanked his arm, nearly wrenching it out of its socket. Bel roared again, in agony.

He fell back on his chair, staring in disbelief at the shaft that had pierced his hand with such force half of it had drilled through his palm and out the other side. Stings jabbed at his nerve-endings and he bit his lip as those parts of his brain not screaming processed the arrow's telltale fletching and bloodstained tip. It was Akkadian.

Shaking, Bel stared in the distance, far behind Sin. There, standing before the largest tent, his Undying sight spotted the lean, dark, bronze-skinned girl with her bow, its string still aquiver.

Bel gasped. No human he knew could ever make this shot from such a distance, and only one Undying could hope to match it. An impossible shot.

"Rather impossible, yes," Sin said, as if he'd read his mind. "But then, you haven't met Nimrod's little princess."

"*Bel*!"

The cry came from behind Bel. He turned. Narama was halfway across the distance from the camp, running, deft fingers arming her bow in the space of a heartbeat.

Bel knew the princess was doing the same even before he turned and saw her do it.

"No!" he cried out. "Stay back, Narama!"

The Huntress hesitated, faltered.

"Please! Stay back! You cannot!"

There was no way even she could shoot the princess at that distance. By the time she got near enough, Aisyah could have gotten a dozen more shafts out. Some would hit him even if he made a run for it. Or she could hit Narama when she got in range. He knew it. Narama knew it.

He saw her grit her teeth. But she stayed where she was.

Bel struggled to control the pain. He steeled himself for whatever was coming, his eyes darting from Sin to the princess.

"A wise decision," said Sin, smiling.

He signaled, an infinitesimal gesture of his hand. The princess lowered her bow.

"Just a warning shot," said Sin, cocking his head towards the arrow sticking out of Bel's hand. "Believe me, I am as averse to taking things further right now as you are. Too many variables. Any of us might die."

"You... fucking..."

Sin sighed. "Insults. The clod's last refuge in an argument."

He got up. "I believe this puts an end to the parley. No shaking of hands, I'm afraid. Seems there will be war, after all."

Bel shot him a look of venom. Sin deflected it with a chuckle.

"I leave you to contemplate your utter humiliation," he said, and started back for the Akkadian camp.

Bel watched him leave, shaking with pain and impotence. He had been played, so cruelly he would not have deemed it possible. He was consumed by a hatred he could not even act on. For at bottom, he knew Sin was right. He had been weak and stupid, and he had ruined what little he had.

Soon his old friend faded from his view, and Bel sat alone, the lone and level sands as vast as his despair.

CHAPTER 9

A WAR CIVIL AND OTHERWISE

The first year of the war flew by. It was, after all, a new war, no matter how enmeshed it was in the sequence of a hundred thousand skirmishes wrought in a rebellion that refused to be crushed. This was a fresh conflict with fresh enemies to hate, and like all new human endeavors, even those drenched in the blood of innocents, it garnered much rejoicing. Banners were waved as troops marched out, fresh-faced and virginal, for by now the Sumer realms found themselves lacking in grown men. Fire-breathing orators rallied the crowds, singing the praises of their side while debasing the enemy to the level of the basest animal, for the only way to fight a war is to believe your foe as not fit to live. Weaponsmiths prospered along with the priests that sent the slain to a better life and the undertakers that put them in the ground.

Sin's tale of him as the redeemer of Ur's throne took root like poison vine in the lands between the twin great rivers. To those that lent him their support, he was the scion of the last nobles of his realm before Anshara sullied its very name and his accursed daughter turned it into a byword for horror. He and his allies in the council were propped up as great men and women rebelling even against the Undying curse Arkhalla had infected them with. The world had had enough of that She-Demon whose legacy still lived in her acolytes, dark Bel and vile Narama.

By the time Bel had risen from the table and, having pulled the arrow from his hand with Narama's help, staggered back to their camp, Kuthan and Fazuz had fled into the night with a hundred horsemen, thus finally declaring their true allegiance. That left Bel and Narama with only Hadu, Anul and Talmas at their side, with all the other members of the Council – Kuthan, Fazuz, Lilit, Erun, and Uthara – pledged to the cause of Sin. It was not only the betrayal that stung, but the resources these traitors commanded and now gave freely to Bel's foe. Horses and weapons and estates, spies and allies, men-at-arms, a vast supply of human cattle from the provinces in their domain, and most importantly, the gold and sundry wealth they'd accumulated under Arkhalla's reign and Bel's regency.

Even worst was the fact that the cabal of traitors had managed to find allies in Nimrod and the Akkadians. Narama was too savvy to think that Nimrod actually believed any of Sin's claptrap, and she assured Bel in no uncertain terms that this was an intimacy of convenience, about as long-lasting and trustful as a cobra bedding a mongoose. That said, however, she admitted that she and Bel had absolutely naught to offer Nimrod that would trump whatever Sin had given him already. And even if they had, Sin had been too successful in presenting Bel as the heir to Arkhalla's cruelty for them even to have a chance of dealing with the Akkadian liege.

"With what you did in Dilmun alone, you convinced Nimrod you are nothing but a mad dog as rabid as its mistress," she had told him bitterly as she dismissed the possibility of sending envoys to Akkad. "He'd back even Asag himself if it meant taking you down."

Bel had said nothing to that, cowed equally by his failure, the truth in her words, and the sting in her voice when she stressed the word *mistress*.

Thus it was with a dire sense of finality that the two sides were ordered during the first year of the war, as well as, perhaps, a dose of irony too bitter to ignore. It was Sin who had doubted the sagacity of Bel's plan to involve the humans in their rebellion against their queen, especially as the wretches were not a factor in his secret plan. Yet now Sin was the one who had brought in the Akkadians with him, in numbers vast enough to even the odds against the military might of Ur. And to rub more salt onto this wound, the councilor and the Akkadian king refrained from fullscale battles on the field, choosing instead to emulate the rebel wretches in the south. Rather than vast invading armies, it was small strike forces that slid inside Ur's territories, raiding and pillaging enough to throw them into chaos, then escaping back across the border, or engaging in skirmishes with Bel's troops in canyons and passes and cave-encrusted ridges which were invariably chosen to ensure small but annoying victories.

The news from the south was just as disturbing.

The human rebellion grew and grew. More wretches fled, deserted or were liberated to the human side as though by the hour. There was a worrying amount of reports calling it The Wretches' War, the word almost an acknowledgment of how this was something that posed a threat to the very heartland of Ur. A rebellion can be suppressed. A war could be lost. This new phase, which had begun, ironically enough, with the defeat of the rebel army and the devastation of Dilmun, became more menacing in the smallest of details: the defeat of the small Urian force sent to crush the fugitives hiding in the desert ridges; the utter failure of the larger forces dispatched to the task afterwards; the growth of this rebel force from a few hundreds to some one hundred and twenty thousand in the space of one year. The fact that this number comprised women and children as well as men was little consolation, for all the able-bodied adults were forged into an armed force whose effectiveness had to be seen to be believed, and even when witnessed was nigh impossible to accept. Time after time, this band of wretches proved as resilient to the Urian troops as reeds against a windstorm, bending and brought low only to rise up again, unbroken. Patrols were followed by militia and these by full brigades under Black Guard command, but each met a singular kind of failure that was just as complete as those that came before.

The wretches wandered throughout the south, raiding estates and provinces with few casualties, their forces often split into several bands that were as hard to track as to pin down, singleminded but allied under their leaders, which included the by now infamous Yssur, a Urian conscript turned rebel general. Stories grew around the man and his cadre, dangerous fictions in their majority for sure, but even more threatening for the tallness of the tales being told. Bel and Narama grew alarmed at the wretch army's defiance and ongoing success, but some of the legends about Yssur and his ilk concerned them even more. Legends about how ruthless they were in the execution of Undying prisoners, in fashions that evoked less a human cruelty and more the Undying's own. About how the wretches did not simply wish to carve out a territory outside of Ur and be left to their own devices, as claimed in some of the original reports, but fully intended to capture the city of Ur itself. And worst of all, how one of Yssur's most fearsome lieutenants was once the She-Demon queen's pet slave, forged by her cruelty and her death into the scourge of all the Undying.

Both Narama and Bel realized who these rumors referred to, though they were loath to voice their suspicions to each other. To give this nameless wretch warlord an identity would mean that they were ready to admit something unacceptable to them both, albeit for different reasons. Bel hated even the idea that Shamath not only lived, but had returned to plague him like a guilty conscience – nay, rather as the very embodiment of it. That the wretch who had pushed him into resenting his queen was out there just as Sin, who had prodded him into bringing her down, was rearing his head as well, were both reminders of his betrayal of everything he had been, and thus both were an anathema to him. Narama, on the other hand, saw the possibility of Shamath's return as yet another memory of Arkhalla, still holding her under, pinning her to stillness and death and the woman she once was. And to the both of them, the prospect of Shamath as one of the leaders of the Wretches' War, coupled with Sin aping the humans' ways to plague them further, was a torment fit for Asag's hell down in the Great Below.

Bel could not articulate what bothered him more; that Sin, his newfound enemy, fought like a wretch, or that the wretches' style of fighting was clearly one he could not train his army to contend with. Ur's sharp-fanged brigades could tear through almost any foe in straight-up carnage. They could descend onto encampments, forts and cities and sweep them all, leaving behind them less than a plague of locusts loosened on a field. But what they could not do was play hide and seek and maneuver through narrow mountain paths chasing invisible foes, nor could they act as protectors to scores of far-flung provinces attacked all at once. A war fought along a definite front line can be won by either side. But a war with no front lines, fought everywhere at once, behind the lines, one act of attrition after another, can only be lost by the side that has more to lose. Ur was an empire of horrors, but all empires thrive on order and fall apart when faced with disarray. And while not much by themselves, all those raided outposts and pillaged granaries and robbed caravans added to a disarray that would soon be crippling. If a poet were asked to wax on the state of Ur in those days, he would probably have likened it to that of a tiger plagued by a twin swarm of bees. No single sting, nor two swarms of them could hope to kill the mighty beast of prey, but they wrought and perplexed it to the extreme, for they kept it from sleeping, from feeding, and from making its way to the waterhole to drink – and everyone knew what happened in the end to all starving and thirsting beasts, even the mighty tiger.

Of course, no poet was asked to provide such a likening, for Bel would have had him rent limb from limb. But that did not make it any less true.

Ur starved and thirsted slowly, kept from waterhole and order. Bel knew it, though he was unable to do anything more than what he was already doing. Sin knew it, too, and it concerned him for altogether different reasons. His concern was one of timing. It was a point of strategy to weaken Bel by taking a leaf from how the humans fought their rebellion down south and use the same tactics to wage a two-pronged war of attrition. But one had to be careful of how long to let this war of attrition go on. The human rebels, it could not be overstated, were fighting an entirely different war, not so much a civil one as the other, more straightforward kind. The slow weakening of Ur permitted the human rebels to grow slowly stronger, which meant that Sin had to balance his actions so as not to bring down one foe only to bolster a new one. In order not to have a full-scale war against the humans on his hands, the civil war had to be played out fast.

So Sin sat to plan the second year of the war as though it were to be the final one. His spies' reports, coupled with his amused imagination, painted the war councils of Narama and Bel as rather sad scenes of an ever-changing string of generals being chastised for incompetence before being led offstage to their deaths, followed by interludes of half-silent, half-suppressed accusations exchanged between the two almost-lovers, rendered even worse by the frustration each of them caused the other. They were creatures of feeling forced to reason, hurt egos made to share something bigger than they were, and thus doomed to fail at both. The councils held by Sin, however, were decidedly more prosaic and well-mannered affairs, especially since no one died after them. With each raid planned in advance and every possible retaliation countered as per Sin's planning, there were very few failures to report, and the allied generals of Akkad and the Shadow Council of Ur tended to walk out of the war council tents with their heads still on their shoulders. Sin planned, while Nimrod commanded; their roles were distinct and thus balanced and respectful of each other's boundaries. There was no love lost between them, only the dogged practicality of a shared goal, which was a pathway to success. Throughout the second year of the war, the lands of Sumer were a board for Sin's and Nimrod's game, and their army was the pieces that they moved in the execution of their subtle plan.

The other members of the Shadow Council – the name chosen on a whim by Uthara, who loved the pointless practice of naming things – were content to act according to their appointed roles rather than vie for a share of the decision making. Spying was Kuthan's game, and he excelled both at providing information from the enemy's side as from the audiences of Akkad and his generals. Uthara and Fazuz threw their considerable wealth and resources behind the war effort, while Lilit and Erun sent scores of priests to fan the flames of discord against Bel and drum support for the redeemer that was Sin in myriad prayer halls and village squares and secret temple meetings across the lands of Sumer. None of them separately could have aspired to Sin's and Nimrod's talents, and even all of them together would be unequal to the task; so they let themselves be ordered and obeyed their orders, guaranteed rewards beyond their wildest dreams.

Keeping the balance, Sin and Nimrod trusted only one person close to each of them. For Nimrod, it was his daughter, Aisyah, who often acted as his voice and conscience and strong right hand, commander of his generals and troops and incomparable in executing even the most impossible of tasks that Sin came up with, while unafraid to speak her mind if she saw a different path. And for Sin, it was Idu, his lover, who had been molded by Sin almost into a younger version of himself, aping his mannerisms and poise and ability to think on his feet while completely obedient and faithful to his mentor even unto death. Sin had appointed the soft-faced youth as his messenger, and counted on Idu to contact, tempt, bribe, cajole and intimidate anyone as well as if it were Sin himself performing any of these acts. He loved Idu for being so resolutely void and selfless, just as he respected Aisyah for having a mind of her own. In that specific choice of confidants, too, Sin saw a balance between himself and Nimrod.

All this and more passed through his mind as Nimrod's field marshals finished their report on all the preparations that were underway. The night, as all the nights before it now that the coolness of spring gave way to long, hot summer, was sultry. The air inside the council tent felt still and stifling despite the rukh feather fans waved up and down by broad-chested slaves. The council members' brows glistened with sweat, and the Undying among them dabbed theirs with handkerchiefs from time to time, conscious of how the tinge of scarlet in their sweat unnerved the humans sitting at their side. Sweating seemed almost a by-product of thought among these men and women of power – a sign that they debated and argued and worried, among as well as within themselves. And what did they worry about? The generals and field marshals, eager to please and concerned about what might happen to their rank and life if they did not, combined in this single act of sweating a powerful angst and a terse desire for self-preservation. The Shadow Council of the Undying, all highly honorable in name and clout, were sweating, their perspiration a signpost of the inner struggle of maintaining that appearance of honor among their human allies while in truth they were naught but ravening, gluttonous beasts, thirsty for power and blood, waiting for the object of their pact to be achieved so they could finally sate their hunger with their allies' blood. In all of this ensemble, only three people did not sweat. Nimrod, because he felt sure in his power, a lion defiant of the jackals surrounding him. Aisyah, the princess, was far more wary of the Undying's capacity for betrayal than her father was, but her brow was smooth and unperturbed because she had trained herself so. And Sin did not sweat because there was no purpose to it, so he simply forewent such a display.

"My lord Sin, it seems the pieces are all in place," he heard Nimrod's gravelly voice say.

The last of the field marshals had finished his report. Vast numbers of men and weaponry, equipment, slaves and supplies had been moved and shifted about the lands between the twin rivers, in configurations apparent only to the mind that had designed their moving. No one but Sin – and Nimrod, to whom he had confided it – could have told that this placement of their forces was a prelude to the big final push and not mere strategic maneuvers. Nimrod's prodding was his cue. Any move beyond this point would be obvious to both subordinates and foes as a move to attack. Now was the time to let the others know.

Sin rose, bowing to the king and the princess before he spoke.

"My Liege. Your Highness. Friends," he began, keeping formalities to a minimum. "Almost two years ago, I asked you to trust my planning, and promised you victory. It is the time now for you to collect."

Everyone tensed in anticipation, except Aisyah and Idu. The two confidants knew what was coming all too well.

"The current placement of our forces has them in an optimal position for attack. We have brigades in the east, west and north of Ur, ready to sweep down upon Bel's domain as fast the talons of the rukh close in around the flesh of a sheep. As soon as his majesty commands –" here he cast a look at Nimrod "– all three contingents can begin to converge, leaving Bel's forces no choice but to meet us in the field or forego their territory altogether." He stopped, letting his words sink in and do their work.

"Where shall this battle be?" asked Erun nervously.

"At Uruch," Sin replied.

Erun gasped. "The Land Before the World," he whispered, his unease even greater.

There was a hush about the tent, haunted by that single word.

Uruch.

"How…" Fazuz started to say, but paused, startled by how his speaking cut through the silence. "How can you be so sure?" he finally asked. "That it shall be there, at Uruch?"

"It is the single furthest spot Bel's forces can gather and advance to before we overtake them. I have left him no time to get anywhere else."

There was silence anew among the council as both Undying and human members fathomed just how precise Sin's planning was.

"Still. Uruch, of all places," Lilit chuckled. Her laughter could not mask a hint of angst.

Sin ignored her.

"It shall be at Uruch," he said calmly. "The bed of the ancient river, long since dried up. We'll have the high ground, coming in from the hills."

There was a susurrus of approval. Their unspoken apprehension about the choice of battlefield aside, no one present could argue about the strategy of it.

Then Uthara spoke.

"Why would Bel not choose a third way? Like gathering his forces further south, closer to the city of Ur, with his choice of ground?"

Sin smiled. This was what he loved about Uthara. He could always count on her to feed him the right line.

"Because of the south, my lady," he said, softly. "The rukh needs no more than three talons when its prey is boxed in between it and a yawning crag."

Uthara's face screwed up, then, on realizing his meaning, lit up, impressed.

"The rebels," she said.

Sin spread his hands, signifying how simple it all was. "If Bel fights closer to Ur, not only does he lose his northern territories to us, but risks the rebel army coming up and attacking him from the back. He has to move up and meet us before he gets boxed in two fronts." At this he paused, leaving the best for last. "And he'll have to fight us with three-quarters of his army at best, because he will have to leave at least a fourth of his forces back in Ur and down South as defense in case the rebels attack anyway."

It was so elegant in its simplicity. The Shadow Council members stared at him, the idea blooming into wonderful outcomes in their heads. As for the Akkadian generals, they just stood there. None of them had opened their mouths during all this. Unlike the Undying, they wouldn't even think of questioning Sin's scheme, not since it was obvious their king had already approved it.

Sin felt the princess' eyes burn into him. Aisyah's stare was not awed. Her eyes, her face, her stance, all spoke quite eloquently. This had better work, leech, they said. Or else.

Nimrod did not even need to look at him. His daughter's stare spoke for him, too.

Aisyah rose, her eyes finally off him. She handed out orders to the generals and to the Shadow Council, appointing each one to a task and setting down the timetable for the push. Her words were chiseled to the finest point, her meaning unmistakable. There was no room for error, neither would any be tolerated. Everyone knew that.

"We set out at midnight," she concluded. "All three contingents. Send carriers with the word."

One last look to her father for final instructions, and another to Sin. None had anything to add.

"Dismissed."

The generals saluted and backed out of the tent, and the Shadow Council followed. Idu was the only one who lingered, invisible, as though he were Sin's shadow. Under the princess' fierce, no-nonsense stare, all the others, even the massive Kuthan, also walked out, their eyes low. Sin couldn't help a smile. Given time, even without the gods' dark mercy, this girl could one day make a queen as formidable as Arkhalla. He remembered the calm with which she had shot that arrow through Bel's hand, and he wondered if her ruthless streak ran as deep as the She-Demon's, as deep as that black pit that had claimed Arkhalla, and he wondered if Aisyah knew just how endless that pit was if she ever fell in it.

Well, the war was on. Soon, they'd know all.

It was just the four of them in the tent now. Sin got up slowly, bowing once more to Aisyah and Nimrod. Idu did the same a fraction of a moment later, a reflection slightly out of tune.

"My dread liege," Sin said. "Your Highness."

"We shall see you at midnight, Lord Sin," said Nimrod.

Sin walked out, his faithful shadow at his side. They headed towards their tent in silence for a while, then, seeing that Sin had let his face relax into non-expressive calmness, Idu felt emboldened enough to speak.

"This is it," he said. "Is it not? The moment. The one after which we cannot go back."

"How well you phrase it," said Sin. "Indeed. We cannot go back."

Idu let a moment pass between them, as was his wont whenever he brought up something unsavory.

"You told me of your plan. Of the contingencies in case something goes wrong."

"Something always goes wrong. That is the very reason for contingencies."

Seeing the frustration in his lover's eyes, Sin broke into a smile. "But that is not what you fear to ask, is it?"

Idu smiled back. "You know me too well."

"What you want to know is, *What if something else goes wrong?* Something I haven't planned for. Is that it?"

"Yes."

Sin stopped, though they had nearly reached their tent. He looked deep into Idu's eyes, into the fear and uncertainty that could have been his own if he allowed himself to feel them. That was another reason Idu was there. To feel, because Sin didn't. "There is always something we haven't planned for, Idu," he said, softly. "Always. One might even say that is the essence of life, though it is not."

Idu was perplexed anew. "It is not?"

"No. Life isn't the unexpected. Life is dealing with it."

Back in the tent, Nimrod and Aisyah let long seconds pass till Sin was out of earshot, and then Nimrod spoke.

"So," he said, his eye on his famed bow on its resting place by his bed. "It begins."

Aisyah hesitated.

"It is not too late, my father," she said after a moment. "Give me the word, and all the leeches shall be dead before your lips stop moving."

He turned to her, amused. "I know that is not fear I hear in your voice. I have taught you better."

"I am wary of them."

"Of course you are. They are monsters. Sin, in fact, is the worst of them."

Aisyah couldn't keep her voice down any longer. "Then why? Why are we going ahead with this?"

Nimrod took her by the hand. It was shaking. He held it until it shook no more.

"Ah," he said. "You fear for me."

She looked him straight in the eye. "You are my father. I would do anything to keep you from harm, always."

Nimrod nodded. "Then heed me. Even in the face of doom."

She made to speak, but he shushed her. "Would you have us face Bel alone?" he said. "Our men are the finest in the world. But they are just men."

She kept looking at him. Two heartbeats passed between them. Then she lowered her head. "I bow to your wisdom, father." And like a little girl, she nestled her head in his chest and put her arms around him. There were times Nimrod might scold her. Such a display was weakness unfit for a princess of the blood.

This was not one of those times.

He was her father. He held her close. Away from harm.

Always.

CHAPTER 10

WORDS TO DIE BY

In the Land Before the World two armies faced each other.

There was the army of men living and Undying that marched in from the east and north and west, three arrows long and vast, made of blades and fangs and sinews. Men of Akkad, dusky lines and lines of them like endless statues cast in bronze and sand, their helms and sickle-swords shined to catch the glow of moon and dazzling glint of sun, walked next to elite companies of gaunt, pale and wolf-fanged warriors who only marched at night. It was a sight unseen in this world before this moment: free men marching side by side with monsters from the pit.

There, too, was the army of the Undying of Ur that marched in from the south, thin black lines of frightening specters that seemed to spread forever along the horizon, led by Black Guard riders whose capes flapped behind them like leathern wings, followed by light brigades of men conscripted and enthralled, whose wills were not their own and whose limbs were but sacrificial meat to be carved and served and burned in offering to the gods of war. The sight of them, alas, was all too known since the beginning of the world: an army of slaves led to the slaughter by the monsters that ruled over them.

To any observer watching as the two armies took their places, the Urians along the ancient, dried-up riverbed of Uruch, their foes along the black volcanic hills that overlooked it, the spectacle was one to take the breath away. This sense of awe was heightened by the very nature of the place it happened in. There was something to the oldness of that land, something that chilled the veins of living and Undying alike. Once the bed of the mighty river that preceded the twin rivers that now defined the lands of Sumer, it had long since been transformed by earthquakes and eruptions from deep within the earth to an arid plain of earth stretching as far as the eye could see, its surface bone-dry and broken into a million plate-like pieces by the desert sun, its edges a crescent of ridges made of stone and earth blacker than coal. It resembled nothing else in all the world, except the remnants of some earlier earth consumed by fire. There were no legends of this land; no wild tales of blood and gods, no ghosts or curses or lost civilizations. It was older than accursed Kur, older than the first men and the Magi, and if men or gods had walked there once, they were no gods known to men, and they were men strange to what we've come to think as man. So old was this land that all the legends of it were long forgotten. That was why the very whisper of it filled everyone with deep and sacred dread.

It was to this place that the two armies came. They came to fight. They came to die. And to the eyes of any observer watching, they came to determine who would inherit the embers of their world.

It was the last day before the battle, and Bel found it hard to sleep. He could recall those campaigns of yore when he'd go into his tent or sun-shelter and surrender to the lethargy that is the slumber of the Undying during the hours of day as soon as his eyelids closed. It wasn't so much that his mind was untroubled back then, but that he knew, like all good soldiers, that a healthy rest would keep the tiredness from weighing down his limbs with leaden weights in battle. It had been the need of victory that eased his sleep, and as he lay onto his camp bed with his eyes open, he wondered whether he had lost that need.

He was not afraid of Sin, or the Akkadians, he told himself. If he died at their hands, that would be it, and good riddance. But still he lay there gripped by a mortal terror, and when he tried to gaze the foe that frightened him so in the eye, he saw only himself.

He had no gods to pray to, for sleep or victory. The Ones Below, who had cursed Arkhalla with the dark mercy, had remained silent since her death, and even if they did speak, it was not to him. There was no one above or below to look upon his army with a kindly eye, to fill his men's hands with ire divine and iron-cast, to make him the sword of righteous victory. And nor was there a soul, mortal or Undying, that he could turn for succor. Narama slumbered – if she did – in a tent some twelve feet from his own, but she might as well be beyond the sea. He had no one but himself, his eye, his hands, his sword, no one to commend his soul to who would take it. Thus he lay in the half-darkness of his tent, shielded from the killing sun, his sickle-sword by his side, alone with his fear and his thoughts, when the tent flap was drawn open and Arkhalla came out of the sun.

She stood before him, as she was, her lithe form covered only by a loin skirt and otherwise as naked as the summer's dawn. Her fangs glistened with blood. Her eyes were blue fire.

Bel stared at her, aghast.

She spoke.

"I shall be with you on your dying day, Bel," she said, her voice crushing his soul. "Look for me, and despair."

Bel made to answer her, but choked. He meant to tell her he was sorry. He tried to tell her he still loved her. He couldn't.

She was covered in her blood, pierced by scores of arrows.

Bel tried to weep, to cry, to scream. He couldn't.

She was a burned husk, charred flesh barely clinging to coal-black bone.

"Look for me on your dying day," she said, her voice ashes. Something else spoke with her, behind the pale, from beyond the shores of life.

Bel started from his dream. A piercing scream rang out, a knife slashing through the curtain of the dark.

Long moments passed before he recognized who was screaming. It was he, his voice restored to him at last. Even more moments passed, to the drum of his heart, before he recognized the word he was screaming.

It was Her name.

Trembling, he tried to shut himself up, closing his mouth with his hands. He could have sworn there was blood on his hands. He could taste its bitter iron tang on his lips.

It was a dream, only that and nothing more, he told himself. It was his coward of a conscience plaguing him, and there was no one in that tent, no one in that whole dark world around him, but himself.

He was the one who had loved her. He was the one who had killed her. He was guilty, and he despaired.

He was alone.

Idu was helping Sin put on his breastplate when Aisyah entered their tent.

"Good evening, Lord Sin," she said.

Sin bowed his head to the Princess. "Forgive my tardiness, your highness." He fussed with the breastplate's straps, making a point of showing just the right amount of discomfort. "As quick I am in wordy matters, I am still a clumsy novice with these things. Is it dusk already?"

Aisyah shook her head. Sin knew it was still a half hour to sunset, and that the princess was not there to summon, but to speak to him. He could see her hesitation, the only sign of vulnerability on her. In her carnelian red armor, with her helm and arms so polished they shone brighter than gemstones, she resembled a war goddess descended on the field dressed in fire and thunder.

"How was your sleep?" she enquired, delaying going into the real purpose for her visit.

"Sweet and without a single dream," said Sin. "A born warrior I may be not, but I promise you a rested, keen, and jocund general tonight on the field."

Her smile may have been ironic, or she might have been amused for real. Her mission, though, nagging at her, made it brief.

"The men are armed," she said. "It is time to give direction." Once more, she checked herself. "My father has spoken to his generals, but..."

"He delegated you and me to deliver an oration to our men."

She nodded, a hint of blushing on her cheeks.

"A wise decision," said Sin, gracefully ignoring her embarrassment. "He heads this army, but no mortal may address an army of both human and Undying, and it'd be just as wrong for him and me to do it, as it'd be as though we were equal in leadership. I'd have suggested this myself, but I would not dare to presume upon you."

She nodded again, this time in appreciation. It pleased Sin. Given time, he might even make an ally of this strong-willed, yet sensitive girl, despite her aversion to him. He was that good with people.

They talked of strictly military matters while he finished dressing, and at sunset they stepped out of the tent to meet Nimrod, who waited for them by his chariot with his generals, a twin-hued, troubled sea of men stretching behind them almost to the horizon. The Akkadians wore the colors of their king and princess, attired in armor the shade of dark carnelian, while Sin's Undying sported the deep indigo of the army of Ur, except with a new crest on their breastplates, a rukh with a bat caught in its talons, which Sin had purported was the symbol of his family so convincingly that most of Sumer could have sworn they had seen it carved in the ruins of ancient temples. Even side by side, the two armies mixed as uneasily as oil and water. If the battle ahead of them was to be won, it was Nimrod's will and Sin's task that these men in red and blue become as matched as foam to wave.

A magnificent white horse awaited the princess, and she mounted it as her father got in his chariot. An attendant handed Aisyah the reins of a night-black steed that was next to hers, and she held them, beckoning Sin to mount it. No sooner had Sin done so than she nudged her horse gently forth to face the assembled warriors. Once more, Sin had to admire the princess' fearless resolve. A lesser girl would have let him speak first, to calculate her speech in correspondence to his or to reserve the last impression for herself. But Aisyah would rather throw herself into a task she was wary of rather than behave in a manner unbefitting.

"I speak to men," she started, her voice steady and strong, "my countrymen of Akkad and my allies standing by our side today, for I ask of you all to stand together as men. As sinew and bronze, merged together. As courage in the face of fear and death. As men."

Smart girl, thought Sin. She courted the favor of Undying and human, binding them in the qualities both would claim for theirs. He couldn't have put it better himself.

"I speak in brief," Aisyah went on, "for time is a leisure forbidden to us warriors. But do remember this as we go together into the night. We have the right cause on our side; the souls of all the victims slain and wronged by the villain that we face and by the bitch that spawned him; and I dare say unto you all, that, had they a mind and will still theirs, even the slave army of thralls that follow

Bel would cheer for us to win instead of him. And so they would, were they allowed to be men."

Her voice rose as she spoke; her horse dug the earth beneath it with its hooves impatiently, like her words stirred it so that it could not wait to get into the fight.

"I ask you, what is Bel? A murderer, a monster, reared on blood and thriving on it. But I do not accuse him of his nature, no, men. I accuse him of his acts. For it is action that brands us what we are. Were I Undying, I would drink blood as I feast on the flesh of slain game, and I would slay as I do now, to feed. But I would not be Bel. Bel and his bitch queen showered in blood. They drowned realms entire in blood merely for them and theirs to feast upon. They ordered their men to act as monsters. I ask you to stand with me as men."

Sin couldn't help stealing a look towards the Shadow Council standing to his left on their horses and chariots, and smiled as he saw Lilit and Fazuz squirm at the mention of excesses they both had indulged in. It was canny of the princess to add that line about men ordered to act as monsters, for it exonerated the Undying about to fight at her side, as well as the Akkadians about to fight beside them. Her words took beasts and made them into soldiers, even if it was only for as long as the alliance lasted. For a moment, he wondered whether the princess would so readily berate all those atrocities if she knew Lilit and Fazuz and a few more of her allies had committed them, but then he decided she'd probably do it anyway. For Aisyah, it was the cause that mattered; that, and getting the men before her to fight for it. Plus, she clearly relished showing that she had no tolerance for monsters. She'd probably enjoy watching Lilit and her ilk squirm.

"Bel killed for pleasure," Aisyah went on. "And just as men who kill for pleasure give other men a bad name, so do the Undying who act as ravening beasts sully the name of the Undying. But you here, tonight, are all men, and Bel is your enemy. If you will fight against the enemy of us all, fight as men! Fight tonight! Fight with me!"

The Akkadians cheered. The Undying cheered with them. Their cheer rang along the black hills, loud as the mightiest thunderclap. Aisyah's horse reared, and she held on to the reins and smiled, a war goddess to them all.

It was hardly an act; it felt true. It was true. And true acts are the hardest to follow.

The cheers went on, and only when they began to hush did Sin nudge his horse forward, taking care to stand next to the princess rather than overtake her.

"If you would follow Princess Aisyah," he began, "you are men after my own heart, for I follow her and the king even unto the lands below and back. If you would shed your blood to bring the tyrant Bel down, you would redeem us all in the eyes of all the gods. If you would fight mankind's foes, your reward would match even your wildest dreams. For you would change the world, and ease its pain, and bring it justice."

He made sure to complement the princess' speech, not to outdo it. He was happy to play satellite, the moon to her sun, if it got him his goal.

"Those of you who fight for loved ones and hearth will find them waiting for you on your return, and you shall be more content than the mighty potentates because you will have claimed the future. Those of you who fight to redeem your kind will find horror a dead word forevermore, and that shall be because of what you did here this day. So, come, mortal and Undying, let us claim the future, and let us rid the world of horror. For me, that shall be reward enough, even if the price is the true death that even the Undying dread. But if I live after tonight, whatever claim is mine you all shall share, from the riches of the mightiest realm to the gratitude of the children of mankind down every generation to come. So sound the alarums and let us march without; for Nimrod and Aisyah! For Ur and Akkad and mankind, cry out!"

There was an even louder cheer, rising up to the heavens like an arrow from Nimrod's bow, defiant of gods and all fears. Sin basked in it, and as he turned to the princess, he saw her face torn between glowering and admiration. He had taken her speech and made it his, just as he had stayed true to her meaning and her words. Whatever victory came to their side tonight – if there was victory to be had – it would be theirs, in tandem, for it'd be tied to this common speech he had so artfully cut together.

For Nimrod and Aisyah, indeed. For Ur and Akkad, by all means, why not?

But most assuredly, for Sin. Always for Sin.

"What shall you say to the men?"

"To win."

"Bel. This is no time for jests."

"Why do you not speak to them, then? Give them a rousing oratory, stroke their egos like base whores fondle old men's cocks?"

Narama looked at him. "It is no time to anger me, either."

Bel winced. "I've botched that, haven't I?" He lowered his voice. "Like everything else."

The slap was fierce. It nearly knocked Bel off his feet. It almost cleared his mind of the wine-laced blood of the youth he'd had after he awoke from the nightmare.

"Seems I made you angry after all," he said, rubbing his cheek. The skin felt flushed and red. Only part of it was the slap. The other was shame. He had wanted her to slap him. The shame hurt more.

"If you had angered me, I'd have taken your head off." Her eyes were even colder than her voice. "That was to bring you to your senses."

They were in his tent. He was still sitting on his camp bed, still half-dressed. She stood over him, armed and ready.

"Have you come to your senses?" she said. Her tone was all too clear. She'd slap him again without hesitation.

He nodded. His head felt clear now. The wine fumes were evaporating, even if the image from his dream lingered.

She helped him finish dressing.

"What can I say to the men?" he asked her. "I'm better with the sword than with words."

Or at least he had been. Once.

She did not answer. He pressed the matter.

"Speeches are more your thing, Narama."

"Not on the field," she said. "Not here. You lead these men. They are about to die for you. You ought to talk to them."

"They are conscripts and thralls. Half of them will go jump in the sea if I tell them, the others would strangle me in my sleep with their chains if they could."

"There are Undying out there. Whole companies of men loyal to you. And your Black Guard. They are still fighting for you."

"They're fighting for *you*, Narama. If you weren't here, they'd have fled to Sin long ago."

She finished adjusting his breastplate, but her hand stayed on his chest. He hoped she wouldn't sense the way his heart was beating.

Her eyes stared up into his. It seemed to him that she was thinking whether she ought to speak her mind or not.

"Maybe," she said at last. "Maybe they would have fled if I weren't here. Maybe they should have. Maybe *I* should have."

Her breast heaved with a sigh. "But I didn't."

A moment passed, and she removed her hand and stepped back.

Bel nodded. He understood. This was the throw they had both gambled their lives on. She was willing to take whatever came, there, tonight. With him.

The least he owed her was to do the same.

"Has the sun set?" he asked.

"There was no sun to see. A cloud cover has enshrouded all for this past hour, the watchmen said."

Bel smiled a wry smile. "And did they think it an ill omen?"

"Some said the gods frown on us. I had them silenced."

"Good." He shrugged. "Why should we care more than Sin? The same clouds shroud his camp as well. What matters is which one of us will be buried come the morn."

He liked that last sentence. It sounded more like a prior self of his, one not shaken by dreams.

Narama smiled. Perhaps she thought so too.

They walked out of the tent into the bustling camp, and pages rushed to them with their horses.

"Let our warlords bring their battalions forth," he told Narama. "I shall lead our men across the plain. Stretch the foremost troops in line to spread our foes' fire. Horsemen and foot soldiers; have the latter be Undying, the faster to climb the hills before enemy arrows make pincushions of them. Have archers follow for support; then our main forces, which we'll defend with cavalry on each side." He paused, out of breath. "How does it sound to you?" She smiled again. "It sounds fine."

They mounted. "All right," Bel shouted. "Let us on, then, each to their task." He clutched the hilt of his sickle-sword with a savage grin, fangs gnashing. "No dream, this. Let this be our omen and our thought. Let this be our reality."

He spurred his horse forward towards the troops arraigned onto the arid plain before them. Narama galloped after him.

Lines and lines of faces regarded Bel as he stopped before them, strange and blank. Conscripts and thralls he had never looked at enough to recognize, and Undying most of whom he should be able to know by name, but realized he did not. The wretches had never mattered to him, but in his state, the mixture of resentment and will-drained submission in their eyes pierced him deeply. It was even worse with the Undying. Fifth, seventh, tenth generation bloods, perhaps, turned these ten-odd years he had ceased to notice, some slavering for blood, fangs out, reared on naught but violence and murder, the others hollow men who were nothing without someone to order them, specters with no soul he could discern. He knew not what these faces expected of him, or what to say to them. All he could see in their eyes as they waited for him to speak was how far he had let himself fall, how far the realm had fell with him. A cold dread seized him then, trickling down his back like clear spring water. He checked himself, forcing his courage up from its hiding place all the long way up to his lips.

"Do not ask me words to fight by," he said suddenly, as though he was lashing back at a silent demand. "What words can I offer you more than my presence and yours here, on the dying of this day? We go to fight, and fight we will, words or not, and some of you shall die whether you get encouragement or not. Were you able to be anywhere but here, you would be, and so would I. But we cannot and we are not. We are here, so we will fight. This was true of both us and our foes on the hills across this plain, believe me. So ask not your leaders to gift you words to fight by, men. All any general can give a soldier is words to die by. For by your death that general shall win or lose a war. And if at day's end you stand alive, it is through worth of yours, not theirs."

He felt Narama's eyes on him, her wonderment at the harshness of his words, just as he saw how it spoke to something behind the eyes of the crowd. They were really looking at him now. They listened.

"Know this, that you go to death, and that you shall live only if you kill those who come at you. Know that they are traitors, scum, and base deserters, for only if you hate them to your guts shall you be able to prevail and slay them. They are naught but bitch-spawn shat out of that cesspool land of Akkad; jackals thronging about that cowardly corpse-eater, Sin. They come to kill you, so you must kill them first. They come to take what little you have for theirs. And if you think me a cruel and heartless lord, then think what life you'll lead under an Akkadian king reared on hate of Ur and a milksop lord so two-faced he would sell friends and country to such a king."

His voice had lowered to a thunderous low roar, yet so silent was the crowd that even his slightest pause for breath was like a hurricane blowing into their ears.

"Fight not for me tonight, but for yourselves. Fight them. If Ur is to be taken, let it be taken by our betters and not by such low men as these. Let them not feast on your blood and take your lives, let them not march on to your homes to rape your wives and daughters. Fight! Cry war, for war is made against you! Do murder before it is done to you! Feast on their paltry lives instead! Ride fast, ride hard! Draw swords and cleave them through their brains!
For tonight, if you do not sleep awash in others' blood, you'll wake vomiting your own in hell!"

No cries broke out in cheer, no voice was raised to praise his name. Instead, thousands of hands drew blades and beat their shields with them. A mighty clang reverberated through the broken plain, all the way up to the hills to chill the hearts of unseen foes, all the way high up to the sky to make indifferent gods sit up pale and frightened, and even down into the lands below to warn demons of men who would spit into their eye even as they were about to shower the earth with their life's blood.

Narama shivered as she looked at Bel drinking up the men's blood lust and hatred. He had done it, just as she had prodded him to. But only now did she realize the awfulness of what he had done. This was no army he commanded, these were not men he inspired. It was a pack of wolves, running together yet each one for themselves, fighting for nothing but survival. She was shocked most of all of how true it was. Another leader would have lied, would have stroked and fondled, as Bel had put it with such venom only minutes before. But he had spoken nothing but truth, all the truth that his pain and frustration and hatred was revealing to him. It was horror, but with truth's beauty twisted into the coils of it. Narama felt her loins afire with lust, for Bel, for blood, for horror, for truth. She, too, like those wolf-men before her, yearned to bury her blade in quivering flesh, to feast on scarlet, pulsing life. She longed to let it all out, her own hatred, her frustration, her pain, out into this purest of all acts; killing or being killed. Without even realizing it, she had drawn her sickle-sword and joined the chorus of death, drumming on her shield along with the army before her.

To war, she drummed. Awash in blood or coughing it in hell.

Dusk fell slowly onto the Land Before the World. The desert expanse stretched, its cracked surface pockmarked by dried-up tar pits, remnants of the ancient fires that had burned beneath the ground those aeons ago. Whatever history was written on this tablet of ground had long since been erased, and it had been left blank and undisturbed by man until tonight.

At sunset teams of men set fire to the tar pits. They'd set out from the two camps with lit torches and carts with barrels filled with pitch, as though oblivious to each other, broaching each crater and emptying loads of pitch into it before throwing their torches after it to ignite the pit. Quickened by the burning pitch, the tar within the craters erupted into flame, and even as twilight gave way to dusk the ancient riverbed turned into a brightly lit inferno. It made little difference to the keen eyesight of the Undying, but Ur's conscripts and slaves and the Akkadian infantry needed the even chance of fighting against a foe they both could see.

Thus was the scene set as the players got in place. Thus were the lights arranged upon it, casting a hellish glow from the ground's depths onto the myriad forms arranged opposite one another. The night's pall came down from above, a black, starless curtain, announcing the start of the show. And an audience of gods and devils took their seats to watch.

As for the play, it was the ancient tragedy of War. And if it had a lead, it was red, blood-drenched Death.

CHAPTER 11

THE SPOILS OF WAR

The air shook with the boom of myriad footfalls as the armies rushed to join together. It was the sole fact of hard reality, the other tenets to the world made changeable according to one's vantage point. To the gods above, viewing the battle in their cold detachment, this war was but twin colonies of ants battling over an arid patch of anthill, distant and tiny lives indifferently snuffed out as one formation ploughed into the other. To the Ones Below, waiting in darkness, there was naught but the rumble of a blood storm, telling them of the red deluge of carnage that they'd soon be feeding on. To the warriors rumbling down the hills, all that was there before them was an angry sea of men and arms that rose in a gigantic wave to drown them. As to the ones climbing from the plain, it seemed as though the barren black rocks themselves sprouted a forest made of men that moved against them. And then the fight was joined, and all the world became clang and screams and blood.

Sin watched, perched on his vantage point, halfway between the rubble and the gods. His men had taken the crag that best overlooked the field and held it, and his blade had been dipped enough in crimson to present him as both the warlord and the general. If forced to, he'd admit having enjoyed this burst of brawn and bloodshed, but it had served its purpose now, and if there was a battle to be won, this was the spot to fight it. The glow from the tar pits lit the carnage below. Sin surveyed the spectacle, aloof from the movements on his board of living pawns just as his mind planned their next steps. Fleet messengers rode up and down the hills, conveying commands, carrying new strategies to captains charged to do or die. It was the simplest truth. No warrior ever won his war by dying; it was how he sent others to their deaths that resolved all. To that warrior, and to him alone, went the spoils of war.

So Sin directed what was happening below, knowing that he, too, was been eyed upon, his performance judged as much he judged that of his men. Nimrod had arrayed his archers along the crag to offer cover to their men as they'd agreed. Showers of flaming shafts rained down onto the Urian lines, the king's own bowstring playing one-note songs of death as each arrow he shot struck true. But Sin did not even have to look sideways in his direction to know that the Akkadian glanced at him at every opportunity.

"Throw everything at them! Push them back up the hill!"

"My lady! Lady Narama!"

"What is it? Speak!"

"The Akkadians! They're descending on our flanks!"

"Sin's men fell back on purpose!"

"Support the flanks! Hold the ground! Fight, damn you!"

Aisyah saw the Black Guardsman swing his axe as he rode at her. She went limp, backwards on her saddle, held only by her weight. The blade swung over her, leaving the Undying's chest exposed, and she stabbed upwards with her own blade.

Her gambit paid off. Flailing, grabbing at his breast, the rider passed her before he fell face forward and collapsed onto the earth.

Another rider came at her as she righted herself. She swung, hitting the man's horse between the eyes. The dead beast crumbled like a wall.

Aisyah rode into a cluster of infantry, stomping onto flesh as hands and blades rose about her like a wave, seeking to bring her down into their depths. She cut them down with wide-arced swings, the warrior's yell out of her lips tearing through her foes' hearts. Gore blended with the dust beneath her horse's hooves, the cracked earth turned soft again by bloodshed. The mount stumbled, either stabbed or bereft of its footing; the next moment, it pitched on its side, and she fell.

Before she found herself trapped under her horse, she jumped onto the ground, rolling with her fall's own force. A tar pit yawned mere inches from where she stopped.

She sprung to her feet not a moment too soon. The two Undying that rushed her from either side thought her a sure prey, for they did not alter their stance but pressed on with their charge as though she were felled and helpless. Aisyah felt the heat from the tar pit at her back. She dodged the first's thrust and swung low, hacking at his leg below the knee. His leg buckling under him, the Black Guardsman went head first in the pit. Aisyah stabbed up and sideways, hitting the second one beneath the jaw as he was bringing his blade down on her. A twist of her hand and the sickle-sword nearly severed the man's head before he even hit the ground.

Few mortals could survive a full-on fight against an Undying. The trick was to use their own force and momentum against them. A truly skilled warrior could make it work again and again. Aisyah had been trained for this all her life. And so had her father's men. Already there were Akkadians at her side, gathering at her flanks.

She glanced about the field, lit from below by the burning pits. A hell of shades pitched against each other, as though the dead down in the Great Below were battling to the last. But it was plain to see how it was her warriors that came at the Undying from all sides, bringing up the rear behind Sin's men as they pressed on. The leech's strategy was working. With Sin's forces as their vanguard, they were pushing the Urians back.

Soon, it'd be time.

Bel saw red. It barely registered in his mind as he rode on, hacking left and right, his arm numb from ceaseless slaying. He could not tell whether it was fury that painted all before him crimson, or whether it was the fires and the blood. He did not care. Each death cry brought back his own when he awakened from that dream of Her – if he had woken up at all. Each foe he felled hurt as though he had slain himself. Perhaps that was his wish. But he did not care. He rode on, his world all red.

"Aid, my dread lady, aid!"

Her men fought on. Narama held her horse, turning to face the messenger. He gasped at the sight of her, a scarlet specter.

"What is it?"

"Lord Bel has slain more than any man and god, searching for Sin or death. He fights alone, boldly, his mount now felled. Help him, my lady! If he falls –"

Nimrod signaled his archers to let loose another storm of flaming arrows. In the firelight from the pits, he looked below and saw his armies sweeping down the hills, routing the Urians. The forest was pushing back the sea. It was more than a fighting chance, now. They were winning.

His eyes fell to the quiver propped up beside him and the gauze-wrapped arrow set apart from the rest.

Soon, now.

Narama saw Bel from afar.

"Pull back," she cried at him. "I'll get you a horse! We must regroup, Bel!"

He hacked on, not answering, a man possessed. Narama tried to reach him through the mayhem. A sea of men held them apart, waves of blades clashing. It was beyond impossible. She cursed through clenched fangs.

That was when she spied the Akkadian witch to her left. She was at the head of the main force routing her men.

Cut off the serpent's head, then. It was all she could do.

With a dead-killing cry, she hacked her way onward.

Aisyah saw her coming. The Urian was a wraith on horseback, emerging from the dust and flame smoke, scarlet, slick with the blood of her countrymen. Time itself crawled to a stop as the hellspawned rider charged forward at her.

She steadied herself, her blade ready, each peal of thunder from the horse's hooves synced to the beating of her heart as it came closer. Aisyah ignored the rider. She focused on her foe's mount, its pace, its rhythm. She became the horse, this great beast that was the Urian's advantage.

And thus linked with it, she struck.

Her blade cut across the horse's legs at just the perfect moment.

The beast neighed in pain as it came down. Its fall threw the rider face first onto the ground. A mortal would have been killed without a doubt. A random Undying would have been crippled.

This rider was neither.

Aisyah saw her land on her feet, catlike. A split second later, she was standing, her sickle-sword ready. There was no mistaking that agility, spoken of in hushed whispers around the Akkadian campfires.

Narama.

The clamor about them seemed to fade; shades fought in a dim background, leaving them facing each other one on one.

They stood still, ready to pounce, limbs balanced, fingers flexing about their blades, eyes gauging eyes for giveaway tics.

"Lady Narama," said Aisyah with a mocking nod.

"Die," hissed Narama.

She flew forward, arm extended, her body a shaft with her blade its tip, and realized at once it was a mistake. The little bitch had taunted her on purpose, made her thrust forth. Even now she side-stepped, parried –

All Narama could do was counter as best she could. It was clumsy, though it saved her from being skewered. But her thrust threw her face down in the dust.

She somersaulted back to her feet just barely before Aisyah's blade hacked her in twain. All the princess' stroke did was slice through one loose strand of Narama's hair.

Narama attacked again, seeking an opening. She found none. Swearing, she tried it again, and again she was countered.

For a mortal, the girl's speed was uncanny. She was neither as strong nor as wiry as Narama, but she was light on her feet and just as skilled, dancing circles about her one moment and making an unexpected move the next. It took Narama all of two more attacks to realize Aisyah was using her own strength and thrust against her. She changed her stance to a defense only to find herself on the receiving end of a flurry of feints and thrusts that tasked even her Undying reflexes. Stroke by stroke, she backed up. Within moments, they found themselves battling on the brink of a tar pit.

The only sure way she could see to a victory was to tire the Akkadian out. No mortal could fight like that for long. She fought to concentrate against the girl's attacks, but it was the ongoing taunts that really rattled her.

"Is that all you have? I expected more from Arkhalla's mare," said Aisyah, thrusting.

Narama parried. "Shut up," she said.

"I guess it's true what they say. She didn't keep you around for your sword fighting."

It was a ruse, Narama knew so, just to ire her, to throw her off. But she couldn't help herself.

She screamed and charged forward, her sickle-sword a hurricane blur, striking in the spaces between seconds, faster than eyes could blink. Aisyah countered, driven back with each blow, falling silent, her full concentration now in staying alive.

The slightest error any of them made would be their last; a losing stroke meant either being run through or falling down into the pit.

The girl was sweating. To her amazement, Narama realized her own limbs weighed heavy with fatigue.

They fought on manically now, each thrust and counter accompanied by an angry cry.

At last, the Akkadian wavered, her side left open a split second too long.

Narama's blade arced wide, slicing towards her midriff; the girl jumped back, a jot too slow. Her foe's sickle-sword tore through breastplate and tunic.

Narama cried in triumph. First blood was hers.

Unbalanced by the blow, Aisyah fell backwards. Narama amassed all her power for a killing swing –

But then the emerald flame tearing through the sky stayed her hand.

Aisyah looked up in triumph.

It was time.

Nimrod positioned the gauze-wrapped arrow on his bow. The wrapping glistened in the firelight, moist from being dipped into the mix of oil, sulfur, saltpeter, and verdigris. With a gesture, he stilled his archers.

It was time.

His adjutant set fire to the arrow, the flame changing immediately from red to deep green. Nimrod raised his bow high, aiming at the heavens, straight in the eyes of the gods themselves, and with a grin, let loose.

The shaft arced through the air, trailing green fire after it like a comet burning through the night.

His troops below recognized the signal.

Sin knew at once something was wrong. He even knew *what*. But he could scarce believe it.

Aghast, he looked below, his movements on the desert board, his faultless planning, all turned to chaos in seconds.

The Akkadians had let his men advance and cut into Bel's army as planned, bringing their numbers in support of this deadly vanguard of Undying. Bel's forces were in a pincer, hammered into backing towards the middle of the riverbed. Victory was within their grasp. Only now, as it happened before his eyes, did Sin realize he had pinned his troops between the Akkadians and the army of Ur.

Before the green-flamed shaft fell out of sight, the Akkadians attacked the very men they'd been fighting alongside. Most of Sin's men could not even tell what was happening. Akkadian spears and sickle-swords cut into their allies' sides and backs; there were howls of surprise, curses; the clang of weapons turned about to engage, too late.

Suddenly, Sin's army found itself fighting on two fronts, their front lines still locked in combat with Bel's troops, their rear hacked to bits by the vast numbers of Nimrod's legions.

It was a bloody free-for-all. The Urians kept on fighting their divided foes; Sin's men struck to and fro blind, in panic; the Akkadians killed indiscriminately.

Sin had expected betrayal. It was a given.

But even he had not expected it right in the midst of battle. Not so finely enmeshed with his own strategy.

He cursed loudly, his voice drowned in the screams and clamor that rose from down below.

Narama vainly sought Aisyah. Waves of warriors had poured between them, pulling them apart in opposite currents. All it had taken was a moment's distraction. That and the battle turning on its head.

They were still not even close to winning. But half their enemies were fighting the other half.

The night was lost. But the war might still be fought. All they had to do was still have an army when the clamor died.

She hacked her way through the men and Undying that came at her, her eyes searching for Bel.

Sin's survival hung on getting on a horse, and he knew it.

His men fell left and right, half of them in the failed act of protecting him, the other scrambling mad for cover as they were plagued by Nimrod's guards. Flaming volleys from the Akkadian archers' bows skewered those who did not get their shields up fast enough. The rest piled onto each other, pushed back into a circle, pinned down.

Sin weighed his chances; there were none. He was about to die.

He laughed as he heard the gallop of a horse. His mind was teasing him with a salvation out of his reach.

Then the cluster of men about him parted and a rider charged through, stomping friend and foe. A hand reached for him, strong. He scarce knew Idu's face from under the blood. He was run through with arrows. Whatever kept him on the saddle was more will than life.

The world lost all cohesion as he was pulled onto the saddle, his arms wrapped about his lover's back.

"Hold on!" Idu's voice croaked.

He spurred their mount and they were out of the deathtrap of bodies, riding hard. Sin held on for dear life. The horse stumbled badly left and right, the hands gripping its leads more unsteady by the second. Twice Idu almost fell, taking Sin with him.

They rode through spears and shafts and gauntlets of Akkadians. Any second now, their mount would be felled, or Idu would fall. It was hopeless.

Sin heard the rumble of thunder at their heels. Hanging on to Idu, he twisted his head about to glance back.

Nimrod's chariot was right behind them, the king erect next to his driver, bow in hand, trying to steady his aim.

"Idu!" cried Sin.

Either in response, or weakened from the blood loss, Idu eased his grip onto the reins. Their sudden slowing down spoiled Nimrod's aim, sparing their lives. But it also brought them right alongside the Akkadian king's chariot. Sin heard Nimrod swear as he drew his sickle-sword to hack at them.

Blind instinct took over.

Seizing Idu's sides, he heaved with all his strength. With a cry, his lover lost his grip onto the horse and tipped sideways, falling straight onto Nimrod's sword.

Idu's eyes stared wide at him as he died.

Sin stared back, aghast, his hands tight on the horse's reins.

Nimrod's blade was lodged into Idu's side. He couldn't pull it out. The Akkadian's driver was trying to control the chariot as it ran side by side with Sin's mount, Idu's body half-suspended between them, keeping them locked together.

A cry of pain and anguish bursting from his lips, Sin hacked with his own sword, cutting at Idu's corpse. One stroke; two; three; all for naught.

Nimrod pulled at his sickle-sword, desperate to free it.

Hacked to a bloody mess, Idu's body finally slipped off the saddle, taking Nimrod's sword with it as it fell forward between Sin's mount and the chariot.

Sin seized his chance; he struck.

His blade caught Nimrod across the clavicle, slicing through his chest.

The same second, Idu's body was caught under the wheels of Nimrod's chariot.

The chariot twisted and veered left as Sin's horse rode free.

Gripping the reins, he fought to hold on.

Nimrod's chariot was dragged away, one wheel spinning madly as it was torn off. Sin saw the Akkadian king fall to the ground, a rag doll rolling in the dirt, just like the youth Sin loved.

It was the last thing he saw through the tears and the night that engulfed him.

CHAPTER 12

WHEN THE BATTLE'S WON AND LOST

"My lady, please. You cannot be here."

Aisyah tore the man's hand off her shoulder. She turned, ready to strike him, her eyes streaming with tears.

The physician winced. His hand was still in her grip.

"Please, your highness. We are doing all we can."

Aisyah's lips trembled. She struggled to make sense of his words.

"Please."

Her grip loosened. The physician gave a pained sigh.

Slowly, Aisyah got up from her father's bedside, letting the physician take her place. The sight of her sire was eclipsed by the figures hunched over him. Bloody rags and bandages were strewn about the camp bed among the king's clothing and armor, clinging to her feet as she stepped back. The smell of blood was as physical as pain.

Feeling sick, she looked back at the men around the bed. Their army's three best physicians were there, as well as the royal apothecary. If there was even a chance of saving her father's life, these four held it in their hands. The physician was right. She was only in the way.

Wiping the tears from her eyes, she exited the tent. It was morning outside, a chill and stillborn day. Guardsmen and soldiers glanced as she passed. She ignored them.

The wreck of the king's chariot was still there on the hillside, surrounded by corpses. Aisyah passed it with a shudder. It was as broken as her father had looked when they carried him inside the tent.

She went down the hill in silence, among the dead. The black rocks were tinged crimson, and bodies lay in the misty grayness of the morn at every side, from the topmost crag down to the riverbed, so many of them it seemed as though the land was no longer composed of rock and earth but of the slain.

Too many of them were her own people. Fresh-faced, bronze-skinned youths, come all this way to lie in shallow pools of gore. As far as her sight reached, she could not escape the view. It seemed to her like more than half of her army had perished.

If this was victory, then she wanted none of it.

That the corpses of the Undying and their thralls seemed twice as many offered her little comfort as she wandered through the carnage. In sunlight, Ur's monstrous warriors were returned to what they were or should have been. A lot of them, turned decades and eons before their final death, had crumbled to wizened old husks of skin and bone or turned to dust outright. The rest, as young as her own slain soldiers, lay gored and butchered alongside them, joined in death. Only their armor told these Undying apart from the Akkadians or the human thralls. All were young men cut down in their prime, all for nothing Aisyah could justify. Not at that moment. Not at the sight of them, or at her father in his tent.

This, then, she realized, would be the legend of this land from here on, carved crimson on the tablet of this landscape. Carved there by her hand, and her father's, and Sin's and Bel's.

The ground beneath her feet muddy with blood, the princess went down on her knees and cried.

She knew not how much time passed before she heard a voice calling her.

"Your Highness," it said, timid with awe.

She looked up through her tears. The messenger was young, not one day over fifteen. He was wounded, his shoulder and arm bandaged.

"My father?" she asked, dreading the answer.

"He lives, my lady. Thank the gods."

A sob wracked her frame. She let it, unable to help herself.

"It was a thin path between life and death," the youth went on. "Your father crossed it many times, the physicians say. But he shall not die."

"What else did they say?"

The messenger hesitated. "Nothing," he said after a moment. "They could not speak of his recovery, only of the present danger."

Aisyah nodded. She rubbed her face with her hands, wiping her tears.

"And what of the battle? Have the dead been counted?"

"They lost more men than we, my lady. That is all I was told."

"Sin's side? Or Bel's?"

"Both. Your generals claim victory."

That made Aisyah chuckle. The youth looked at her, perplexed.

"Victory," she said, her voice hoarse. "Yes, I see."

She let her eyes wander the land of the dead. "They told me Sin fled after he struck my father down. Is it confirmed?"

"Aye, your highness."

"What of Bel and Narama? Are they among the slain?"

"They were both seen heading the Urians' retreat, alas."

Aisyah sighed. "It was too much to hope for," she said.

So the war was still on.

Just with a whole lot less men on each side.

She lifted her eyes to the boy. "You look pale," she told him. "Go to your unit, what of it's still there. Rest. And on your way, tell the generals to start setting up pyres for the dead."

The youth turned to leave. She stopped him.

"All the dead, tell them. Our men and theirs. We leave no corpse to rot."

He looked at her for a long moment, fathoming her words.

"Yes, your highness," he said, and ran off.

Over the following days, news of the battle and its aftermath spread far and wide across the lands of Sumer. Sin's army, it seemed, had suffered the worst casualties, to the point that, bereft of the Akkadians' numbers, his cause was irretrievably lost. In direct reflection of this fact, the Shadow Council had disbanded, its members scattered in the wind with as many men as each of them could muster, on the run from the Urians and the Akkadians alike.

Next in the number of casualties came the army of Ur itself. The battle had left their forces a mere shadow of their former might, now barely able to match the Akkadians, though the Undying still made up for that in terms of strength. It was still a war of Undying against mortals, and the mortals would always be in a disadvantage. As Aisyah thought, the war was still very much on.

In betraying their allies like they did, in the midst of battle, the Akkadians had not won the war. The truth was that Nimrod had hoped he'd be able to deal a decisive blow to both his foes, and in the end his troops had been only partly successful. At best, they had decimated one faction bound to become their enemy somewhere down the line. At worst, they had only delayed the inevitable, and merely faced a better chance against Bel's forces when that time came. Some of Akkad's generals criticized the king's bold decision, though none did so in the open, not with their liege bedridden and

Princess Aisyah in a mood that could charitably be called unforgiving.

Whether the strategy followed thus far had been right or not, what was undisputed by all was that the war had to be won – or lost – sooner rather than later. Bel had fallen back to Ur to regroup, and Akkad could not afford to let him do that. They had to press on into Ur's borders and advance all the way to the city itself, or die in the effort.

Without Sin's Undying, "die in the effort" seemed the most likely outcome.

CHAPTER 13

THE FUGITIVE KIND

Of all the things Erun could have recalled at this low point in his long life, he kept remembering a saying Narama's people had, lost with them in the sands of time.

"Judge not a man's path by the size of his tracks, but on whether he ran making them."

Narama had told him that lifetimes ago, and at the time he knew not what she meant. Only now that he was on the run, the trappings of the power he had amassed in eons reduced to worthless baubles as he fled for his life, did he realize the wisdom in the words.

One literal such bauble was tucked among the contents of a small chest in his tent. The magus almost laughed at the thought of Arkhalla's scarlet scepter stone. The key to the power of the Ones Below could have turned the war they had lost; it could have granted them victory. Except it was nothing without Arkhalla's blood, and Arkhalla was dead. None from the Council had claimed it all these years, right to the time when they left Ur for Sin's side. Erun did not even know why he bothered keeping it, other than as a reminder of how filled with false promise his life had been. All his days he had chased after the Magi's lore, and the mastery of the world that it would bring him. And all he had to show for it was failure.

The sun died on the horizon, its blood turning the sky red, and Erun felt old and tired. A reversal of fortune would do that to a man, as would long weeks of trekking across the desert. Of the followers and resources once at his command, the magus was left with but a paltry detail of three dozen men, and even they would stay at his side as long as the gold he paid them lasted. He had poured everything else into Sin's mad vision and had lost it in one cast of the die. All these one could deem as factors to feeling the weight of his years so acutely.

Or perhaps he simply was tired, and getting old.

He wrapped his cloak tighter about his thin frame, cursing Sin for the umpteenth time. Around him, his men were busy breaking camp. They had been crisscrossing between enemy borders – another humiliating reminder of how Ur and Akkad were hunting for the remnants of the Shadow Council now – heading towards the only territory not held by them: the South. His men had not asked how Erun planned to evade the rebel scum running rampant in those parts of Sumer, neither had he any idea what he'd answer them if they did ask. The chance of them slipping undetected across the chaos to the southern ports was next to nonexistent. Calling what Erun was fast running out of "hope" was probably an insult to the word. But what else did he have?

He straightened up, already feeling the cold of the coming dusk in his bones when one of the guards called out.

There was movement in the horizon. To mortal eyes, it'd be hard to tell whether it was a mirage or not, a cloud of dust trailing after nothingness or after something out there. But to the Undying, the shimmering was fast coalescing into substance.

Riders. A dozen of them for sure, perhaps twenty at the most.

Slowly, the riders came into being, edging closer across the desert out of the mirage for long minutes that seemed like forever. Erun's men waited for them with blades drawn. In the desert, one ought to be ready for friend or foe. And truth be told, Erun no longer counted on seeing friends anywhere in this world.

The riders stopped at last before the camp. Under the dust that caked their garments, Erun recognized familiar colors. Whoever these warriors were, they had fought beside his men at the Land Before the World. The one that seemed to be at their lead was very slim, almost jinn-like, wrapped in the robes and headdress of a desert tribesman. Erun was intrigued when the stranger dismounted and bent the knee before him, but not nearly as much as when the newcomer unwrapped the swaths of headdress to reveal a thin, tender-lined face and long, wavy hair that he knew only too well.

"Well met, Erun," said Lilit. Her smile was only halfway there, as though she was too exhausted to form it. There was something about her features that was more sharply drawn than usual, and her lips seemed chapped and pulled further back from her fangs.

"We are starving," she went on. "Been starving for days now. Almost as long as we've been in this godforsaken wasteland."

Erun could see no mortals of any kind among her train. He and the Undying among his escort had survived on frugal rations, taking care to do nothing worse than bleed their short supply of thralls. A smile creased his long face. The dumb bitch must have drunk hers dry.

"I beg of you, grant us sustenance and shelter," Lilit said, her head bowed.

Erun almost laughed. An augur bending the knee to a magus was too rich.

He had an immediate inkling to refuse, as much to humiliate his erstwhile rival as because he was loath to share his blood supplies. But as soon as the fantasy took shape in his head it was tempered by clear and present need. If he played it right, he could add close to two dozen swords to his. And humiliating Lilit would taste twice as sweet if it prolonged it.

Avoiding Lilit's eyes, he gave curt orders to his men to help to the other newcomers' needs and told his captain to bring the priestess to his tent. There, he slashed open a slave's arm and let her feed just tantalizingly short enough of sating herself before he ordered the slave and his captain away, leaving Erun alone with Lilit. He eagerly scanned the augur's slim face for anything from frustration to anger as the slave was led out of the tent, but she betrayed no emotion, turning her eyes low as, with an unsteady hand, she wiped the blood from her mouth. Erun had no doubt she was fighting hard not to lick the slick stain of crimson off the back her hand while he was looking. He felt a rush of satisfaction at that.

It took her a while before she lifted her gaze to him. Her doll-like face was still pale. Erun was surprised to see her eyes shining with unshed tears. He had not expected to see her so rattled already.

"It must have been rough out in the desert," he told her, barely holding back his glee.

"What..." Her voice was thin, emaciated, a slender twig breaking beneath his boot. "What will you do with me?"

"Well, your men are a welcome present, my dear," he said. "No doubt they shall readily switch allegiances to me in exchange for being fed and all." His smile turned to a sharp grin. "I may even leave you alive to starve. Or burn if you can't bear it, that's up to you."

She was shaking. He had broken her. Or the desert had done it for him, but it came down to the same thing.

"You... hate me that much, then?"

Erun laughed. "My dear girl, I have no feeling toward you whatsoever. Never did. But time and again you stood between me and what I wanted. Your followers rivaled mine; you vied for the influence I craved; and you undermined me at every turn."

She tried to protest. "It... it wasn't personal," she said. "I thought we moved past that. We were allies. Against Arkhalla. And Bel."

"While it was to our mutual benefit. And even then, there times you attempted to thwart me."

Tears were streaming down her face, scarlet with blood.

"In truth, it wasn't personal for me, either," he went on. The sight of her reduced to that state excited him. "After all, what more to expect from a stupid little bitch digging for prophecy in boys' entrails? Your whole faction was a bunch of bothersome nitwits. You wouldn't know true arcane power if it slapped you in the face."

He chuckled. "So no, nothing personal. Though I'll admit it gives me pleasure to see you grovel."

"P-please," Lilit blubbered through her tears. Great sobs were wracking her slender frame. Her breasts heaved from beneath her desert tribesman's tunic. "Please. Spare me. I'm at your mercy."

Erun felt a stir of excitement that was patently erotic.

"You have won," she begged him. "I have nothing. Spare me. Please. I'll do anything."

He eyed her for a moment, her despair in every limb and quaking curve of her body.

"Come here."

She obeyed, taking two steps forward. Her face was inches away from his.

It was the cruelty of it that made him hard with lust, he realized. That, and how completely at his mercy she was.

"You went down on your knees before, for blood," he said. "Bow down before me now. For your life."

She did it, trembling. His pleasure swelled. He felt it stretch against the fabric of his britches.

"Show me how much you want it," he said, unfastening his belt.

He took her there, on the floor of his tent. She had not even offered resistance, not when he forced himself into her mouth nor afterwards when he plucked her rags off her pale flesh like petals from the stem of a desert flower. So complete was his victory over her. She was a thing for his needs, a rag doll he punished for its insolence of having thought it was alive.

So it was with considerable surprise that, when he awoke from the lethargic slumber he had fallen into after that vigorous exercise, he found himself in what he could only define as extreme discomfort. He was sitting on the floor of the tent, propped up next to one of the support poles, his right hand chained to it. His wrist and back hurt him with the dull ache of bondage, and his throat felt as though he had swallowed ground limestone. A sharp inhale of breath brought the acrid taste of smoke, and he choked on it, coughing furiously.

It all felt wrong. What was *right*, what he remembered, the very last thing, was Lilit chained where he was now, bound for his pleasure. He shouldn't be here. He ought to be in his camp bed, waking up to the sight of his trophy all trussed up instead.

A second fit of coughing shook him. He could actually see smoke now, seeping in through the entrance and from beneath the tent itself. Something was burning.

The tent flap was pulled open and someone walked in through what seemed to him like smoke and fire. It was Lilit.

For one long, awful second, Erun was sure he was dreaming. There was no resemblance between the broken thing he had taken for his – was it even an hour ago? – and the harridan scowling down on him now. Lilit wore attire he recognized through bleary eyes as the same as the outfit his men wore, except it was crimson with blood, as was her face and lips. There was a scarlet-stained dagger in her hand, too.

"I thought I heard you coming to, dear," she said, stressing the last word in unconcealed mockery.

It was scorn's sting that finally pricked Erun to full consciousness. "Oh gods," he whispered. It was no dream.

"What... did you do?" he asked, his voice in pieces. Each word hurt his throat.

Lilit laughed.

"You really are pathetic," she said, and then she pulled open the tent flap.

Hell stared back at him from the opening. The shades of devils passed back and forth, howling, stabbing, and feeding the fire that was eating up the tents and corpses of his men.

Erun howled in horror, to which Lilit responded with another cackle.

"The funny thing is, Erun," she said, closing the tent flap, "that I really was weak, me and my men. We really were at your mercy. All you had to do was slay us."

She strode over to him and crouched down so that her eyes stared straight in his. What he saw inside them made Erun flinch.

"Except I know you too well, you vicious old fuck," she said. "I knew you wouldn't resist making it last. All I had to do is let you have your jollies and wait for my men to free me while you slept."

Her hand caressed his neck. Only now did Erun feel a sharp stab of pain where she touched him.

"Only took enough to have you sleep through it," she said softly. "Wouldn't want to spoil the surprise now, would we?" "Filthy whore!" he screamed back at her.

The backhanded slap almost took his head off.

"That is the last time you call me that," she said.

Erun tasted blood on his lips. It brought him an acute sense of his mortality.

"No!" he cried out, desperately fighting against his bonds. "No! No! Please!"

It only made her laugh again.

"Idiot," she spat out before she got up.

It was when Erun saw her rummaging through the tent that he began to realize. But only when she had already found his gold and kept on looking did he grow sure.

At last she found the jewel at the bottom of the chest. With a cry of triumph, she held it up. The scepter stone caught the flames' glow in its facets, burning like the eyes of a cruel god.

"Tell me," she said, looking at him again as though she'd just remembered he was there. "Were you ever going to do anything with it? Or were you going to let it go to waste like Sin and those other fools?"

Erun swallowed hard. "You know it doesn't work," he blurted out, weakly. "The ritual; it needs Arkhalla's blood."

"And you know *I* told you that, even before you found out," she retorted, all scorn. "I told you all. But *you* thought me worthless. And after you failed, high-and-mighty Sin would not even bother listening to me. So I stayed silent. And I waited."

She stared deep within the jewel in her hand now, and to Erun's eyes, it almost seemed as though the shadows in the stone stirred in response to her lingering look.

"I am a blood augur, you fools," she said, her voice low and deep with something that spoke through her. "If there is one thing I am the mistress of, it is my craft. You think it impossible to use the stone. It is only next to impossible."

Her laugh came from somewhere dark and cold inside her. "But none of you can see that."

Erun struggled with his chains, frantic. "How? Tell me!" he cried out, hoarse with smoke. "Lilit, please! How?"

She turned from the stone to him. "You are forgetting your place," she said. "You're at my feet, Erun. Grovel." He cursed, vilely.

All it did was make him feel even more impotent.

Lilit's smile widened into a grin.

"Let me tell you why you still draw breath," she said. "I've burned down your camp and murdered those of your men that would not follow me. I have your gold. And I have the stone. To kill you now would be a mercy."

She paused. There was no sound except Erun's labored breathing and the crackle of flames.

"So I'll tell you what I'll do to make this last, my dear," she went on. "I'll leave you alone here after I set this tent on fire, and then I'll ride out with your men and your gold and the stone. Your fate I leave to you. Perhaps the fire will finish you, or if you still live, then the sun will when it rises."

At this, she lifted her index finger, stressing her next words.

"Unless, that is, you choose to free yourself."

Erun's heart pumped so hard it ached within his chest as he stared back at her. He could find no meaning in her words, none but a vague dark horror that seized at him and would not let go.

"You may choose to," Lilit went on with a shrug. "And perhaps you will make it out of here in time. And then you will be in the middle of the desert. Without your followers. Without your thralls. Without your power. And with naught but enemies at every point in the horizon."

She turned to leave, pausing in the entrance for one parting remark.

"You know, I actually hope you make it. Then your humiliation shall last forever."

And like that, she was gone, and Erun was alone.

He had only half-listened to her, his mind torn between his abject terror and a nagging need to know what she had meant.

Choose to free yourself, she'd said.

How? How could he?

A crackling sound made him jump. She'd done it. She'd set fire to the tent.

He struggled with the chains that bound him to the pole. There was no breaking them.

What did she mean?

A rumble of horses came over the sizzle of the flames. She was riding off, taking it all. His men and gold. The stone. And then the galloping died away and all he heard was the fire.

It was getting hotter. He fought to free himself anew. He was getting so despaired he tried to break his hand. All it did was make the chains cut deeper in his wrist.

He cursed at the pain, at her.

His wrist.

Choose to free yourself.

Oh, no.

He looked at his wrist. He felt the pain where the chains had broken the skin. He felt blood, metallic, dry, like the blood in his mouth, tickling his fangs.

Oh, gods.

It was all it'd take. If he did, he could get free.

He could see flames now, peeking through gaps that opened in the fabric of the tent. Thick beads of sweat flowed down his brow. There was no telling if it was the heat or horror.

He lifted his hand as much as the chains let him, looking at where in his wrist he'd have to –

To –

Choose to free yourself.

With tears in his eyes, Erun bared his fangs.
A moment later, he bit down on his hand, howling with pain.
He could not stop. If he did, he’d never finish.
Choking on his flesh, he bit down again.

CHAPTER 14

STALKING MOON

What made the desert a safe place to hide was that it seemed so empty. Somewhere in all its desolation, though, there was always a well, which was why it drew the nomads to it in the first place. To untrained eyes, a never-ending desert with sand dunes that towered like palaces and vast flatlands of limestone and fossilized rock was just that, and nowhere was this impression more apt than in the lands to Ur's southwest. Of all the places Ur's and Akkad's hunting parties searched for the fugitive members of the Shadow Council – and there were many, for the world was a far greater place to trek through in those early days of man – none could seem less likely to support and harbor them than the Empty Place. Which was the very reason why Lilit chose to hide there.

In those lands that hid her from her hunters, the heat hovered just short of boiling point at midday and was barely more tolerable at sundown. That made this part of the desert all but unreachable to the Akkadians, and even the Undying, who could withstand the sandstorms and the ice-cold winds that whipped these lands from dusk till dawn, would have hiked less than a thousand cubits in an hour before their lungs filled with sand, gravel, and dust. Humans could not survive the Empty Place, and any Undying not knowing exactly where to head would find themselves at sunup stranded on a wasteland without end that was the gods' frying pan.

But there was one secret that the Empty Place kept closely guarded to its bosom, and Lilit knew it. She had learned it early in her long life, before the desert tribesmen, since extinct in one of King Anshara's wars, sold her to slavery in Ur and she was taken and initiated into the priesthood of the augurs. Her people, wiped out by the desert raiders, called it The Sky Goddess' Tears; reached only through a grueling night's trek across the western borders of the Empty Place and only thanks to landmarks that were next to invisible to anyone not wise in the desert nomads' ways, it showed up as a well in the center of a dry riverbed. Those who managed to climb down its limestone, fossil-covered walls, the only sign this land was once at the bottom of the sea, found the Sky-Goddess' Tears, the underground caves filled with pools of water. The legends of her people had it that the Sky-Goddess wept for the loss of her daughter who fell to the earth, and that her tears seeped deep into the earth to form eternal underground lakes. From what Lilit could tell, the water seeped in and formed the pools from deeper underground, but how that happened was as magical to her as tears from heaven. In the days her tribe still roamed the earth, these caves had been hideouts to raiders, trekkers, even kings that waited out attacks from invaders.

Here it was that Lilit waited, hidden, with her men and thralls, till the Urians and Akkadians either tired of looking for her or slaughtered each other, whatever happened first. She would not bleed her thralls dry and repeat the error that had brought her to that sorry state while she had sought out Erun. Here in the coolness of the caves, she'd be sustained, safe, until it was time for her to reemerge. Not only could she think of no one who knew that she had made it here, but even that this place existed. She was here, alive, and with her prize. The stone she kept always by her side, in a pouch fastened to her belt, and at night she'd take it out and watch the reflections from the water pools play on its facets. Arkhalla, whose blood powered it, was gone. The blood of those Undying she sired, even the Twelve of her Council, was too diluted of the essence of the gods' power after their eons of feeding and siring others in return. But Lilit believed in the power of blood. She had studied it and its intricate secrets, how memories of victims were passed to the Undying through the bite that bonded them, carried in riverways of veins, how deep connections formed between the Undying and their thralls that bound them across space and time. Erun and the others had it all wrong. They had tried sacrificing droves of humans to the pit to energize the stone and open the doorway to the gods, while all it'd take would be the blood of even one living soul that the Queen herself had fed on. That blood, still tainted with her bite but untouched by the change brought by the turning, could contain a trace of her, as much, perhaps, as to energize the stone. For eons, while she was Queen, Arkhalla left no victims alive or unturned, so it had been impossible. But then she fell, and had to change her ways.

Lilit had seen the boy, the slave Arkhalla had fed on to survive, when Narama brought him to Ur and used him to hunt her down. If that boy still lived, he or any other human bitten by the Queen before her death, then not all was lost. All Lilit had to do was stay alive long enough to seek them out. The thought warmed the cold nights in the cave as though it was a warm flame cast by the scarlet facets of the stone. She lay basking in it, her eyelids drooping with sweet lethargy. And while she was here, she was safe.

It was impossible for anyone who didn't know its location to reach the well above, so no guard was placed either up top at its mouth or at its bottom. So no one was there to see when, near the end of that night, so close to morn that a pale wound began to bleed along the black and grey horizon, a lone figure stumbled out of the storm of sand and into the dry riverbed. Lean and clad in a black desert tribesman's outfit turned golden brown by the sand blown on it, the Undying – for no human could have ventured thus far in the raging elements – paused on the well's mouth like a tiger coiled to strike. The storm was already abating, the heat around the riverbed rising with the coming of the day. Mere minutes later and the Undying would have been caught uncovered in the sunrise and burnt to cinders.

Wasting no time, the figure climbed down inside the well, lizard-like, hands and feet gaining precarious purchase on the minutest holds onto the rock. Its climb was fast, no-nonsense, yet graceful. By the time the sun shone on the mouth of the well, it was out of the light's reach. But it did not slow down, yet continued on. The walls were slippery, almost flat. Twice, it damn near lost its hold and fell down the abyss. Yet even as it managed to cling on desperately, its hands stayed steady, betraying not even the slightest sign of fear.

Even aided with ropes, Lilit and her men had taken twice as long to reach the bottom. By the time the climber reached the caves, one hour had passed.

The figure moved in stealth, blended with the dark, from shadow to shadow. It needed no light to guide its way, only a tracker's instinct. Lilit's followers and thralls were scattered throughout the maze, the Undying among them shrouded in blankets and asleep, the thralls sitting awake beside them, ready to guard them with their lives, as instructed, even against no apparent danger. The figure crawled past them among the rocks, as close onto the ground as a snake on its belly. It crept behind them, silent as a feather carried on the wind. And where there were no rocks for it to hide behind, it crawled along the ceiling of the caves, above the thralls' heads. Nobody saw nor heard nor felt it.

Lilit and two of her guard were in the furthest cave, on an islet of ground surrounded by a dark underground lake. These men were Undying like her, but did not sleep, their keen senses alert to anyone and anything that'd dare approach their mistress during her day's rest. Shrouded in darkness, the lone figure crept to the lake's edge and slipped into the water without stirring the tiniest wave. Instead of swimming to the islet, it let itself be submerged in the black pool, then walked across its bottom without letting out as much as a bubble of breath to betray its coming.

Slowly, it reached the islet. As it began to emerge from the water, it slowed its motions even more to total stillness, so that only the top of its head peaked out of the pool, two dark green eyes scanning the guards from the gap between the folds of its headdress.

The guards had their backs turned, none the wiser to its presence. The figure knew it was too close for silence now. Every movement it made would cause a rippling of water which an Undying's hearing was bound to pick out. It coiled itself, ready to spring, aware of the strength it'd have to put into the leap to counter the effect of the water.

Like a knife unsheathed, the figure leapt; even as the guards turned, alerted by the sound of its breaking through the surface, it knew they'd be too late. The first guard had but half-drawn his sword before the figure's blade sliced across his neck. The second man was able to see the sickle-sword, stained red from his comrade's blood, as it cut a red-streaming arc through the air before it struck him right between the eyes. Blinded, he opened his mouth to cry out, his sword flailing at the air. His blade brushed the figure's cheek just as a second stroke severed his head from his neck.

Lilit, wide-eyed, awoken but still half-lying down and covered by her blanket, stared in terror as the figure came closer, undoing its headdress.

There was no whisper or gasp of recognition from Lilit as she saw the Undying's face. As for Narama, she only stared at the terrified augur, emotionless. There was a single cut on her face, a long gash caused by the second guard's blade.

Lilit tried to think of something to say. The moment of one's death seemed to warrant it. But nothing came to her. Her limbs trembled as she got up, slowly, like a desert rat caught in the gaze of a cobra.

She had hoped – she only now realized – that it would not be Narama herself to come after her, that with Sin and Kuthan and all the others on the loose the Huntress would have not deemed her worth the chase. A lilting pang in Lilit's heart told her she was almost gladdened she was worth it, even at the cost of that long life she had fought and gone through so much to hold on to. She was important, after all. For some reason, whatever it was, she was worth the time of one of the significant ones. A bitter smile came on her face from underneath the terror, caused by her realization and embittered by a taste of ashes. All her efforts, her tracking down Erun, her hiding in the well of the Sky Goddess' Tears, her dream of power in the future, all had been in vain. Narama had hunted her down. Lilit might as well as run from the huntress moon, stalking across the sky.

Narama's dagger slid between her ribs so softly she almost never felt it. Lilit reached up, twitching, her hand touching her killer's cold face in one last brush with life. The augur's fingers felt the gash on the Huntress' cheek. Narama's blood burned hot, firing the flames of vision one last time in Lilit's mind.

"I'm sorry about your daughter," the augur said, death a fast thief stealing her voice.

Narama held onto the dagger lodged in Lilit's heart as her free hand drove her sickle-sword upwards through her neck.

CHAPTER 15

THE GHOST AND THE DARKNESS

For close to three weeks now the ghost plagued the village. It had started like all terrible things start, small, with sheep and goats taken in the night and found the next or following day far from their pen, pale and bloodless and with their throats torn. To be clear, that was no small matter for the villagers. Their tiny settlement had changed hands so often this past year, the land surrounding it taken by the Undying, then retaken by the rebels and back again, that raids and pillaging had left it with its population halved and their grain all but looted. So something claiming what little livestock they still had was cause for alarm. Still, the matter's graveness paled before their terror when the ghost began to take their children.

A dirt farmer's daughter was discovered first, the five-year-old child's body found mangled in a ditch, its throat eaten clean through in a botched effort to mask the kill as one done by an animal. But the lack of blood on and about the corpse gave the thing away. Then another child was taken and found dead, and another, and no one in the village doubted what the ghost was anymore.

The rebels came the very next afternoon they were summoned, in force. Yssur himself led them, on his way to raid the lands of Ur and secure the territories of this part of the South, and the villagers' messenger had found them that dawn as they were breaking camp. Even in the grip of terror and grief, the villagers' hearts cheered at the sight of the rebel leader whose name had grown to that of a hero for all under the Undying's boot. And his arrival was tied to their urgency, for just the previous night a new victim had been taken from her bed, a young girl only four years old.

Yssur decreed he'd lead a hunting party to the monster's lair before the hour was up.

Shamath drew him aside and questioned the wisdom of this move.

"There is only one place the leech can be hidden," Yssur countered. "The caves on the rocky hills just outside from here. We'll corner the brute and have its head."

Shamath nodded. The hills on the other side of the settlement were the one place in this patch of desert an Undying could crawl inside come the dawn. That wasn't what concerned him.

"It's near dark," he said. "The damned thing has had the child for a night and a day. She is done for."

"You cannot know that, Shamath. Not for sure."

"Neither can you. But the leech will be up soon. Let us not face it in its lair. We'll set up a cordon around the village, gather the children where it cannot –"

Yssur scoffed. "And show fear?"

"Caution. I would not risk even a single man's life. Not when we can scour the hills come morn and catch it helpless."

Yssur frowned. He knew his second was right. Shamath was ruthless in war and even more so with the prisoners, more than Yssur cared for, but he was as keen in mind as a warrior born. For a moment, he considered giving in. But the order was already given, his men ready to ride, and the villagers were watching.

"We cannot fail these people," he objected. "There is a chance the child might be alive, however slight. They expect us to act now. We are committed."

Shamath flared up. "*You* are committed. To the idea they have of you. Your men –"

"Must follow orders," Yssur spat back, incensed. "As must my second."

Shamath stared at him.

"We are committed, Shamath. And we cannot give in to despair while there is still hope. We have to keep up their idea of us because that is who we are. That's how a war is won."

The young man looked at him another moment before he turned and headed to his horse. "That isn't how a war is won," he said, almost under his breath.

The hunting party set off within the hour, keeping Yssur's commitment, and the rebel leader was at its head with Shamath riding silent at his side. By the time they reached the small cluster of hills, it was dusk. They left their horses and began to search for the leech, split into teams of four men. Yssur was no fool. The search was methodical, conducted in strict army protocol. The men uttered not a whisper, moving as shadows in the growing dark as they signaled an area to be clear after they'd combed it.

It was a half hour later that they heard the laugh.

One moment, all was silence. The next, the hills and the caves that pockmarked them rang out with a sound that chilled the men to their marrow. It was not quite a laugh, nor was it truly human. There was a sob there in it, underneath, drawing it out, a cry of pain that only repetition turned into anything that could be thought as laughter. There was no mirth in it, no reason. It was the laugh of a thing gone mad, one that had gone through too much even to remember sanity.

"Kill you," the hills reverberated all about them between the fits of laughter. "Kill you all!"

There was no telling where the voice came from. It was too dark, and the rocks too cluttered and hollow. Yssur swore under his breath as he signaled the men to take extra care.

The laughter ceased. They went on with the search. Minutes later, one quartet of men found the cave with the remains of the kidnapped child inside. The other teams converged onto the spot and filed out again from there. Yssur's team waded through a narrow passage and the rebel leader took point, his sword drawn. His face was crestfallen. He really had hoped, to that last moment, that the child would have been found alive. Shamath followed, and the two other men brought up the rear. The passage narrowed even further as they went on, its shadows growing deeper. Any moment now, they'd have to turn back.

A shrill cry tore out from the dark ahead of them. A thing flew out, pale and in rags, a wraith, wailing, insane.

Yssur plunged his blade forth through air and rags, missing the ghost's heart by a second as it leapt onto the side wall of the passage. He twisted in mid-thrust, bringing his sickle-sword upwards to cleave the thing in twain when it caught in the narrow walls of the passage. The next moment, the creature was on him.

Shamath stabbed at it just as he heard Yssur's scream cut short and the thing cried out when his blade caught it in the arm. Leaving Yssur onto the ground, it tried to leap above the three men. Shamath reached up and grabbed it at the last second and threw his full weight on it. They smashed together on the wall and Shamath held on as the thing tore at his face and arms. He thrust his head forward and his skull smashed into the monster's face. They fell down together on top of Yssur. Shamath cried out at the two men. He knew there was no room for a clean stroke. They had to subdue the thing before it freed itself. Already he felt it slipping his embrace.

One of the men brought the hilt of his sickle-sword down onto the thing's head, and all of a sudden it went limp and was still.

Panting, Shamath threw the leech off him. His two men grabbed and helped lift its weight even as Shamath reached in panic for Yssur's still body.

The rebel leader was dead, his neck broken.

Shamath held his comrade's face in disbelief, feeling the warmth of life dissipate from it.

They had fought these long months together, against odds beyond impossible, untouched, as though the gods had favored them and their cause. All these battles, all these warriors, Black Guards, in numbers that dwarfed their own every single time, and now Yssur lay dead at the hands of one single leech.

His face scarred by tears, he looked at the motionless form of the thing in the grip of the two dumbstruck soldiers. It was a skin clothing bone, burnt and parched, drawn tight about a mouth filled with broken fangs and limbs that were nigh spider-thin. This half-dead thing, driven mad by hunger and exposure as it crawled through the desert to this village, had killed one of the bravest, kindest souls Shamath had ever known.

"Bring it with us," he said to his men as he lifted his slain leader in his arms. "Alive."

The Undying snapped its jaws, its neck stretched helplessly forward as it pulled at its chains. All that was left of humanity in its yellowed eyes was rage. Shamath looked at the thing across the torchlit tent, the thinned strands of hair glued to the skull, the dried stump that its right arm ended at instead of a hand, the hollowed, fleshless face. Only the rags that still clung to its burnt, skeletal form bore even a hint of the tall old nobleman with trimmed beard and vinegar tongue that he recalled from his days at Arkhalla's court.

"So much for the ambitious and the mighty," Shamath said, as much to himself as to the chained thing. "Wouldn't you say, Lord Erun?"

The thing blinked at the sound of its name. It opened and shut its mouth a couple of times, as though it was trying to repurpose it to speech again. Shamath wondered how long Erun had wandered in the desert, crouching into the shade of rocks and burrowing into the burning sand to take refuge from the sun. The mouthful of broken fangs told him it had been too long. The madness of hunger had driven the magus so desperate he'd tried biting into the stones of the wasteland.

"You... know me?" the thing said at last, its words coming out garbled and deformed.

Shamath nodded.

"...Undo these chains, then."

"Or you'll do what? Kill me? Like you killed my friend?" At this, Shamath paused, controlling his anger. "You are not among your thralls, Lord Erun. Get used to that."

Shamath got up from his chair and crossed the tent, stopping a few feet from the prisoner with his back to the entrance of the tent.

"If you won't free me, kill me," the old man said. "Anything to spare me your prattle."

He cackled then, quite unexpectedly. Whatever effort he was doing to sound like his old self, he was too far gone for it to work all the way.

"Goats and monkeys," he said, the laughter twisted into something bitter. "Ha. That's what I'm reduced to." A bloody tear rolled down his cheek.

He had spoken the word *monkeys* with such abject hatred, Shamath realized that was how he thought of the children of the village. It took a lot of strength not to end the old bastard right then and there.

No. Not yet. Not before he knew.

Calming himself, Shamath stared at the living dead thing's face.

"The Magi," he said. "You knew their lore, their secrets. Asag's forbidden knowledge."

Erun let out a drawn-out cacophonous laugh that lasted several moments longer than it should.

"If I had a gold coin for every idiot that pried," he said, "or every trollop that slept with me for scraps of the power; heh. I'd be wealthier than Arkhalla in her prime."

He chuckled. Shamath ignored his mockery.

"The Magi," he insisted.

"You have no idea," the old man spat at him. "No inkling of how deep it went, their knowledge. Their power."

He started repeating that last word, rolling it on his tongue in all the ways he could. Then he laughed again.

"Tell me how to get to the Lands Below," said Shamath.

Erun's laugh died like it had been cut by a blade. He stared at Shamath, blinking.

When Shamath realized the old magus wasn't going to speak, he repeated what he'd said.

A misshapen grin broke onto Erun's face. "The Lands Below," he chuckled. "You want... to know how... to go there."

"Yes."

"Die."

He started on another mad laugh when Shamath lifted up the tent flap.

Sunlight poured in. It was high noon, when it was at his strongest.

Erun fell backwards on the ground, reeling from it. His face was twisted in a grimace of unimaginable pain. His leg, caught in the bright noon's light, began to decompose.

An Undying caught at sunrise will blister and simmer and burn beneath the skin. One caught in the noonday desert sun, even an elder of Arkhalla's strain, will turn to ash in minutes.

Shamath closed the flap again. Erun's whimper reached his ears just as a stench of roasted meat tickled his nostrils.

"Tell me how to get to the Lands Below," he repeated. "*Fuck you*."

Shamath drew the flap aside. The beam of sunlight fell on the Undying's leg once more, slowly, agonizingly crumbling it to thick dust. Erun screamed and twisted about his chains as he tried to crawl away. His eyes were bloodshot.

Shamath's hand pulled the flap down.

"Talk."

"I don't *know*!"

More sunlight poured inside. Erun's body arched and fell to the side; he howled in agony. His fall had brought his left hand straight into the beam's path. Brittle bones began to fall to pieces, then to naught but dust.

Again the flap came down.

"Please," the old man whispered weakly. "I do not know. I never... knew." He sobbed. "Only Arkhalla knew. She... she left only... pieces. And even that little... she left... was taken from me." Tears flowed on Shamath's face at the mention of Arkhalla. He did not even know why he had asked the old man that, and only now did he realize that the demand had always been there, in the back of his mind, that wish to defy death itself and step into its cold and haunted realm to bring her back, back into the light.

He believed the old man. No one in the pain he was could keep on lying. Erun did not know.

For a moment, Shamath almost pitied him. Then, remembering, he lifted the tent flap.

A blade of light separated Erun's hand from his arm. The old man writhed, another long howl drilling into Shamath's ears.

"You helped murder her," he said. "It was your poison that Narama used."

Erun tried to crawl back, twisted, fell. Shamath opened the flap a little wider. Sunlight hit the Undying's face; he tried shielding it with what was left of his right hand, screaming.

The tent flap fell down again. There was thick smoke filling the entire tent now, the stench of roasting mixed with that of rot, unbearable.

"Wasn't it?" asked Shamath, his voice shaking.

The old man whimpered.

"WASN'T IT?" Shamath screamed. He reached for the tent flap.

"Yes," Erun said, his voice ashes. "Yes." He whimpered again. "I did it... I... made it. That... poison. Please... Anything. I'll tell you... anything."

Shamath lips trembled. "Anything," he heard the old man say, weakly.

Once more the idea writhed in his head, fully grown.

"Tell me how you made it."

He had to reiterate his demand again, his hand tightened about the fabric of the flap, before the old man could make sense of what it was that Shamath wanted of him. Shaking, twitching with pain, the living dead thing spoke in slow, drawn-out sentences. With each breath he took so agonizing Erun thought it to be its last, he told its torturer what instruments he'd used to craft the poison that had brought Arkhalla down.

When he was done, at long last, Shamath asked him if that was all.

The old man said yes.

Shamath nodded and tore the tent flap open. Light washed over the Undying's face, past the stump of a hand he threw up, past his arm. Howling, cursing, he burned, till his face was nothing but grey rot. Still Erun screamed, a skeleton on fire, his skull crowned in flame. His body burned, decomposed, like hers on the pyre, so long ago. His rags contracted around dwindling bones. What was left of the once fine fabric grew caked with ashes and dust as Erun melted.

Erun was nothing but a pile of dust in tatters now. A tuft of hair blew with the breeze from a skull that was there no more. The draft coming in the tent dissolved it all into nothingness, the outline of dust that was a hand, a head, a face.

Even then, Erun still screamed in Shamath's head, his cries mixed with hers.

And in his head, they did not burn in light or fire. They burned in darkness.

CHAPTER 16

A LEADER OF MEN

The flames on Yssur's pyre hadn't even died down yet when a lookout cried out that a company of riders was approaching.

"Undying?" asked Shamath.

"Not by their colors," the lookout replied.

Men. And judging from how they used none of the agreed signals in their approach, they were not rebels. What was a company of strangers doing there?

He told the guards to meet and escort the riders through the Shaft, the narrow gorge that snaked through the mountain to the rebels' camp, and waited at its mouth, the wind fanning the pyre behind his silhouette.

"Should we expect trouble?" he heard Dumu's voice at his side.

His smile was bitter. He didn't have to look at his friend's face to know that hers was the same. "There's always trouble."

She hummed in agreement. "So the question is what kind." Shamath sensed her tense up. "And here comes the answer."

About thirty riders came out of the Shaft, counting out the guards that flanked them. Enough for a raiding party if they were good enough. Or an infiltration squad plus reinforcements, or a delegation on no less than a king's business. Their colors were strange to Shamath and Dumu, but from their duskier skins and the shape of their eyes, they doubtless came from afar. The warrior at their head was not dressed in any different kind of armor, but the way the others stayed a half-length behind this rider's magnificent white steed marked him as a less a captain or a high ambassador and more as the prince they were escorting.

"Princess," Shamath heard Dumu say, as though she had read his mind.

He turned to her. "What?"

Dumu raised an eyebrow. "Look at the bearing. How light she seems on horseback, even in armor. If that's not a high-born woman, and a young one at that, then I'm an old man." She shrugged. "I've known one queen in my life. This one carries herself like that. Except she doesn't dress the part, and she moves like she's too young for it. My money's on princess."

Shamath smiled. "When did you become a magus?"

She scoffed. "The magi know nothing of body language. Girls in my line of work had to."

The riders stopped a few feet from them. As their leader dismounted, Shamath could see Dumu was right. The high-born woman did neither try to make her motion masculine nor added to it any tropes of femininity. She just was what she was; her grace was natural.

She did not remove her helm until she stood before them. A cascade of dark hair adorned a face as Eastern as those of her men, and beautiful enough to justify all of them dying for her. She stared back at Shamath with interest, studying the young warrior almost as though she sized him up as an opponent on the field, except not quite so.

"I am Aisyah of Akkad," she said, her words rich with the accent of some foreign tongue that made her voice as sensual as her face. "I am here on business of High King Nimrod, my father."

Shamath nodded. "We know of your war with Ur. You are welcome, your grace."

He had addressed her with a proper greeting, but neither he nor Dumu bowed. If Aisyah took notice of that, it did not show, except if it was in the smile that played fleetingly on her lips.

"I seek your leader," she said.

Shamath's face twitched. He pointed to the burning pyre.

"There he is," he said with a sigh.

Aisyah's smile broke. She stared at the flames for a moment, their glow casting shadows on her visage. "How?"

"An Undying, the night before last."

Shamath and Dumu followed the princess as she approached the pyre and stood before it. Looking at her, Shamath thought he saw her lips move briefly, as in a greeting, or a farewell. She seemed to sense his eyes, and turned to face him.

"While we sought out your camp, the people of the towns and villages all along the South from here to the borders spoke nothing but praises for Yssur," she said, her voice betraying how moved she was. "They spoke of a warrior with a dream of peace. There are not many like him."

"The world shall not see his like again," said Shamath. Her words had rekindled the injustice of his friend's end. He would have followed Yssur to the gates of Asag's hell, all for that dream of his. And now he was awake, the dream burning on a pyre, like all his dreams ended.

Aisyah saw the darkness in his heart, but probed no further, respecting it. "I am sorry for your loss. And for our importune arrival." She paused, one brief, careful moment. "But our wars go on, and time is of the essence. Will you speak with me?"

Shamath was taken by surprise. "Me? I am not these men's leader."

The princess glanced at Dumu, then at the faces of the rebels gathered about the pyre, turned towards them. "The way these men look at you, I believe you're wrong," she said. "If you don't mind us staying, we can talk after the burning."

At this, she nodded, and with a second nod to the direction of the pyre, she withdrew to the side, where her men had dismounted and waited for her.

"A princess, all right," whispered Dumu, turning up her nose. "She says jump and we are supposed to ask how high. Still, that doesn't make her wrong."

"She couldn't be more wrong," Shamath objected. "All that nonsense about how you all look at me."

Dumu smiled. "We look up at you, Shamath. Even Yssur did, in his way. You noticed how everyone listens to you since he died?"

"What?"

"Who gave instructions for the pyre? Who had the guards escort the little princess and her thirty swords to the camp?"

"I was Yssur's second. I'm just handling things until we pick a leader."

"Well, we have."

Dumu cast a look towards the princess. "Guess princesses know body language, too."

"I am sorry we could not meet under more fitting circumstances, General Shamath," said Aisyah as she settled by the fire. "I understand how my manner may have appeared brusque at what must be a hard time for your men and for yourself."

She hoped the sentiment behind her apology did not sound as studied at her words.

"No offence taken," said the young warrior. "And please do not call me General."

"Ah. Commander, then?"

"We do not have ranks, your grace."

"Ah."

There was a naivety to this young man's manner that might have come off as a lack of intelligence if not for the experience she could see in his eyes, so Aisyah decided it was his manner, and that he was as honest as he was not a fool. His way of addressing her was rather old-fashioned, as though he had learned it in some ancient court, but she kind of liked it. He spoke the word *grace* as though it was meant for her, not her status.

She cast her eyes about them. The camp was well chosen, with the rock wall behind them offering both shelter in its caves and as many natural vantage points for archers as the embrasures of the best war tower. And that gorge they called the Shaft meant no army could advance to their position except in lines of one to two men wide, at a pace that would allow the camp's defenders that shoot them full of arrows before they made it half the way in. The plateau above the wall, if well guarded, would be nigh impregnable, and the mountain above that offered multiple avenues of escape in case of a siege. Aisyah could understand why this rebellion had not been crushed, and the sight gave her heart a warmth she sorely needed after the wounding of her father.

"The south of Ur is yours in all but name," she said. "You have done well."

Shamath smiled. "That's good to hear."

Aisyah felt her cheeks flush. "I did not mean to sound superior. Yours may be a ragtag army, but you have accomplished much."

It was the second time she apologized to him within an hour. Embarrassment was not something she was used to, and it felt strange.

"Thank you," he said, with feeling, as though he meant to put her at ease. "We heard of your victory at The Land Before The World. I would have thought it next to impossible for Bel to be bested in the field, and even less for Sin to be double-crossed. Your strategy was masterful."

"It was difficult," she countered, speaking truth rather than niceties. "And costly."

"How is your father?"

"Ailing. But he lives."

There seemed to be genuine concern in his voice when he asked her. In this, too, he treated her not like a royal born, but like a person. Two people talking to each other. Aisyah could not remember the last time she had experienced that.

She cleared her throat. "I am here to talk of an alliance between us. Bel is weakened. If we can coordinate a joint attack, you pushing from the South, we from the North and East, we can finish him."

"What about Sin?"

"His forces were annihilated. He's on the run. And there is no way Bel would ally himself with him again. I think we can erase him from the picture."

Shamath stroked his beard, thinking. "We are not a regular army, your grace. A big push could end up decimating us."

Aisyah leaned forward. "This is the moment. We need to engage him on two fronts. He will never be able to send his full forces against you while fighting us, but our advance means nothing without you pushing forward at the same time."

The passion in her words made him look her in the eyes. Their color was almost as changeable as Arkhalla's, and in firelight, they seemed golden as honey.

"Perhaps you are right, your grace," he told her. "You offer strategy while we have none, and a joint advance seems like the only way for both of us to win. But I will not send my men into the dark of death without thought."

Aisyah was taken aback. "Nor will I," she protested.

There was a moment's silence. She took a breath before going on.

"I... saw nearly half my father's army slaughtered at The Land Before The World. All those men dead, their lives stolen, their families bereaved. All because of orders my father gave and I carried out."

She lowered her eyes. "I was born and reared to lead, with no more choice in the matter than you have now that your commander was slain. And with my father bedridden, I must be the one to make the hard choice of sending my men to their deaths. But I only do it because the alternative is the annihilation of my people. And I will never do it lightly. That would make me as dark and dead inside my soul as those we fight."

"I am as dark and dead inside as those we fight," he said. "That is the only way to beat them."

It was her turn to look at him. "You cannot mean that."

"I do." He sighed. "Yssur thought like you did, that we are better than them, that we have to do better, and he is dead. I used to think like you did, lifetimes ago, and it cost me everything."

"But you do care about your men," Aisyah objected. "You said so just now."

"I said I will not send them to their death without thought. But not because I wish to spare their lives. You know as well as I that is not possible, your grace."

"Why then?"

"Because to have them slaughtered will lose us the war."

Aisyah made to ask something, but what she saw in Shamath's eyes silenced her.

She wrapped herself tighter in her cloak and stared at the flames awhile, perplexed. Her question still bothered her, but rather than ask him, she chose to give her own reply to it.

"I wonder sometimes what I'd be if I was not royal born and pledged to fight this war," she said. "What life I'd picture for myself if I did not owe so much to blood and the future."

That seemed to move him. "What did you picture?"

"A quiet life on a farm," she said. "I'd rather be a farmer's wife, toiling the land with him, scraping a living from it. I'd rather have that than all the jeweled thrones and glorious wars of man." She looked at him again and saw him deathly pale.

Someone called out to the young warrior from a nearby fire, and as he turned to answer, she studied his face. It was still youthful, handsome, but lined and scarred with hardship, and his beard covered what seemed to be scars amassed over a fair share of fights. The scars she studied, though, were ones beneath the skin. There was a darkness there, a black mass of cicatrices she felt she could almost touch if she but reached out and touched his cheek. It was a wound that had never healed right, only scarred over, that made this quiet man utter such cold and cruel pronouncements. She knew, deep within her somehow, that he tried so hard not to feel it was killing him. But he still felt; of that Aisyah was quite sure.

His eyes fixed on hers as he turned to face her, and she looked away, uncomfortable. But she still felt his stare.

"There is something you wish to know," she guessed. "But you hesitate to ask."

"Yes."

"Ask it."

"I've heard your people are wise in the ways of the Undying. That you have long experience in dealing with them, and a drive to end them that is second to none."

"That is true."

"And it is known that to learn their strengths and weaknesses, you have studied the lore of the Magi, the legends of the Undying's creation in the pit of Asag's hell, more than any people on this earth."

Aisyah frowned, unsure of his intent. "Yes."

"Do you know how to cross over to the Lands Below?"

She was startled. "Why in the gods' name would you want to do that?"

"Is there a way?" he insisted.

There it was again, behind his eyes. A darkness, edging him on, grappling with his humanity in a fight to the death.

She drew a sharp breath before she answered. "I know how Asag cast his mirror from his own accursed flesh and powered it with the blood of his own daughters, and I know how that mirror birthed Arkhalla and her children. These I know because I need to understand my enemy. I know a thousand ways to kill the Undying, and have mastered them all, because I need to defeat my enemy."

At this, she got up, wrapping herself in her cloak. "But the only way I know for any man to cross over to Asag's hell is through the darkness of their heart, and this I refuse to know, because I shall not be my enemy. Tell me when you have thought over my proposal, Shamath."

And she turned and walked off, leaving him to brood by the fire.

She couldn't sleep. He vexed her, this quiet young warrior, with his handsome face and his troubled heart and his chilling words. She had no inkling why she felt so uncomfortable around him, or why she had reacted so fiercely when he asked her that odd question. Not at first. Lying with her eyes open, Aisyah tried to make sense of her behavior. Perhaps she did not like this man Shamath, and she reacted to his coldness out of vehemence against what he stood for. It seemed to be the opposite of everything she stood for... but was it?

No, that was not it. She did not dislike this man, and she could see the good in him, locked in battle with the dark. In truth, what they stood for was not all that different. They had both been hurt because of it. But she had taken this hurt and had tried to make something of it, or at least she was trying. Perhaps he had tried to, just not anymore. Or the world had hurt him much worse.

After all, who was she to speak of hurt? A princess who had seen one battle too many? A daughter who dreaded losing her father like she had lost her mother? What had Shamath gone through, and who was she to judge him for it?

He was a good man in pain.

It was his pain that seemed to bring him so close to her, that experience of a dark and savage world that they both still had to fight for, and that same pain that, a moment later, tore him away. But even with only a shared moment, it hurt her to be torn away from him, by pain, by hatred, by the dark. It was nothing her father nor her life up to this point had prepared her for, this fear of losing a kindred soul once one had found it.

With shock, Aisyah of Akkad realized she was genuinely touched by this quiet young man that she knew next to nothing about. She was touched by his feelings that he kept down, by the spark of life still fighting the darkness growing inside him.

The knowledge did not help her sleep.

His sleep was fitful and filled with awakenings. He was haunted, like every night, by dreams of Arkhalla suffering in darkness. They all started the same, with them living that perfect life, the one Yssur and the princess and Shamath himself had dreamed of, each in their own way. He and Arkhalla were at his farm, living together and in love, and he was coming back from a day out on the fields to find her waiting, and he tasted her kiss and found it sweet like honey. Then she was taken from him, always, by fire, by darkness. The darkness always came for her, alive, reaching out with a myriad cold hands of shadow and tearing her from him. And she would scream his name, burning in darkness, calling to him from the depths of Asag's hell, and he woke up.

Awake, his eyes flowing with tears, he panted, trying not to scream. It never went away, the pain. Tonight, it had felt even worse, doubtless by what Aisyah had shared, her fantasy of a dream life so close to his. It had shaken him, this affinity, this common dream they had. It was a reminder of the ways of the human heart, the ways he struggled so hard to stifle, because of the dreams, because of his inability to save his beloved, back then, and even now. It was an affinity he had no use for. Feelings were useless if they did not help him rescue Arkhalla.

Another man might have buried the past. He might have found the affinity he felt with this bright, beautiful girl, this kinship of their souls, appealing. A sign that he need not be alone. But he was not that man. And this girl was not Arkhalla.

Another man might have ended his life. He might have found the world unbearable to live in without her and fallen on his sword. At least the dreams would stop in that sleep of death, perchance. But he was not that man. And he would honor nothing of what Arkhalla was, what she had become there at the end, by such an empty sacrifice. No, Shamath had to live in this world. She would have wanted him to.

His path was clear to him now. He'd take on the princess' offer in the morning and he would lead his men to the heart of Ur. It was the right thing to do, the only thing. If they died in the attempt, so be it. Like Yssur, like all the men lost in the war against the Undying, they all lived on borrowed time anyway, and if there was a chance to make that time worthwhile and wipe those monsters off the earth, Shamath had to take it.

He knew what he had told the princess was the truth. Inside, he was as cold and dead as those fiends were. But he'd use this to bring them down. And he no longer fooled himself about the secret hope that he cradled and nurtured in whatever dregs of soul he had left in him, the hope Erun's words about the power of the Magi had rekindled. One day, in the ruins of Ur, he'd find the way. If he had to go that far to find the Magi's secrets, he would, and more. He'd bring Ur's ziggurat down on the leeches' heads. He'd brave the jaws of hell itself to bring Arkhalla back, to end his pain. There was no room for anything, anyone in his heart, except for her.

A WORLD TO DIE IN

CHAPTER 17

A LIVING LEGEND

The gods begin fully formed, writ large as life and larger, shaped and empowered by belief and the bottomless pit of man's fears. But demigods, heroes, and legends begin the way that everything stemming from the human heart begins; very small.

Something changed in the Wretches' War with the new season, and it grew obvious what that was once the combined offensive on Ur began, with the Akkadians advancing from the North and East and the rebellion pushing upwards from the Southwest. Not even the news that Yssur, the vaunted leader of the rebels, had been slain could curb the surge of pure rage and terror throughout the provinces threatened by the humans' advance.

In Kish, the rebels attacked first and at daytime, catching the human thralls of the day watch unawares and slaughtering all the Undying in their sleep. The strike had been timed and planned to the hour, and the border fort of Kish proved to be woefully indefensible, standing on the edge of a low and swampy approach that discouraged a frontal attack yet also prohibited an exodus or retreat if the need arose, and with hills on its rear side that the Undying had considered too steep and a natural wall of protection. Yet down those very hills the rebels chose to come nonetheless, making their approach at dawn, during the changing of the guard, and under cover of bushes and tree branches held before them, invisible until it was too late.

At Nippur and Isin, the rebels fell on the twin outposts like swarms of bees, attacking and retreating, and when two companies of Undying gave pursuit to the fleeing wretches, they overplayed their hand and let themselves be lured into a narrow, grass-grown valley adjacent to a river and thick with reeds taller than a man, and there they were set upon by hordes of rebels that had stealthily closed in on them by crawling through the long grass until they were on their positions.

What happened in the battle of Sharrupak no one could tell, for no man, mortal or Undying, from all five companies that formed Sharrupak's garrison, survived it. All that was left there for the scouts from Ur to see before they fled right back to the capital in horror was a field of corpses mounted and tied spread-eagled onto long twin spears crossed together, greeting all who cast eyes on these scarecrow-shapes with a deep, hollow warning. The rebels had left them there indiscriminately, for death and daylight to sort them out, the Undying among the corpses burnt to a crisp by the morning sun, the thralls rotting and nibbled at by feasting carrion birds.

So went the war as Narama gathered her army to face the invaders within Ur's inner borders for the first time. Not since the Wretches' War began had the realm been in so clear and present a danger, so much entire companies of men had to be moved from fronts widespread along the borders to form a shield of men around the spot where the Akkadians and the rebels would converge. What made it even worse was that of all the places it could have been in that vast eternal desert, the invaders chose Larak. For the one thing that put the fear of the rebels into Ur's Undying was what was said of the wretches' leader.

The rebel leader *was* a man from Larak, it was whispered throughout Ur, hushed. He had been born in that nation that was no more – one of the last that Arkhalla had annihilated before her own demise. And he remembered.

In one fell swoop, with these victories and others like them, this mere man had overcome the terror that had long crippled all armies to battle the forces of Ur. No human soldiers could contend with the Undying; that much was known. The most inept of strategists had tried, time and again, to attack Ur's troops by daylight, while the Undying rested, only for their plans to backfire when, by the day's end, their men would be exhausted from fighting conscripts and thralls and be slaughtered by the Black Guardsmen once they rose from their slumber. But then had come this wretch and showed them all one could take on the Undying, with trickery, with guile as well as courage, with leverage as well as raw force.

In two-something short years, this wretch had grown into more than just a man, his tales and names striking terror across Ur all the way to the capital. He was the Wretches' General, the Scourge of Ur, the Bane of Bel – this last name spoken in low whispers and on pain of death, yet even less fearful than the man's true name, forbidden in all official messages yet always there in terrified conversation. Shamath, the dead queen's slave, as rumor had it, who had come back to burn the Undying for the evil done to him. He was Arkhalla's sins, the whispers said, back from the grave to haunt them all.

Narama, who knew the truth behind it, knew Shamath was much, much worse. He was becoming legend.

As news of the humans' advance reached the capital, Narama heard and saw with her own eyes how that legend grew among the people. She saw it in the eyes of wretches that looked back into hers as she passed, even in the moments' pause in some thralls before they carried out a command, and each time she felt the cold claw of fate seizing her heart. With Shamath edging ever closer to the gates, it was a given that she and Bel could not both lead Ur's forces to battle. Someone had to organize their home defenses, ready and hone the troops for that decisive moment that would come if Larak, too, was lost. Bel could spare her to lead the charge at Larak, he had told her. It was essential that she hold off the humans' advance there while he rallied their regiments back home. But Narama struggled with this decision, partly because she sensed that, behind his logic for it, the truth was that Bel was not up to the task of leading the attack. In the end, she acquiesced – Larak was a long shot that could go either way, after all. Still, it galled her. And what really stuck in her craw was that boy who would be legend. Even if she killed him tomorrow, that wretch of a man whose face she barely remembered – *a man! Ye gods!* – the damage would still be done. For legends can't be killed. They can only grow.

Of this apprehension she spoke to no one, even Bel, especially Bel. For what Narama was even less liable to admit was that, even as a wretch she had once made her thrall was growing into a man she could not fathom how to stop or defend from, Bel, her Bel, slowly turned into less of a man.

They had come together at last, after the battle at the Land Before the World, the worst night of their long lives. They had fled, alone with what remained of their might, their allies divided and dispersed, their pride smarting worse than their wounds. And left alone in a tent, the two of them, when they finally stopped fleeing and set up camp, they had stared at each other, really stared at each other, for the first time in years since that awful night when Arkhalla's ghost had come between them. He had been dressing her wounds and she had been dressing his, the two of them too hurt, too proud to let a thrall or a slave near them in this dark hour, in their shame. And so it was then that they looked deep in one another's eyes, and saw each other's pain, aye, and the loss. They had lost so much.

"I cannot hate you anymore," she had said. Bel had avoided her eyes. *"You should."*

"I tell you I cannot."

He sighed. *"It is only your hatred that I deserve. I am undone, Narama, like I undid us. Do not kill me with compassion now."*

"I have no compassion left in me, Bel. But no hate either. Not here. And not for you."

"Let me die, then."

Her smile was wry and bitter. *"If you do, I shall not exist a moment longer."*

He looked at her, then, and saw that she meant it, and they embraced.

Their lovemaking was silent, surprisingly tender. Neither of them hid or dissembled their hurt nor punished the other. Like their bloodied, broken armor, that other armor they had on around their hearts was stripped from them, by fate, by chance, by each other. Whatever was left, all that remained of who they were, was naked, offered. They were broken, in pain. Love, at last, was healing. He was hers. She was his.

So bittersweet that this would happen as the world was coming to an end.

The Akkadians advanced from one side, Shamath from the other, and nothing they tried had stopped them. With each day that passed, every piece of worse news they received, Narama saw Bel sink further into a black pit of silent despair. He'd get drunk on blood laced with wine without saying a word, and show no expression as he put subordinates, slaves and random-picked wretches to death on the flimsiest of pretexts. Guilt was the demon at the bottom of the pit, she knew, and all he clung to as he drowned was her love.

Seeing him like this was a knife in her heart.

Her adoration of him was undiminished despite all that – or perhaps, she secretly feared, because of it. Still, this life was far from what she had dared hope for in those years she burned for Bel. Now she had him and it was all ashes. Especially now that another ghost from their past came to haunt them.

Narama could almost sense Shamath coming. She had made him her thrall once, after all. Though her control over him had been broken, some traces of their bond still had to be there. His face had faded in her memory, but she recalled everything else – the way his will fought hers to the end, the words he had spat at her, how his soul felt. None of it could have prepared her for Shamath returning to Ur and to her life, or for how this world had changed him. And yet here he was now, inexorable, like a cold season returning. One had to give it to him. A slave turned general. A wretch rising to end the Undying. She'd almost laugh at the irony of it if laughter did not feel like a distant country.

It was passing strange after all this time, their connection. And him grown to such a warrior almost begged belief. The tales of his prowess that reached the capital rivaled Bel's, and Bel had grown into the greatest warrior of his time in eons rather than mere years. An Undying admitting admiration for any wretch was anathema, to her and Bel both, she knew. But if pressed, she sensed that even Bel respected what this wretch Shamath had become – and against all odds at that. But it'd gall Bel even more. Some of the blame for it had to be laid at their door, after all. The two of them had helped make him the man he now was. And Arkhalla. Always Arkhalla. In a sense, it had been the three of them that birthed him. Their boy, grown to so much more than just a man.

The memory of Arkhalla was always bitter fruit to her, and Narama soured once more at the poison of its taste. She realized, then, the other thing that disturbed her so about Shamath returning. More than the respect she felt for him as a warrior, more than her amazement at his becoming so much after starting out with less than nothing, more even than the fact that he gave Bel pause. Narama remembered Shamath's voice when the boy spoke of Arkhalla. She recalled, with crystal clarity, how he had crossed a gauntlet of archers with nothing but a shield in hand to sweep his beloved out of danger. The scream he gave out when Narama's poisoned blade cut the bitch.

Narama knew Bel could never love her that way. She loved Bel like that, perhaps. Perhaps. But it was not the same with him.

Shamath and all the love he felt for the dead Queen almost made her want to be Arkhalla.

And with these thoughts, Arkhalla's own poisoned blade striking back at her from the grave, the dread and forlorn Lady Narama prepared for war against a legend that she had helped make.

CHAPTER 18

BLOOD AND SAND

It was the violet hour. Twilight stalked the sunset onto dusk. The wasteland of Larak yawned like an empty hell-mouth, bordered by the armies facing each other across it. There, after more than two years of advance that had passed in what seemed like days – so fast and terrifying the humans' campaign was – the Akkadians had at last joined with the rebels for the first time the wretches would face the Urian army straight on.

Nothing remained of Larak from Arkhalla's day, when the queen had razed it and its people, leaving only desert. No roots grew nor branches sprouted out of its sandy ruin, nor had they for the past twenty years. Where the Land Before the World was haunted by nothingness, the sight of Larak caused dread of a wholly different kind; a terror born of the evil that men did to other men. The people of Larak had wrestled their land out of the desert, fighting the arid soil for generations to grow their mean patches of turf and pasture, and after their demise, the desert had been taking the land back. Twin decades of sun and sand and wind had beat onto the broken remains till they had claimed Larak completely, and now Larak was naught but this void hell's mouth. Its trees and fields were dug and buried under sand. So were the bones and ashes of its people. No shade gave shelter, no bird or beast drew breath, and no cicadas sang in it anymore. Long stretched the men's shadows across the emptiness, and lonely, facing their foes into the distance as a wind rose, tearing wisps of fear out of the dust.

Narama could see the terror in the eyes of her soldiers. For the first time in all her long existence, she saw the Undying afraid. Larak stretched before them like unto a reminder of the reckoning day that was coming, that would come to all when they passed into the Lands Below and judged according to their measure. She could see the horror of this reckoning as they saw the evil they had wrought. And like them, she saw this reckoning across the sands, and knew its name was Shamath.

Her men watched her as she mounted her horse.

Fear was the one factor she neither could counter nor deflect, the one no strategist could beat into submission. It had festered into the hearts of her troops on the march from the capital, and grown malignant by the time they reached the cave-ridden hills onto the wasteland's edge from where they set out at sunset to face Shamath's army. Fear and repute were Shamath's allies, fighting her troops before the battle had begun. She had to wonder to what extent fear and repute had caused the outer garrisons to lose their battles, at Kish and Nipur and Sharrupak. Fear and repute and legend. The only way to conquer them was face on. And the only time was now.

She put on her helm and raised her blade, thousands of eyes turned onto her, armed worshippers of a bronze goddess of war.

"Forward," she cried, and charged.

Shamath saw not the emptiness nor heard the silence of the desert. His eyes and ears were assailed by white, bled bodies cast on the crimson-damp earth, rattled not by the stir of life but by the scurrying of rats among the dead, while screams and wails in the horizon signalled the coming of more adding to their number.

Unable to look upon the massacre, he opened wide his eyes. The screaming ceased. The dead were taken by the desert along with the past.

All it had taken was one blink of his eyes. He remembered it all as though it was still yesterday. But it was all gone. Only the sandstorm rose at twilight, like it always did this time of the year. It was the one constant, then and now. That and the treachery of the sands.

"Shamath," he heard Aisyah's voice at his side.

He turned. She was on horseback, awaiting his signal. A sea of men, Akkadians and his own, were lined behind her.

"We let them charge first," he said. "The infantry take the brunt of the attack and hold. Like we planned."

"I know," she told him. "It will work."

He bit his lip. "I hope so. Your father believes in it."

Aisyah shook her head. "He believes in you. So do I."

Her hand reached out, light on his forearm. "It is a good plan, Shamath. You and my father have shaped and formed it for days on end now. And no one knows this land like you."

"I knew it once. As it was."

"You still know it. It is your land. It is as much a part of you as your heart."

He nodded. She was right. The sands had claimed the land, not changed it. The autumn sandstorm still came as if on cue. The soft places would still be there under the dunes, buried like secrets. Like his past was always there, bubbling deep in memory.

Shamath turned towards the plain as he heard it now. The distant rumble of horsemen rising with the dust. No time for thought now. It was do or die.

He raised his hand.

Ur's Black Guards and ground troops charged first across the wasteland, a wave of dark shapes out of the sandstorm. Shamath saw this sight that had stopped so many a brave man's heart and cried out.

"At them!"

He ran forth and the mass of rebels and Akkadians charged before and with him and about him as one body made of thousands. The battle was joined.

The first line of men was lost fast, falling beneath the blades and hooves of the Urians. Those that comprised it had volunteered, laying down their lives of their own will so the rest would have a chance. Rushing forward with the second wave, Shamath felt their death tear into him and redoubled his speed. Their sacrifice would not be for nothing.

The sacrificial line of rebel infantry was the first thing that lost the Urians their momentum. One after another their horses stumbled and reared, their charge halted by both the rows of dead and the living charging to take their place. Against impeded progress, the riders' advantage turned into its opposite. Swarmed from all sides by demon-wailing men, the Black Guards had no room to maneuver. Tens and dozens of them found themselves unhorsed.

That was the humans' single saving grace during that first wave, for those of them found straight into its path fell by the score. The Undying were neither weak nor readily opposed by men, and fighting one on one, it was the men that fell.

The sandstorm was the second thing to come to their aid. Rising in savagery by the second blew the desert winds, the battle's fierce and bloody sight obscured by storms of dust. Gone in this dust cloud was the advantage of the Undying's superior sight and speed, their senses as vulnerable to surprise as their mortal foes'. And for an army of superior numbers the storm heralded doom. At six feet in all directions the world became a blur. There was no discipline of line, no balance and no center held within the tumult, the winds raging and blowing so hard those hit by them felt their bones creak with the strain and the hair singed on their heads.

Fighting in this inferno of dust was worse than battling drenched in hurricane and thunder. Their balance precarious by the storm's full force, the massive troops were troubled by their own size, while the small tactical units of the rebels pricked their sides like small, sharp, gathered thorns.

Soon allied rebels and Akkadians fought the Urian troops on sand hills muddy with bloodshed as well as shifting with the winds. Like the heads of the Mushmanhu severed by the hunting god Ninurta, more rebels seemed almost to spring renewed from where their brethren fell to plague the Undying anew. Their sacrifice was total, their gamble desperate. At the rate they lost men, defeat was certain. But it would be at the cost of too many of the Undying for the Urians even to think it as a victory.

It was a wonder of wonders that the humans held, but that they did.

For almost the full length of twilight turned to dusk this battling at close quarters claimed hecatombs from both sides. By attrition's odds alone, the human side was doomed, and time, too, worked against them. The onset of the dark would tip the battle's scales on the Undying's side once more and then all would be lost. And yet the chaos of the sandstorm and Shamath's thorn-units still kept the chances of the battle balanced on a blade's edge.

In this hell of blood and sand the Huntress of Men sought her foe. Riding the maelstrom of the chaos she slew all that came at her, her eyes peering through the inferno for a glimpse of Shamath.

Something was happening again now. Narama could not believe it. All about her, she saw her men driven backwards, as though pushed by some invisible wave hidden in the storm cloud.

Damn it all, she thought. They are bursting through. What was happening? How?

"Rally!" she screamed at the top of her lungs on sight of the men fleeing to the right and left of her. "Regroup, gods damn you!"

The desert sweated blood under the warriors' feet. Raised in the whirlwinds together with the dust swelled bursting sprays of red, turning the sandstorm a dark copper. Faces and forms appeared and vanished in the all-consuming cloud, scarlet and screaming among the hooded hordes that swarmed and stumbled on the godforsaken plain. Anyone but Narama would have given up the search when at last she caught sight of him from afar.

It was him – it had to be! Sense memory, Undying, preternatural, mapped flashes of movement and mien onto the living image of the youth that she recalled, and she knew him at once.

He was magnificent; his wrath alone seemed to drive her men back.

As though the very will of his erstwhile enthraller called to him, Shamath turned and saw her at that moment.

The world ceased to exist about them, all but the blood storm hitting them now with a rush of feelings.

Narama's breath slowed to a muted hiss. There he was, Arkhalla's wretch, her will and testament plaguing her, incarnate.

Shamath gritted his teeth. She had not changed, the witch. Under the armor and the blood of men she wore like unto a cloak, there was she, as she was on the day she sent Arkhalla to her doom.

Dust choked the cry that burst forth from his mouth as he charged at her through storm and men – And then hell's tide turned.

This is what happened as the storm of the battle was bringing Shamath closer to Narama.

The plan had worked so far. But the ashes of defeat were just one false movement away. Through the mayhem about her,

Aisyah of Akkad more sensed than saw the onset of the night and knew that the moment was now.

She gave the signal; a fiery arrow burned through the dust cloud, turning the sky aglow.

The left and right wings of her cavalry, thus far consigned to the edges of the battle, converged within its center in a great push. Like a rogue wave dwarfing the ones that had come before it, the Akkadians hit the Undying. The rebel archers led by Dumu lent support, loosing one lethal volley after another. Now the Urians fought exhausted from the sandstorms and the constant onslaught of humans that kept coming at them no matter how many of them they'd slay. A fresh onrush of them was too much to bear and hold the line, and they began to back away.

That was the surge that had brought Shamath and Narama within view of one another. By this time, inch by blood-soaked inch, the Undying had started to retreat in disarray deeper into the wasteland, the Akkadian cavalry chasing them as they fled in panic.

It was then that disaster came. Not by chance, as the Urian communications tried to spin it afterwards, but by design and cunning thought up by Shamath.

Behind her Narama heard the screams, distant at first, then horribly, rapidly near, like they too were a wave rising as it got closer.

By Asag's hell, what was that? The foe was to their front, not back. What had gotten her men screaming so?

There was something else wrong, too. She felt it beneath her mount's feet now. A subtle shifting, like a tremor along the surface of a lake.

No!

Tearing her eyes off her prey, she glanced backwards. Through the storm cloud, she glimpsed the screaming men. It was worse than she feared.

In their attempt to rally and regroup at the far side of the wasteland where the rebels and the Akkadians pushed them to, the Urians had marched straight into quicksand.

The hollow ground began to cave and give way under the weight of the Urians' heavy armor. Losing their footing, the Undying slipped and stumbled onto each other and down maelstrom pools of sand breaking forth onto the desert surface. The dust mire swallowed men by the dozen, the combined weight of their retreating numbers causing more and more whirlpools to form beneath their feet. Horses and comrades stumbled and fell with them. Narama saw them disappear into the desert hell, dragging more and more down its myriad mouths.

"No! Hold your ground!" she cried out.

None listened; her cry was drowned by screaming horror.

Roaring with rage, Narama faced front again. She picked out Shamath at the head of his troops, calling for volley after volley from his archers. Her men were pinned like cushions or driven backwards to horrific death.

He had planned this. She just knew it. Somehow, it was *him*.

"Wretch! Face me!"

She rushed towards him and saw him charge to meet her. Now, at last!

The ground caved beneath her mount, and in the sand it went. Even as it did, Narama leapt clear. Unhorsed, she struggled to find her balance. But now the horse, already swept into the hungry sand up to its neck, fought to break free, its movement widening the chasm about it. Under her foot, Narama felt a sudden, shocking tug. One moment there was earth and dust and then there wasn't. Balanced on solid soil with her other foot, Narama jumped clear of the pool a split second before it closed about her leg. Another step backward took her to safety, though precarious.

Before her and to the right the pool opened and widened into a gyre that drew everything in it to a swirling abyss.

She stepped to the left, missing a new pool by inches. About her, some of her men tried to do the same. The battle, the arrows, all forgotten, they fought for their lives, leaping between widening pools of sand.

"Back! Back to the left!"

More of her men were lost to the desert even as they leapt to safety. Their screams deafened her; she shut herself to them, bent on survival.

At last she felt steady earth, but still she backed away. Ten cubits, twenty. With each step, the ground felt real again.

Panting, she looked up. The plain before her was an abyss of sand, pools and pools of it still moving like waves onto a sea of desert. Amidst them she could see the drowned and drowning, holding on to nothing, stray hands and heads vanishing under the rising sand. Some of them still lived, screaming as their screams drove them deeper in the shifting hell till its mass clogged their throats.

She looked aghast at the company men about her. They seemed so few. The desert had claimed the rest.

Across the divide of treacherous sand, she saw the Akkadians and the rebels. The quicksand was between them and her men. Across the wide divide, she saw Shamath, his eyes burning her.

There was nothing to do. Already another volley of shafts came, driving her men further back. So few of them left. She could not believe it. The disaster passed understanding.

Darkness descended from the hills. Her hand rose, giving the sign for retreat. The battle had been lost, almost in the blink of an eye.

Running from the next volley, her men backed from the desert into the shadow of the hills. She glanced back through the sand cloud, at Shamath's form, receding in the dust and the dark.

It *had* been him. Only the men of Larak knew where the quicksand lay, and all but one of those men were long dead, only their ghosts left behind to cheer at the massacre. And in the most vicious manner possible, Shamath had repaid his people's doom in full, and shamed her.

Around the nothingness that once was Larak closed in the night, as pitiless as the sands.

He would pay. If it was the last thing she did in this blasted long existence, the bitch's cur would pay.

Shamath stood deaf to the cheers of his army. He remained fixed at the edge of the shifting abyss, his eyes avoiding the glimpses of stray blades and helms roiling slowly in the sand, but staring ahead into the sandstorm and the night. "What is it?"

He turned. Aisyah stood there. Her smile froze on her lips as she saw the tears in his eyes.

"Shamath? By the gods, what is it?"

His voice was dark, hollow. "You gave the signal."

She was taken aback. "As planned," she almost stuttered.

"It was too soon. I had her."

"What?"

He almost screamed it in her face. "You took her from me! I had her! You took her away from me! You took her from me!" His

fierceness drove her back a step. "Shamath!"

Now his rage scared even him. He threw his hand onto his face. "I'm sorry," he managed to say through a sob. "I'm sorry."

"Shamath..."

But he had turned and was gone from her, back towards the camp, as though Asag's demons were after him.

Aisyah stood aghast. Watching him walk away, she did not even notice Dumu behind her until the fair-haired girl spoke.

"Let him, Princess," she said. "There are some things you do not know."

CHAPTER 19

REFLECTIONS IN A SLEEPLESS NIGHT

The weeks rolled on with the miles that brought them closer to Ur's capital. It was the night before they'd reach Eridu, and Aisyah could not sleep. She lay on her camp bed with her eyes closed for what felt like an hour before she gave up and dressed and went outside her tent. It was getting to be her wont more and more, and nights were naught but four-hour rests anyway in their breakneck race to get to Eridu before the Undying. So she'd get up and throw a cloak over her soldier's outfit and pull her hood down over her face, and she'd take long walks, her mind heavy with thought, glancing fleetingly at the faces of the sleeping men as she passed by their campfires. Life in a camp never stops on the eve of battle. For every twenty men between shifts trying to catch a half-hour's sleep, there were ten others sent on errands and delivering messages, loading supplies and polishing and stacking up weapons in the armory, heading off on scout missions and patrols, or just wandering to the next campfire to talk through a sleepless hour. In the dark and without her armor, Aisyah was just another trooper among the hustle and the bustle around her.

She saw the light burn behind the canvas of her father's tent, so she made her way there, allowing his guards a glimpse of her face to let her through. A chuckle clear and thin, like the tinkle of shattering glass, was joined by the king's throaty laughter as Aisyah walked in and saw her father sitting up on his rug-draped divan against the pillows that propped his back while Dumu sat across from him.

"Aisyah, my light," Nimrod chided her with a mock frown, yet still smiling, "you ought to be in bed. Youth is a candle that burns quickly. Once done, its wick is spent forever."

"You should be resting as well, father," she replied.

"Alas, child, I have an old man's excuses for staying up. Sleeplessness and pain. Those old wounds of mine are acting up again." He nodded at Dumu. "Thank the gods, your friend here has the gentle heart to keep me company, a kindness I repay by regaling her with a couple of old war stories."

He pretended to frown again, at Dumu this time. "Now, where was I, little girl? You keep interrupting me with your entirely inappropriate fits of laughter."

Dumu tried to be serious. "You were telling me how you captured Lugal of Zaggisi and led him to Akkad in a neck-stock, sire."

"Oh, father," said Aisyah. "You must have told this story a hundred times this month alone. And Dumu must have heard it at least half those times."

Nimrod shrugged, which made him wince with pain. "That doesn't make it any less of a great story. Does it?"

"No, Sire," Dumu said, smiling. "Besides, it is different every time you tell it."

At this, the two of them laughed again, and Aisyah chuckled with them. It brought an unrushed joy to Aisyah's heart to see them thus. Dumu had grown into a close friend to her these past few weeks, but to Nimrod, she had been like a balm, and Aisyah was twice as fond of her for that. The wounds her father had received at the Land Before the World were grave ones, and though he had managed to pull through, they had never quite healed, leaving him changed. Three years on, he was older than he had looked in most of Aisyah's life, plagued by crippling pains in his worn-out joints, a pale shadow of the dread king he once was. Aisyah, who had assumed the kingship in all but name in his place, feared for more than his physical well-being for a long time after. Shorn of his vigor, Nimrod had been growing glum and silent, though being relieved of the burden of duty had also made his disposition gentler than Aisyah had seen it in years, from back when her mother still lived. It was, alas, another sign of her father's faded strength. When Nimrod had insisted that he joined the Ur campaign, if not in battle, then in the war tent plotting strategies with his still keen mind, Aisyah did not object, for she dreaded what the onset of depression might have done to him had she refused. In truth, her father's advice in the campaign had proved indeed invaluable, and it did their men good to see their king lead on the march, even in his horse-drawn litter instead of a chariot of war. But until they were joined by Shamath's men before Larak, Aisyah still caught her sire wiping a quick tear of pain or dejection from his eye in moments he thought she wasn't looking. She felt guilty, about her assuming the duties of a queen while he still lived, about his pain that she could not soothe, about how her new role meant she could not spend the time with him that she knew he sorely needed in his state.

With Shamath, though, something had changed in her father's mien. He had as much told her so the very day he met the young warlord, after his long talk of strategy with Shamath had ended and Nimrod and Aisyah were alone in his tent again. Aisyah recalled his words even now.

"I like this young man," Nimrod had said. "He's not a warlord born, but for me, it was always how war forges men that mattered, and this Larakian's mettle rings as true as his mind." "You approve his strategies," Aisyah said.

"Approve? I tell you I have not seen a keener strategist in all my days, and I have seen a few. He's as good at it as that cursed leech, Sin. I think he may even be as good as you."

"Then he is second only to you, Sire."

Nimrod's smile was wide and pleased. "Daughter, I am a softer touch in my twilight years, but not an old fool open to flattery. The lad is good. He may even be great." At this, he paused. "Besides, you like him too."

She felt the blush coming on and fought it with a steady voice. "Of course. I met him long enough to know his worth."

"You know that is not what I mean."

Her blushing deepened. "I hoped it was not showing that much."

"It was not. I took a chance on a wild hunch. You only proved me right just this moment."

She frowned. "Why?"

"Well, I like the lad. From the first moment, when all his cortege bent the knee and he only bowed his head. I could tell it was not empty brass, but the sign of a free man who respects all but prostrates himself to no one. Haven't seen that in a while." He paused, reflecting. "His warrior's worth is already more than known; it stands proven. I was prepared to ally myself with Yssur, but after meeting his successor, I am willing to throw my lot in with these rebels, all the way. And I am an old man, daughter, and you may be a lonely queen and wish to marry. It's worth knowing that a man like Shamath catches your eye..."

"Father..."

"... and it is worth for you to know that I'd approve if that is the case."

She struggled for an answer. "Father, the thought has not come to me."

He looked at her. "You may lie to yourself, child. You cannot lie to me. And to me, the way you look at him speaks volumes."

"You would approve? A commoner from a nation rubbed off the face of the earth?"

"I was not born a king. And by the time this war is over, kings and queens may be made. If we live to its end."

Those had been her father's words, and keenly did Aisyah feel them on this night. Nimrod had spoken truly. The thought of Shamath had been in her head ever since that night at the rebels' camp, no matter how she had tried to deny it up to now. But her sire had seen through it, like he always saw into her heart. And these months they had been together, those feelings had simmered, and surged. With Shamath's coming, not only the war's course had changed, but Aisyah's as well. Here was someone who represented all that was best in man; all it was worth fighting this war for. Even that flicker of darkness she could glimpse in him, even that made him feel closer to her. They shared this weakness of having been touched by the terrors of this war and the strength to rise from it to the light. She really believed that. With him, everything was changed.

And with Shamath had come Dumu, who she had known briefly at the rebels' camp in the Shaft. Back then, the fair-haired warrior had been cold and standoffish, but the dawn after the victory at Larak, Dumu had chanced on her as Aisyah looked on the men's celebrations from a distance, her soul too heavy from the carnage to join in.

"I'll forget you're stuck-up and highborn if you'll forgive my low manners, your highness," Dumu had said, her voice slower from a couple of cups too many. *"Way I see it, we're both women in a man's game."*

"So we are," Aisyah had agreed.

They were firm friends afterwards. More than that, it had gladdened Aisyah to no end when Dumu, even as she grew warmer towards her, managed to bring the smile back to her father's face, almost by the sheer infectious power of her vivacity alone. It was as though Dumu had sensed beyond Aisyah's need for friendship, as though she had seen the worry in the princess' heart, and had taken on the mantle of a second daughter to the ailing old man as unreservedly as Aisyah had taken up the obligations of command. Dumu had told her she had never known a father, so perhaps she saw one in Nimrod, too. As for the king, though he was still ridden with pain, he had embraced life again, more so than even in his days of power. The princess struggled to recall him laughing in years before. More than once – a lot more – she had seen the two of them as they were now, with Nimrod launched into his umpteenth retelling of some lewd off-color anecdote from his days as a reaving, barbaric warrior before he claimed his jeweled throne. This was one change in him she welcomed.

Now, however, Dumu got up to leave. "We ought to leave you to your rest, sire. Our night is short, and the day tomorrow our most important yet."

Aisyah could tell something was on Dumu's mind, but if Nimrod noticed, he made no sign of it.

"True," he admitted. "If only I was as fit as you both, children. There'll be poems written of the battle joined, and I so wish I could fight it with you."

"You shall, Sire," said Aisyah. "We fight to your instruction; to your plan."

If we get to Eridu in time, she thought. But she did not voice it.

"You know that's not the same, daughter," said the king. "But that is what the gods give, so I'll take it. Doesn't mean I cannot lend an extra hand, at least in spirit."

At this, he reached for his legendary bow, which even now never left his side. "Songs sang of how the sky goddess herself crafted this bow for her favorite among the great kings." He chuckled. "The truth is far more prosaic. But this is a weapon fine enough to birth legends, and I do refuse to let it go to waste as an old fool's ornament."

His hand, still sinewy and strong as his nether limbs had grown weak, held up the heavy bow. One could believe just by the sight of it that it would kill gods if used right.

"As great as you are an archer, you are too good with the sickle-sword for me to burden you with this, my light," Nimrod told Aisyah. "And a king's bow may weigh heavy on our young general. He has too much responsibility as it is."

With this, he held the mighty weapon out to Dumu. "I witnessed your might in Larak, child. An archer you are, and you excel at it. You are fast and your eye is keen. If you can string this, it is yours."

The bow was great, a composite marvel of craft made from horn and wood and sinew. To look at it was intimidating, for to the untrained eye it seemed as though it needed two grown and brawny men to string it.

Dumu took and balanced the weapon in her hand with a slight smile curling her lips. Her eye was not untrained. The bow required skill and leverage to string it rather than brute strength. With the speed of lightning she turned and twisted it, using her legs and stance to help her in the task rather than just rely on her hands, and in moments, the great bow was strung and ready.

Aisyah looked on with approval as Nimrod smiled. He had chosen wisely.

Aisyah and Dumu left him chuckling as they left together.

"Have you told Shamath yet?" said Dumu once they had cleared the tent.

The suddenness of the question shook Aisyah, though she knew its meaning at once. "What? No," she said.

"Then you must."

"I shall do no such thing."

"Princess, you protest too much."

The fair-haired girl looked straight at Aisyah, the weight of Nimrod's great bow slung across her back not making her hunch in the slightest. "I've noticed your feelings for Shamath. Ever since that night at the Shaft."

"And you've told me so often. Father says they're hard to notice. Next thing I'll have the troops making fun of me."

"Do not evade the matter, Aisyah. Noticing them was not easy. You're both as tightly shut as clams. But my noticing how you feel for him is what brought you closer to me." Aisyah looked at her, surprised.

"What?" Dumu said, smiling. "You believed that us being women in a man's game was all it was? Shamath is my friend, my comrade. I want what is best for him. Frankly, Princess, you annoyed me at first."

"Well, thank you."

"Let me finish. You come on strong and standoffish, so it's easy to dislike you. But anyone with eyes can see the person that you are inside. I just had to look harder. Shamath did not have to do that at all. He knew at once. He convinced me."

Aisyah thanked her again. This time, she meant it.

"And I saw," Dumu went on. "And saw Shamath, my friend, too, and how he suffered being alone. If you have feelings for him, and you do, then you can be the balm his heart needs."

Aisyah struggled hard to ignore the flutter in her breast that Dumu's words had stirred. "A balm," she countered. "For the wounds *She* gave him."

Dumu sighed. "You never knew Arkhalla, Princess."

"I know enough. The whole world does."

"The world knows legends. I knew her. Shamath knew her."

"You've told me that, too. And all you've told me I find hard to believe."

Dumu nodded. "Because they are not possible?"

"At first. But then I found it hard because you are the one who told me, and I know you would not lie."

"I do not lie when I tell you how true and deep their love was, too, Aisyah. I saw it, and so would you had you been there." She paused. "And neither do I lie when I tell you it left Shamath a broken man, and that I thought there was no mending the hole in his heart. Not until I saw what you are like, and how you look at him."

She paused again, pivoting slowly as she turned towards the part of the camp where her squadron was stationed.

"I see what the two of you are, and how you feel, and what you could be to each other, Princess. Tomorrow night, any of us may be dead. If I were you, I'd tell him before it was too late."

And like that, she was gone, her step spry as she vanished in the darkness.

With heart lightened somewhat, almost despite herself, Aisyah resumed her walk. Dumu's words echoed deep inside her, but each reverberation tinged them with her own hesitation.

How could she? How could she say it, do it?

She fought hard to purge the thought, to lose herself once more in other things. Slowly about her, the camp stirred to life. There were more voices whispering, and hopeful for anything to get her mind off Dumu's suggestion, she gravitated to them, her cloak disguising her as she passed each work post and campfire to hear snatches of talk from those men not asleep.

"Sky's graying in the horizon, lads. Morn will be breaking soon."

"I don't look forward to it."

"I do. What I don't care much for is tomorrow night."

"I'm not scared of them being undead. A foe is a foe, if felled by sword they can be. I'm scared of them being quiet. You cannot hear them come at you, so silent they are."

"What thinks the captain of our chances?"

"Slim as a strumpet's honor."

"I'll bet he did not say that to the general."

"Or the princess! Ha!"

"Who *doesn't* wish we were back home and this war left behind us?"

"I wish I was."

"So do I."

"If not for threat of execution, I'd flee tonight."

"Shamath himself would, if he could." "Right."

"Fie on you both. He'd stay right where he is. He's one of us, he is."

"That's his misfortune. He can die right there with us, then."

"He scares me, lads."

"I know what you mean. He's a dark one."

"Not dark like Bel. You're talking shit."

"No, not that dark."

"But close."

"Aye. That he is."

"She doesn't fight like a princess. That I respect."

"That I'll lay my life on the line for."

"That, my lads, I'd *lay* period."

"You'd lay anything on legs, you drunken sod!"

"And a couple of things without!"

"I wish they'd settle this themselves. A duel, man to man."

"Many poor men's lives saved, I'll tell you."

"I'll settle for even a few men's lives, if I'm among them. Let them fight."

"Who, the king and Bel? Come off it!"

"The leech would slaughter him."

"Shamath, though. He might take Bel."

"You want to broach that with him, perhaps?"

"We follow orders. That is our lot."

"Our cause is just."

"And if it were not, you think they'd let you off? Out of the army?"

"Some of the lot on the other side must be like us. The grunts. The conscripts."

"Some of them have blood for breakfast."

"They'll kill us all if they can."

"We kill them first. That's cause enough for me."

"Or die trying. We'll die well."

"No one dies well. And not in battle, that's for sure."

"They'll get us all killed, Shamath and the princess."

"On their head our blood be."

"They purpose not our deaths, lads. Just our arms."

"We need to do this."

"They fight alongside us; they might be killed as well."

"We have to do this, lads. Our bodies are our leaders' to command. But our souls are our own."

"Aye, and I like it that way. We have to slay them all."

"We must."

"For our wives and families."

"I'll tell that to your widow."

Aisyah listened to these and lots more words like them spoken as she walked the camp, some in hushed whispers, others loud and anger-fuelled, and each and every one of them all too human. That was humanity offered to her ears, the good and the bad of it. That was what the monsters of Ur sought to hunt down and enslave and wipe off the face of the earth. That was what she'd fight for.

It was these thoughts that burdened her step when someone brushed past her in the dark. She mumbled a pardon and walked on, not looking, but then a voice spoke to her.

"Who goes there, then?" the voice said, familiar. Its tone bore just a tinge of amusement, as though its owner knew full well who she was.

"A friend," she replied.

"Same here, your highness," said Shamath.

They faced each other. Aisyah raised her hood to look at him while Shamath smiled at the sight of her soldier's outfit peeking beneath her cloak. "I wouldn't have pegged you as the slumming type."

"They do say the world surprises us all," Aisyah retorted. "Do you have trouble sleeping, too?"

He didn't answer. "Walk with me?" he suggested instead.

They fell into step and went on together.

"So what is this?" Shamath asked after a while. "A low profile?"

"A quiet walk," she said. "Plus, disguise is a leader's prerogative. One hears things one wouldn't hear otherwise. You ought to try it sometime."

He chuckled. "I'm sure that works better for royalty."

Aisyah waited a moment before she spoke. "So how hard do you find it?"

"What?"

"Leading."

His face darkened. "Oh. You mean having peoples' lives and souls laid at your feet and on your head? Their futures, families and faults? That kind of thing?"

She smiled. Even this way he put it, with humility and humor, endeared her to him. "Exactly."

"Hard."

Aisyah nodded. "You know what I envy about them?" she said, cocking her head towards a group of sleeping, huddled men.

"Being able to sleep so easily?"

She chuckled. "In part. Don't you?"

"I didn't sleep well before anyway."

At that moment, Aisyah realized it. She had not lost her sleep just because of the battle all these nights. It was what Dumu had said, too, that had kept her awake. The thought of Shamath, of her feelings for him. And how they might not survive tomorrow night.

It was then, too, with a pang of sudden ache, that she realized why he did not sleep well. He panged for another. Someone dead that Aisyah did not know, and could never know. Not like *he* had known her.

"Did you –" She checked herself, a tad too late. "What?"

"Did you sleep easier when you were a slave?"

Shamath glanced at her. "Well, one rests easier when one has survived another day. That is what slavery is, day-to-day, your highness. Survival."

"All other worries seem petty."

"They did." He paused. "There were horrors aplenty when I was awake. But sleep, the little we got, that came fast."

"Horrors." Aisyah paused, the word lingering between them. "Of the Undying?"

"Yes."

"And... Arkhalla?"

He looked at her for a long moment. "Dumu told you."

The way she had asked it had betrayed her. There was no use denying it. "Yes."

"And? Are you repulsed? Horrified?"

She wasn't. The realization had always been there, but it was clear now. Like everything seemed to clear when he was with her.

"No," she answered. "I... wish to understand."

"Why?"

"Because..." she hesitated. "Because... I feel the way you do about so many things. And if... if you felt... feel... like that, about Her, I mean... I would like to know why."

It was truth, most of it. There were other truths in there, too, hidden. Aisyah had no inkling of whether they were glimpsed by him.

She sighed, trying to turn the conversation elsewhere as trepidation seized her once more. "Tonight... tonight I feel I could exchange all the pomp and the flattery and reverence, the bended knees, the crown. All that, and the silkworm-weaved sheets, the lapis lazuli and gold chambers and the vast, soft beds, I would exchange for a slave's sleep. For that survival a slave achieves at the end of a day."

"Some would call that an offence to the gods."

"And me a vain, gold-spoon-fed noblewoman? Would you say that?"

He did not hesitate. "Not about you."

Aisyah almost thanked him. It was not princely pride or decorum that stopped her, for around Shamath she felt not the stranglehold these had on her at other times. It was the fact that she did not have to thank or apologize to him. He knew what she felt. The knowledge, the understanding, was there in his eyes. She wondered if she ever would know him so well.

"There is something to be said about going to one's bed with an aching body and an empty mind," Shamath went on. "Isn't that what you mean?"

"Yes," said she, pleased to hear her thought from his lips. She felt flush again, all of a sudden, as though from his lips, though meant to be as innocent as she had used it, the notion of going to bed took a meaning wholly different to her ears. With effort, she checked herself again. "A laborer rises with the sun and sleeps the sleep of gods, day in and day out, till that day he sleeps in the ground," she went on. "He lives free of care, because he lives to survive. And he lives free, with those that he loves, faithful only to those that he loves. But for the pomp and circumstance of it, I'd say that laborer is happier than a king."

"But the hours when a slave rests are more fretful to a king."

"Or a leader."

His smile was wry, bitter. Her words, too, had struck home. She had tried to say something else, too, but it had slipped away, she feared, unnoticed.

One of Shamath's lieutenants came running, and her dread increased. Now she would not tell him. Now he would be taken away on some errand and she'd miss her chance. She cursed herself for a fool.

The man got near enough before he caught a glimpse of Aisyah's face under her hood and stopped, unsure of what to say.

"Please," she told him, stifling her disappointment. "Don't mind me. Speak your errand."

"Your Highness," he thanked her with a bow of his head, relieved, before he turned to Shamath. "The men look for you through the camp. You said to tell you when it was a couple of hours till dawn."

Shamath nodded. "Tell them we'll get together at my tent in an hour, with the princess' generals --" He paused, giving Aisyah a quick look. "If you agree, your highness."

The princess smiled. "I do."

"We will be there then, Kahlil," said Shamath to the man.

"I'll tell them, Shamath." The soldier bowed his head to her again and took off as fast as he had come.

"Your men love you as well as they obey you," Aisyah said to Shamath a heartbeat after.

"I was one of them. I do not forget that." The

look on his face told her more.

"And that makes it harder to send them to their deaths," she spoke his thought for him. "Though not less necessary."

Shamath sighed. "I wish I had gods left to pray to, for these men's sakes. I'd pray for them to show courage in the face of fear." Something in his words made him wince. "Or for them to go blind to the odds against them. Perhaps that is what a general prays for." He paused. "An hour left. Shall we walk some more?"

They resumed walking. Their pace was uneven, too slow, as though they'd rather walk backwards in time and have a little more of it to themselves.

"I wish I had other things to pray for than the blood spilled. The blood on my men's hands, and on mine."

"Blood must be spilled. Or it would not be blood." Shamath's jaw was firm with determination. "Life means death no matter the times we ask forgiveness for it."

Once more Aisyah glimpsed the hidden wound that ached him; the pain that twisted his words so. Once more she yearned to soothe it.

"Please do not say that," she said.

"Why? It is the truth."

Her hand was on his before she even realized it. "It may be. But you are better than that."

The emotion in his eyes moved her even more. "I do not deserve better, your highness."

Her hand moved up to his face. He did not pull away. His eyes closed as though her touch did soothe him.

The impulse drove her forward, and her lips touched his. His mouth parted. The kiss was soft, tentative, as though it could bruise their flesh. She yearned for him to bruise her, to take her. Her breath hoarsened; so did his.

Another sudden flush overtook her, filling her not with embarrassment, but something warmer, deeper. She smiled and opened her eyes the same moment he did, and saw the fire on his cheeks as well.

"We have an hour," she said, softly.

He hesitated, fighting himself.

She let out a soft chuckle. "I would wait for tomorrow if I was sure it will come," she said, trying to ease the tension. "You are worth waiting for."

"Aisyah, I..."

Her bliss at hearing her name spoken by him like that was tempered by what she heard in his hesitation.

"I can't."

She drew back a step, hurt. "You won't," she countered.

Despite herself, she glanced about her. They were far from the campfires, in darkness. No one could have seen. But even that hurt her more.

"Because of her," she whispered, reading his face. "Arkhalla."

He did not have to answer, or even nod. He only lowered his eyes.

Aisyah tried to hate him. She tried to hate *her*. To her surprise, she realized she could not.

"It's her, is it not?" she asked, taking another step back. "Why you want to know how to get to the Lands Below."

This time, he answered. "Yes."

"You are still in love with her. You want to get her back."

He admitted it freely. "Yes." No hesitation at all now. Not for Arkhalla.

"I know you cannot understand," he went on.

"I am trying to, Shamath," she said, fighting back tears. And she was.

"I love her."

"How can you?"

"If you knew her, truly, as she was, you would not wonder."

"I know you," she retorted. "And because I do, I... I think... she must have given you reason to love her."

She believed that, too. Because she did know him, like she knew Dumu. Neither of them would lavish love or friendship, *that* love, *that* friendship, to the monster of all those tales. Either Aisyah did not know anything anymore, or those tales were, somehow, as impossible as it was even to think it, wrong. She did not know what to think.

"I'm sorry, Shamath," she said, flushed with embarrassment now. "I made a fool of myself."

"I kissed you, too," he answered. "Believe me, I'm the fool here."

She neither agreed nor challenged him on it. There'd be little use in either.

They fell to walking once again, in silence at first, then, once they reached the campfires, with tentative exchanges about the preparations for the day to come. It was the hardest thing for the both of them, acting like nothing had happened. But there was nothing else they could do. Only when the council tent was on sight did she dare speak something true and hurtful.

"I fear for tomorrow, Shamath."

She wished she could have told him that in his arms, the two of them lying together after an hour of warding the world and all its death away, instead of now and with the pang of his refusal still inside her. But in that, too, the world would not wait for tomorrow.
"So do I," he admitted. "We must take Eridu, or all is lost."

"It's not just that I fear."

"Then what?" He studied her face, and she knew he could see the dejection eating at her.

"I cannot put aside how costly our victories have been, Shamath. Larak, Kish, all of them."

It was the deepest fear in her heart, the one she had hoped his kisses and caresses would drown out.

He pursed his lips. "And I cannot put aside that they were victories, your highness."

So it was back to 'your highnesses.' It was her turn to let out a sigh.

"Our strategies favored us, as did fortune," she admitted, determined to voice her fears. "But cunning and intelligence will get us so far. Our strength is halved."

"Their casualties are just as high."

"So that is all? Men dropping like flies until one side hasn't any more to send to slaughter?"

His voice rose, very slightly. "What would you *have* me do?"

It was the first sign she saw of how what had happened – or not happened, in any case – was distressing him. Whether he wanted her or not, he was not cruel. It hurt him saying no to her as it hurt her hearing it.

When he spoke again his mien had becalmed, at least as far as he would let her see. "It is the toll. You pay it as much as I do. We are soldiers."

"And deep inside enemy territory. Within range of villages and towns, not just forts. We reach Eridu tomorrow. What if our plans don't work where the people living there are concerned, Shamath? What if their fortune runs out?"

They were getting close to his tent. One of the men thronging outside it saw them and cried out to him.

"Shamath!"

"Aye, brother," he said, acknowledging the greeting. He gestured Aisyah towards the tent, and followed her inside.

The princess' question was left unanswered.

CHAPTER 20

ONLY MONSTERS

Eridu was a town of some fifteen thousand people, and the only area that was inhabited in the great distance between the capital and the wastelands of Larak. That made Eridu both a crucial line of defense where the Undying were concerned and a vital springboard for the human side, both for the same reason, which had only become apparent after the massacre at Larak. If the Undying held the town, even with a token garrison, they'd have a base for Bel's army marching out of Ur. They would be able to coordinate their attacks from there, to dictate the narrative of the last battle rather than subject their fortunes to what had been unthinkable in Arkhalla's day – a siege of the capital, with them behind the city wall and Shamath's army on the offensive. Their numbers and might was still larger. With Eridu as their base and the blood of the town's population as supplies for the Undying troops, they had a chance to come out ahead. One final and far from best, yes, but a chance nonetheless.

With Larak a disaster, Narama convinced Bel that the whole war now hinged on holding Eridu, so she gathered her riders and charged out of the city gates to get there first. Shamath and that bitch Akkadian strumpet, no matter how hurried their advance, could only march an army so fast through the wilderness. Bel would take about the same time setting out of the capital. They were swords, heavy to lift and draw, though their heft and weight were devastating. Narama and her men were the quick stab of a knife. If they got to Eridu first, the humans' chances would be halved in one smooth stroke.

The trek was as grueling as it was swift; the black riders rested not throughout the dark hours, but spurred their steeds through the desert so hard they drove them to the brink of death. She had hand-picked her company from among the most ruthless of her soldiers and the most battle-hardened and ruthlessly loyal of her thralls. Their mission warranted that these be men that'd be unflinching. With mere minutes to spare the riders dug their sun shelters at dawn, and dug out of them even while the solar disc was still being gobbled up by the dark horizon, with blisters on their hands and arms and the hairs on these sun-touched forelimbs singed. But so it was that a four-night journey was cut to a ride of two and the black riders came from the sand upon Eridu, silent, no clash of hoof and clash of spear and shield heralding them nor trailing in their wake, and they fell onto the sleeping settlement. Again in silence they performed their task, the sole wild shouts and tearful cries issuing from the human men, women and children of the town as the Undying herded them all into the main square that'd be barricaded to serve as their pen. Most of the children and the old had not even realized what was happening on being dragged out of their beds and homes; so quiet is evil when it comes, swift on a wind of sin.

Narama looked upon the herding and corralling of the wretches with a detached interest, her mind on the fight to come. All was done as it should be, and just on time. Her decision to forge ahead with her riders had been a gambit, but it had paid off. After her defeat at Larak, it just had to. They had barely finished fortifying all points of access to the town when the lookouts signaled the enemy approaching from the horizon.

"Light up the gate," she commanded.

At her signal, torches were put to braziers set along the battlements. The warm deep red and orange glow revealed the children lined up along them over the gate, tied to posts made of bundled reeds. It was the sight of them and the armor-clad platoon of Undying Narama had posted at their side that would tell the tale to the enemy's watchers. She watched as the lines of troops gathered in the distance, doing nothing. She noted the passing of the time as they dug up trenches and set up camp to block lines of advance attacking from the city, but making no advance toward it themselves. Only then did she allow herself to smile, imagining the wretch leaders' frustration. The Undying had Eridu in their grip. Fifteen thousand captives and just as many wells of blood, held in reserve for Bel's army which was itself fast approaching. And the wretches could do nothing but wait for Bel with her.

Aisyah oversaw the digging of the entrenched camp with her heart heavy and sick. They had marched as fast as they could and still they had been too late. For the humans, getting to Eridu first had been half the battle, and now half the battle was lost before it had even been fought. The city lost meant fifteen thousand souls lost as well. And that was far from the final toll, or the full implications of this strategy. With the hostages of Eridu giving them nourishment, the Undying would be at full strength in the battle when Bel's troops came. She knew whoever commanded the Undying garrison that held the town would have standing orders to start executing prisoners at any sign of an advance, and enthralled soldiers in reserve to carry these same orders out at the onset of the day. It was what Aisyah would have done in this commander's place. The strategy was ruthless in its elegance. These hostages were the very people they were here to liberate and now they were being used against them. It left a single choice to the attacker. To sit and do nothing while the besieged town awaited reinforcements... or to commit to action that was unthinkable.

This was the darkest hour of the war. The humans had won every single battle since they had breached Ur's inner borders, but now they risked losing it all. Losing Eridu did not just tip the scales, it brought them crashing down under a weight of dread and loss so heavy there was no lifting it.

Even as the princess' mind was overrun with the darkest of thoughts, her eyes sought Shamath. She had an awful feeling all the way from Larak to here, a premonition of something ghastly and inexorable that they were on their way to. Now that they were before the gate of Eridu and her portent of doom had been confirmed, that dark foreboding *still* worried at her insides like some ravening beast, as though whatever she feared was yet to come. This time, though, her feelings seemed to center around Shamath. When he had laid eyes onto the site of the gate and the hostage children on the battlements, it looked to her as though he had seen a ghost; so haunted did his face seem.

"Oh gods," she heard him say, his voice a death rattle. And the next thing he said she did not understand. "Carcosa," he whispered. "It's Carcosa."

And afterwards, as Aisyah and the other generals realized the hopelessness of the situation and ordered setting up a camp and digging up a trench so that at least they'd occupy the men and fortify a position for the coming battle, she had noted how silent Shamath had stayed throughout it, his gaze still possessed by whatever demon was gnawing at his heart. Not even the warm glow of torches and braziers lit up about them could disguise how his face had gone pallid in an instant and the knuckles of his hand were so tightened on his sickle-sword's hilt that they had gone white. Aisyah's attention was drawn to some maneuver her generals needed her approval on for not more than a minute, but when she turned back to Shamath, intent on finding out what had upset him so, she realized he was nowhere to be seen. Aisyah asked after him, but what she heard gave her pieces of an account far from complete. Shamath had been seen riding off far from their lines on his own; later, he had been witnessed riding back to the camp, and then inspecting the front lines of the rebels in the trenches till he was lost from view somewhere in the darkness and the multitudes of men laying there in wait. But there was none to tell her what he had done outside the camp. Aisyah wondered, her heart sick with foreboding.

Her hand snaked its way down his chest as she hugged him from behind. Shamath let it happen without opening his eyes, allowing her caress to draw him out of the depths of sleep. He woke up slowly to the warmth of her body embracing his, as close as a sheath hugging a sword. Her lips were the next sensation he felt, a soothing welcome in her kisses that brushed against the skin of his neck. Then she shifted and moved upwards to his face while he turned, his limbs stirring in response to the lust that stoked him like a breath on kindling, and his mouth opened to hers. Her body was a warm sun-kissed shore that he was washed out on, but her lips were another ocean, and he fell. Only when they both came out for breath, pulling back from each other, did he look at her. Her eyes were an azure dawn and her smile the sunlight.

"Good morning," said Arkhalla.

"It is now," he told her.

She laughed and he felt the tingle of her laughter breeze down her body and saw her naked as a spring morn. Clearly she felt his desire pressed hard against her, and with a smile, she kissed him again, and now they fell together. She was on her back now, guiding him to her, ready for him.

"I love you," he said.

"I love you, too," she whispered.

Their bodies came together, joining in ecstasy. Their limbs were a single being's attuned to the rhythm of their sighs, each soft moan taking them deeper inside each other. It was as though their passion bled the colors of the morn about them, drawing the day's glow to them alone, and with each moment, the light grew paler and the shadows beyond them deeper. They cared nothing for the world that vanished, lost in one another. The shadows lengthened, dark limbs growing from them like tendrils, closer and closer, embracing them. They were tentacles of darkness entwined with their limbs, more with every thrust and motion, and all of a sudden they were hardening around them, and Shamath couldn't move. There was fear in Arkhalla's eyes now, and he saw himself in them and realized he was screaming but he could not react, there was nothing he could do but scream in silence as the dark tentacles pulled her from him and he could not move, he could not *move*, the darkness was taking her into it and he screamed without speech, without a tongue, with no mouth to scream with. The darkness swallowed her, a black swamp of pitch deep as forever, and she called to him.

"My love," she cried out. *"Hold me! Don't let me go!"*

The dark claimed her; she was a face; a hand, held out, drowning, desperate.

"Save me, Shamath! Don't let me g—" And

then she was nothing.

Shamath opened his eyes with a jolt like he had been lashed. He was in his armor, seated in the trench, in the real world. He couldn't have nodded off for more than a second, the tiredness of the long march and the sleepless nights having caught up with him at last. But he still felt it all, his throat hoarse from the screaming, his eyes stinging with tears and rage, his body still hot with desire, so much that it hurt. He shook his head, wiping his tears. There were soldiers all about him, getting ready for battle, none of them wise to his dream or the agony he felt. Already the fear and the hurt and the tenderness taken from him were getting twisted in the bitterness of anger.

Limbs still shuddering, he emerged from the trench and headed for the company of archers and spearmen arranged alongside it. He saw the princess there talking to the chief spearman, but paid her no heed, calling out to Dumu and the chief archer of the Akkadians, who were standing nearby.

"Line up your men for attack," he told them, hoarse-voiced.

"Attack?" queried the chief archer. "When?" "Now."

"What?" Shamath heard the princess' voice behind him. Again, he paid her no heed.

"You heard me," he told the chief archer. "Line them up at shooting range. Flame arrows."

The chief archer could have been felled with a feather. "Their battlements are mud and... and brick fortified with... uh, with reeds," he almost stammered. "Their houses are just bundled... *reeds*. They will go up like tinder. You... you must know this." "And you must know an order when you hear it." The man looked at him, dumbstruck.

"Shamath –" Dumu began, but the look on his face shut her up.

Shamath felt Aisyah's hand on his arm and almost knocked it aside. She sensed him flinch, but did not withdraw it.

"What is this, Shamath?" she asked.

He did not look at her. She pressed his arm, gently. "Shamath?"

"Unhand me, your highness."

"Not until you face me."

He did, his eyes slowly rising to meet hers. She let go. Even if she had not promised, what she saw in his eyes would have made her release her hold.

"Flame arrows," he repeated to the chief archer without unlocking his gaze from her face. "Do it now."

"Shamath, I cannot allow this," she said.

He paused for one brief moment. "Fine."

Tearing his eyes from hers, he shouted to the gathered men.

"Those of you not Akkadian, ready your arrows now!"

"Shamath, stop!" she cried out.

"I'm not your man to order, your highness. Neither are my troops."

She stared at him, shocked. "Please," she said. Her voice trembled. "Reason with me."

"What *about*?" he snapped at her.

She did not flinch even though it pierced her like a spear. "Set fire to the battlements and the city will burn to the ground. All those innocent people in there –"

"Bel will use them all to feed on," he cut her short. "His army will be here, and they'll feed, and hunt us down refreshed."

"But if you –"

"If I do it, they'll be weakened. Days and nights out of Ur without nourishment."

"You'll *massacre* these people for – what? A fighting chance?!"

There was a moment's silence balanced between them, their eyes locked again like swords in a duel. The men around them waited with bated breath. Dumu looked disconsolate with grief.

"A chance to end this war," he told Aisyah, his voice a dying breath from a corpse's lips. "We can do it now. We may never be able to again."

"Shamath –"

"If we do not," he cut her, "these people are done for anyway."

"You cannot know that!"

"If we have the power to do it and we do not, then every life Bel and his leeches claim after now – and not just these people's – every death will be on our heads. If we allow these people to live, we allow the Undying to go on committing atrocity after atrocity." Aisyah realized she was shaking. She did not try to hide it.

"So we *commit* it *first*?" she asked. "We become like *them* or *lose* the war?"

There was an untold sadness in his eyes as he answered her.

"Only monsters win wars."

He turned and snapped at his archers, who, though numb with dread, began to line up at shooting range, whipped to action by his cold command.

"Shamath," she pleaded. "I cannot let you do it."

"I am doing it, Princess."

It was as though they were two different people to the ones they were mere minutes ago. She had felt closer to him than ever a mere night before, and now she could not believe she heard the words leave his mouth. It was even harder to fathom when she heard herself, even as the order sounded through her lips. She made no sense of what she had said, only of its effect, like something in a dream. A dozen of her spearmen barred Shamath's way, and only then did she realize it was at her command.

There was a moment's silence, frozen and terrible.

Then, a motion of Shamath's hand; a soft-spoken command she did not catch. Suddenly there were rebel archers pointing their arrows at their Akkadian comrades. At her spearmen.

At her.

Aisyah looked at Dumu. She was the only one who hadn't raised her bow. Dumu avoided her eyes. She was not able to stop her men, not against Shamath's orders. Aisyah wondered if the fair haired archer would dare it even if she could.

"Stand down, my lady," Shamath said. "Or let us kill each other now and win the Undying's war for them."

He fell silent, letting the standoff drive his point home.

A part of Aisyah's mind screamed for her to wake up as the rest of her brain raced through outcomes, all of them impossible. Her heart beat madly, like a ruptured drum.

There was only one choice that did not mean their mutual destruction or an outright end to humanity's cause, right then and there. For a moment, Aisyah wished her father was there to shoulder this burden instead of her. It was a wish born of fear. She felt ashamed of it the second after. Her father would have carried the weight of the decision. He would have known what really mattered in this war, the only thing that mattered, at any cost.

Not losing it.

She held her hand up, ordering her men to stand down. The command was silent, the words ashes in her mouth before they were even spoken. But its meaning was clear. The spearmen lowered their lances.

Shamath avoided her eyes as he turned to his archers.

"Ready."

Dumu and her men obeyed, lighting up the oil-soaked tows tied below their shafts' heads and setting them onto their bows. The fair-haired archer's eyes were bright with tears.

"Aim."

Dozens of bowstrings were pulled back as one, the arrows' flames lined along the darkness like an army of jinn poised to attack.

Aisyah looked at Shamath, willing him even now to turn, to see her, to stop.

The warrior stood his ground without meeting her eyes. His voice, when it sounded, was no louder than a whisper, yet in the silence it could have dwarfed a clap of thunder.

"Fire."

Narama knew what was happening as soon as she saw the flames lining up in the darkness. It was the only thing that could be happening. Too late, she realized it was what she would have done in Shamath's place. Once more, she had underestimated the wretch's utter ruthlessness --

No. Narama realized she was deluding herself. It was what *She* would have done.

Arkhalla.

The shock cost her a second of numbness. Time slowed to a crawl as her Undying sight registered the arrows rising in the night sky like a hail of comets.

A roar of rage tore through her gritted fangs. There wasn't a single thing she could do but watch as doom came down on Eridu. About her on the battlements men scrambled madly looking for cover, slow as flies wading through amber. The hostage children saw the fiery death raining down and screamed, their cry drawn to an eternity.

Down came the arrows in a storm of flame and heat. The battlements shook from their impact and time sped up now, exploding, the night ravaged by deafening crackle and flashes that erupted in all-consuming fire. Faces mortal and Undying glimpsed each other pale and screaming through blinding peals of thunder.

Great bursts of fire gutted the battlements and ate through structure and flesh alike. Narama cried angry orders through the flames for her men to put them out before they had an inferno in their hands. It'd have been futile even if they had heard her. Volleys of new firestorms came down almost by the second. Fire caught and spread to what could feed it. Before they knew it, they were its fuel.

The hostages burned with their jailers. The braziers and tar barrels overturned by panicked warriors spilled their contents over whatever was not already up in flames. Narama felt the deep and roaring impact like the savage blow of a beast as the battlements exploded. A hot wind took and blew her high, throwing her off the wall and onto the ground as mud and reed and brick and burning limbs rained down around her.

Deafened, she struggled to her feet. The inferno had swelled to the town all about her. All that could catch fire was burning. Screaming figures ran past her in flames, spreading the blaze to all that they touched before they collapsed. The boom of new explosions mingled with the screaming and maddened those few among her men that still held on to their sanity. Every new fire burst opened another mass grave.

Everywhere she looked, Narama saw the beast that was the fire or the carnage it left in its wake. Men stumbled, caked with burns, shaking, dying. Women wailed for their children till another blast of fire silenced them. Grown warriors doubled over churning their guts and blood in fits of vomit. One man, crouched in a corner, was biting his arm, feeding on his own flesh. Wherever her eyes turned, there was blood and fire, driving the Undying to frenzy. The town stood riddled with holes and pits and mounds of dirt from the blasts.

Eridu burned to the ground around her as Narama raised her eyes to heaven and screamed the wretch's name.

CHAPTER 21

DUEL AT THE GATES OF DAWN

Aisyah thought she had run out of tears. She had stood with them flowing down her face as she heard the screams of fifteen thousand souls crying out in agony before they were snuffed out for all time. It was a sound she had never dreamed of hearing in all her life and would not forget till her dying breath. And now that the screams were dying down at last, her tears dried on her face and she thought her heart had dried too, forever.

All through the burning of Eridu she had not dared look at the sight, nor at Shamath. Only now did she turn her eyes to him and found him gazing at the flames, alone among his men and hers, who stood about in huddles and, like Aisyah, had turned away from the inferno, unable to watch. But Shamath stood and watched as though he waited for something, like a prophet waiting for a god. Something other than screams called out to him from the flames, and he waited for it.

It was in the change in his eyes that Aisyah realized what that was even before she heard the sound of Eridu's gates thrown open.

She turned just in time to see the nightmare burst forth out of the inferno.

Most of the men that rode out of the gates had to be dead; flaming corpses erect on burning mounts, the only life left in them the keening cry that tore through scorched and wasted lips. Yet still they rode, brandishing sickle-swords, Undying horrors riding out to prove their name before they dropped. Among them were half burnt warriors, the dregs and remnants of Eridu's garrison, the once and past pride of Ur's black guards making a last dash.

And at their head, wailing like a demon born, rode the nightmare-death-in-life herself, leading the charge of a brigade of dead.

Narama, the thought screamed in Aisyah's mind even as she sprung to action.

"To arms!" she called out to her men. "They are making a break for it! To arms, Akkadians!"

Her cry rallied her troops and they poured out of the trench and onto the field, joining Shamath's men as they met the riding dead. Divided mere minutes ago, they stood together, fighting their own fear and dread together with what came at them. Akkadians and rebels alike, they had new purpose. To slay the horror and live, for Akkad, for humanity, aye, even for Eridu's slain. If even one of these Undying lived, then fifteen thousand had died for nothing. Every blow dealt was more than itself; it was a blow to end the Undying once and for all time.

Aisyah drew her sword and threw herself against the dead tide with a warrior's yell.

Narama hacked her way through an endless forest of limbs, unstoppable. She saw no enemy but one; no blade but that of the bane of her existence. Shamath had bested her again. He had set fire to the town, to her plans, and he had burned her last hope to the ground along with her men and with fifteen thousand of his own people. And now she finally knew why. Shamath was still *Hers*. He was Arkhalla's final weapon thrown at her, and she'd cleave and break and sunder it or die. Even if it meant Narama's doom, Arkhalla would not prevail.

Now at last she caught sight of him from afar. Even as she charged forward he saw her and turned his horse to the side, goading her to come after him.

"Face me, wretch!" she cried out, maddened by the taunt. "Come and die!"

Men fell before her like leaves burnt away, but Shamath kept the distance between them. It enraged her all the more. She fought through foes and the pain from her burns and finally she broke through their lines, yet still he drove his horse back.

"I'll chase you till the ends of the earth, wretch!" she yelled at him.

He yanked at the reins of his mare and the horse rose on its hind legs before it broke into a gallop across Eridu's plain. Narama caught sight of his face for a mere second in the glow of a campfire, but that silent glimpse had called back to her. It was that look she remembered; the defiance; the resolve that just would not be broken. He was challenging her.

Narama rushed after him.

They rode like mad across the plain, the battle and the world falling behind them. None but the night and the gods would be witness to their final showdown. She realized she desired just that. For the desert alone to hear her cursing Arkhalla's name one last time.

She slapped and kicked her horse as though she meant to drive it to its death and at last she began to close the gap between them. Even in moonlight, she saw thick lather foaming on the coat of Shamath's mare. Any second, either his horse or hers would drop down and die, and the chase would be decided for them. She had no love lost for the gods of fate. If she was to catch up to him, it would be up to her – and either now or never.

Fight me, you coward!

Whether Shamath read her mind or not, that was the moment he stopped and dismounted.

Narama saw him waiting and stopped.

They had ridden for what had to be miles. The country spreading out about them was a wasteland, all dirt and thick thistle bushes so dry they tumbled in the wind. An old well going some forty feet deep and a crumbled mud hut long since abandoned by whoever had tried digging the well to farm this godforsaken piece of earth were the sole signs that humanity had ever stepped its foot here. Other than these, there was nothing around them but desert and faraway hills, and none of the clamors of the battle could be heard in the sudden silence. Even the moon had sunk behind the horizon, naught left of the full round disc but its eerie glow, bathing the night silver. They were alone.

Shamath stood by his horse, waiting, his sickle-sword in hand.

Now Narama dismounted, too. Wielding her blade, she drew closer. He waited for her, not a muscle on him moving.

No. Not cowardice. He had led her here by choice, at an arena just for the two of them. Defiant to the last.

Even at this moment, so close to the point of dying for one of them, she found herself impressed by his courage. Such a *man* he has become, she thought. So much like what Bel was... or had been once, at least. A surge of unexpected feeling flowed through her, mixed up, unfathomable, the feeling of a woman before a real man, perhaps, or that of a mother before a grown son. This was a man she had wrought. This was a man waiting for her at the point of dying.

She almost wished things were otherwise between them then, even as she knew very well they could never be. He was an enemy.

Worse still, he was *Arkhalla's*.

"You still have that same look in your eyes," she said, willing herself to follow her words with a spitted insult. "Still a defiant wretch." She paused, letting a breath pass between them. "This time, I will *rip* your eyes out of your face".

He gazed at her in silence. That rattled her more than any spoken slur. It wasn't just that he had the unmitigated gall not to answer her, that he was robbing her of the satisfaction of one last exchange between them. No, the wretch was attempting to direct these final moments they had together on this earth. He was choreographing this dance of death. He had picked the site of their duel, he had determined it would be this barren place that no one knew or would ever know and that had never yielded anything, not to the long gone farmer, not to a warlord claiming it, not to any man alive or dead, as though he was shoving it into her face that if she died here no one would ever know she had lived, and if he died here he simply did not care.

Well, *he* would die here that night, and Narama was determined about that.

To this swell of rage that built inside her, Shamath paid no heed. He had staked his piece of ground and stayed on it. That was his gesture. What came next he left to her.

Narama began to circle around him, her movements calm but scurrilous, meeting his defiance with a taunt of her own. She looked for an advantage and an opening. Shamath's eyes followed her, but other than that, he did nothing. It was almost as though he knew he needed no advantage. The thought was scurvy to Narama's mind, and she cast it out, focusing on her dance, the dance of the lion in the desert. She had her prey in her sight, unmoving, while she stalked. They were linked, the two of them, predator and prey, fixed center to narrowing circle. He was the star around which she turned, her destiny. She was his doom.

Her eyes studied him, relishing every fold and pore in this face that was youthful and handsome yet as unmoving as granite. She chose him now, to be her nemesis, the ultimate foe she would defeat. The stone-hewn features that were his face matched the fixity of her purpose. Tonight her age-old feud with Arkhalla would be ended. Washed in his blood.

They stared each other down now.

Her eyes, narrowed slits, shining a true snake-green in the pale grey light.

His eyes, a cool, calm sea.

Her hands twisted slowly around the hilt of her blade.

His hands flexed around his, ready.

A bead of sweat glistened on his brow.

Her lip curled, ever so slightly.

Then, with a heart-stopping cry, she pounced.

Her blade tore the night air, seeking his heart. His sickle-sword parried. Lightning-fast, she attacked anew, but again his thrust was there to counter hers.

Narama's lips parted in the sharpest of grins as she reassumed her initial stance. The wretch fought smartly, like that little bitch princess of Akkad. He was versed in the Undying's ways. He knew their style, the hits they went for. Inhuman speed was of little advantage when one's target could be anticipated.

Again she charged, switching from one attack to the next, changing and combining moves, trying to tire him out, like she had tried with the Akkadian. She pressed and pushed and hounded him, every bit his superior, but he almost held his ground, giving inches where even Undying swordsmen would give yards.

Uncanny, she thought, even as she doubled down on her offensive.

This was the legend, then. The best mortal men had to offer.

He was almost up to her challenge.

Fine by her.

Changing her tack, she charged him now with none of the rhyme and reason of her style till now. One move led to its total opposite, one attack a mere feint before the next. It was a tactic only the finest swords could sustain without some fatal error. Bel himself had taught it to her. A madman's style, yet rich with secret method.

At last Shamath began to give her ground.

Narama pressed on her attack, her blade pounding his with no quarter given as she drove him backwards. Into the thistle bushes they walked now, step by slow step, clang by spark-lighting clang. Shamath backed down, slowly but surely. She saw the sweat pouring down his brow, the slight trembling of his sinews as he raised his blade again and again and it was heavier each time.

It'd be any moment now, Narama knew. Soon he'd stumble and leave himself open; or he'd be blinded by sweat, or slowdown that split second.

Soon now.

She pressed on, forward, through the bushes.

There it was; the stumble.

He sidestepped, tottered back. She thrust forward.

That was when the gripping trap closed about her foot.

Toothed jaws of bronze snapped on bone and sinew so fast she did not even sense it happening until the bone was smashed and her leg almost severed in twain.

The pain was a surprise; an unexpected, uninvited friend.

Her scream shocked her.

Shamath looked at her, panting, but steady on his feet.

A feint. The trap was his. Through the pain, she saw his ruse clearly.

It took the strength of more than ten men to stop her shaking and speak over the agony. Narama had that strength.

"You..." she spoke, a breath between this word and the next, "think this... can... stop me... wretch?" She gritted her teeth in a supreme effort. "You think... me... a cur... that you can... chain?"

Even as she said it, she sensed something was wrong. Pain she knew. That she could handle. But... she had not lost blood enough to feel weak. Not yet. And yet... *weak*... was what she felt.

She looked at him in rage, filled with it, spitting it.

And then the wretch did the oddest thing. He

smiled.

"No, I don't think it would stop you. But something else will."

Narama's brows twitched into a frown.

"That foul smell your heightened senses must be picking up now," Shamath went on. "Is it not familiar?"

Narama looked down at the metal jaws, at the green, rustlike tint smeared onto the teeth, clear against the bronze and the darkness of her blood.

No.

"Yes," said Shamath.

"P-poison," Narama stammered. It all came back to her now. "M-*my* poison."

Shamath shook his head. "One of Erun's."

"Tell me how you made it."

He had to reiterate his demand again, his hand tightened about the fabric of the flap, before the old man could make sense of what it was that Shamath wanted of him.

"The poison that killed Her, old man. The one you gave the Huntress."

"Arkhalla's bane," Erun stuttered. He remembered. After all these years, he remembered.

That was when he knew he was going to die.

"Tell me how you made it."

Shaking, twitching with pain, the living dead thing spoke in slow, drawn-out sentences. With each breath he took so agonizing Erun thought it to be his last, he told his torturer what instruments he'd used to craft the poison that had brought Arkhalla down.

There was a frog, of all the lowly little things that can fell and kill the mightiest of giants. Not even a snake, a scorpion, or a spider, hunters all among the creatures of the gods. A frog, a dweller of swamps that festered all over Ur, those same swamps the fallen queen had been hunted through like the lowliest thing. The slime that coated its glistening black and yellow skin was the sole defense the gods had given the frumpy little thing, and it could kill the fiercest of predators and save it one more day of its mudfilled existence. That was the vile liquid, secreted from its boiled carcass, mixed with the most appropriate of herbs, that Erun had chosen to gift Narama to slay their queen with, in what was sure to be a final insult to her power. And with what he sensed to be his last breaths, he yielded that royal-slaying secret.

When he was done, at long last, Shamath asked him if that was all.

The old man said yes.

Shamath nodded and tore the tent flap open. Light washed over the Undying's face, past the stump of a hand he threw up, past his arm. Howling, cursing, he burned.

As the invasion army marched through Ur, Shamath had waded through those swamps and he had sought out and found the damned frog the poison had come from. He had found and picked and gathered the herbs the dead leech had specified. He had mixed the poison himself, long hours, until it took on that hue and stunk of that foul smell he still recalled as though the night he had seen Narama dip her blade in it had been mere minutes before. And he had done it all so he could savor this very moment.

That was when Narama glanced at the glow reddening the horizon and realized that Shamath had dueled her to the break of dawn.

She was stuck with her foot in a farmer's trap, out here in the open. And the day was about to break while she had been poisoned with the same poison she had used on Arkhalla.

The bitch would have her vengeance after all.

Pain swelled into a sob in her throat. She stifled it and held it down till it was no more.

"It is not you who kills me, Shamath," she said, the words coming out slow and painful. "The bitch slays me from beyond the grave. You are just her hand."

He looked at her, pained. She was glad she hurt him.

"That night, so long ago," he said, "I promised you I would kill you before I let you lay a hand on her. But I failed. And for ten years of my life, I suffered for what you made me do."

His voice trembled with anger. "A part of me died with her that night, Huntress. I could not save her... but by all gods, I will avenge her."

Burning eyes met hers. "I *live* to be her hand," he threw back at her.

"Her hand, her pawn," she spat out. "She still uses you, wretch. I should know. She uses you like she used me. Like she used us all."

"You still hate her."

She scoffed. "And you still love her."

Like Bel, she almost said. But she did not. That last shred of dignity she meant to keep.

"Hate is the lesson she taught me, Shamath," she said instead. "I've learned it well. She was a fine teacher."

Shamath's hands tightened into fists. He pointed a finger at the trap and her bleeding leg.

"You taught me this," Shamath said, his voice shaking with emotion as he looked at her. "That I should use the best thing in my arsenal to catch my prey. Even if it was something foul and beneath me!"

His words were coals under the cauldron of rage bubbling inside her. A soul-slaying cry tore through her gritted fangs. It sent lizards scurrying to their holes half a mile away.

"I'm not prey, wretch! I'm the *HUNTER*!!!!"

She thrust herself forward to grab him and the strain almost split what was left of her leg in twain. A sword of pain wedged itself in her to the hilt, and she collapsed.

It was almost the gods' pity that the sun came out at that moment. Light touched her skin, red, soft, hot.

She burned.

It was a slow thing, slower even than Erun's dying. The blisters first, then the smoking sores, then, at last, the flame igniting, the flesh roasting from the inside. With the burning came her cry, a sighing breath rising to a moan and then, when no residue of will could hold it back any longer, a scream.

Shamath watched until she was on fire. Then the moment he had waited for all his days since that last dawn soured.

Again he saw *her*, burning, at dawn. It was *her* form he saw writhing in the flames. *Her* skin he witnessed peel from decomposing sinew.

Narama burned, but it was Arkhalla that he saw.

And that sight was not one he could endure again.

He shut his eyes and the image burned in his head. A wild panic seized him. He backed away from the burning woman, his hands pressed to his ears to shield him from her piercing screams.

He was there again, at the square of Dilmun, helpless as she died again. Panic and guilt and helplessness thronged up on him, clad in the dusky robes of nightmare, enwound within his soul like serpents coiled together – away! He had to get away from them!

His eyes still tightly shut and his hands clasped to his ears, he stumbled to his horse pursued by these hellhounds of his mind. Behind closed lids Arkhalla burned; black blood dripping from her eyes as she screamed her final scream into a forever morning.

Away! He could bear it no more!

Shamath struggled onto his horse and spurred it on; the beast lunged forward with a neigh of fear, almost as though it too beheld what only Shamath could. Hooves thundered, a mad gallop rushing the both of them away. Tears streamed down Shamath's cheeks as he rode away, the thunder of his mare joined by his own cry in an effort to drown the screams that hounded him.

Already far behind him, in the golden brightness of the new day, Narama's body burned. The rider had reached the horizon and the hoarseness of a death rattle crept into her screams when a shade came running out of the desert towards her.

Its shape was manlike but deformed under the thick animal hides thrown onto it. Whatever protection they offered it was not enough, for there were wisps of smoke and the smell of burning coming from underneath them.

The hide-covered shade stumbled to the burning woman and fell on its knees beside her. Steaming hands came from underneath the mass of skins and threw part of its covering onto her. Strong arms ignored the burning heat and the welts beginning to bubble onto them and pressed the furs tight about Narama's writhing, fragile form, putting out the flames.

"Hold on," the shade's voice said, so dear to her.

Narama heard it from death's distant shore and feared she'd dreamt it.

"Hold on, Narama," it called to her again. "Hold on to me."

Arms opened the jawed trap, releasing what was left of her leg. They lifted her, hot and sinewy.

"B-Bel," she croaked.

He'd die, he'd burn with her. She couldn't let him.

Staggering, he tried to walk with her in his arms. The skins were not enough. Now he was steaming, too. Soon, he'd burn.

He took one step. Another now. And another.

She tried to warn him off her, tell him to let her die, but the pain did not let her. He could not make it.

The heat and her weight dropped him to his knees. He kept moving, on his knees. The stench of burning, rotting meat rose with his sweat from beneath the skins.

They'd die, they'd both die –

He couldn't do it. He was crawling now, dragging her with him, inch by screaming inch.

Narama waited for the fire. They'd burn together. It was the end.

Her senses fading, she surrendered herself to him.

He dragged her on. With one hand he held her to him under the skins as with the other he dug into the dirt and inched forward. Together they crawled and crawled along the sand.

Towards the well.

Ten feet away. It felt like miles.

Bel gritted his teeth. He'd have to endure it, or they were both dead.

His sweat sizzled as it evaporated from his burning skin. A scream built in him and he held it back.

The mud hut was crumbled, roofless. Even if they got there it'd offer no respite from the sun. The well was their only chance.

Six feet now.

He was sure he was on fire under the skins. They were the one thing that kept them from erupting into flames.

Four feet.

It was agony.

Three.

Bel pushed himself along towards the yawning mouth.

There! His fingers grabbed onto the edge of the well. He heaved with all the strength left in him and hurled the two of them forward.

They fell, two shapes steaming, from light into the darkness, hurling down the rough rocky walls till they hit the bottom.

Neither of them moved.

CHAPTER 22

THE UNFORGIVEN

The pain was a sign he still breathed, and Bel woke to it with gratitude. He was unable to move for the first hour after he opened his eyes, still weak from the effort and in agony so intense it crippled him. But his ears picked up Narama's breathing too. It was uneven, shallow, and too akin to the rattle of death for comfort, but it was life nonetheless. As soon as he could move, he pulled her close to him, warming her cold, brittle, coal-like flesh with his body. His blood was thick and coagulated like globs of mercury, yet he managed to press some of it from the cut he made on his hand down her throat. Embraced like that, with him holding her just off the brink of death, they waited out the day in the deep darkness of the well.

He had forged ahead of the main body of his troops with a squadron of riders, eager to get to Eridu and join Narama as soon as it was possible. But all they had managed to catch sight of was the far-off glow of the flames, coupled by the echoes of the massacre of the last that had made their exodus from the burning city's gates. His scout caught sight of Narama in pursuit of Shamath across the desert, too fast and far from them to do anything but follow. Even at top speed, they had not managed to race the coming sunrise, and as the sky turned from black to grey with a hint of purple in the horizon, Bel had ordered his men to the hills to find shelter in the caves and had continued the pursuit alone. All the protection he had was the skins from his saddlebag that served as blankets. He knew what he was doing was suicide, but he could not leave Narama to face her fate alone. And yet, fast as he went, though he swooped ahead to the deserted clearing with what seemed the first rays of the dawn, he was too late. Already his skin wilted in the rising sun and the hair on his head began to curl with the heat despite the skins. A rider fled from what seemed to be a pyre, but Bel knew what it really was even before his keen eyes told him. Bel knew he was as dead as her. But all he thought of was Narama. He had grabbed another animal skin blanket from his saddle and raced towards her with no notion of how they'd manage to pull through this, and it was only halfway through that desperate run that he had seen the well.

He would have been content to die. But not to take her with him. He owed her that much. He owed her love that much.

With all the feeling he could muster in his wounded heart, Bel held Narama close until the day finally faded and he heard the hooves from his men's mounts thundering up above.

Narama had been scorched so badly she was more burn than flesh. As Bel's men roped and lifted her out of the well, she looked like a woman of coal and ash about to crumble, and the sole sign of life on her while they wrapped her in blankets and on a litter of reeds was her eyes, fluttering between this world and the next. Bel was half-burnt and holding on to consciousness by sheer will alone, but the sight of her wracked his soul worse than his body. Two unseeing, faded green eyes in a maelstrom of burnt off features was all that was left of the great Huntress of Men. It'd be a wonder if she lived, much less recover.

Without fresh provisions, the imperative was getting closer to the capital again to keep the army fed and strong. His men took them both to shelter in their encampment in the desert caves, from where Bel sent word to the rest of his troops to join them and make their way back towards Ur to regroup for the final battle. His wounds were severe, but treatable, and bandaged from his head and face down to his feet, Bel was able to shamble about by the time they made camp after the first night's march, drawing furtive frightened glances from his men before they looked away again as though they had seen a corpse walking in its shroud. Narama, however, remained at death's door. He had slaves cut and bled to provide her with a steady replenishment of blood every other hour and he gave her his more than three times every day, but it brought only the slightest change in her state. The burns refused to heal. Her dressings had to be changed constantly, for the fresh influx of blood seeped from her open wounds to them.

The worst thing was looking at her. It was the sight of that nigh formless shape of burns that brought to him flashes of that square in Dilmun the night after they burned Arkhalla. Back then, it had been the smell and the glimpse of the ashes left from the pyre that had cut him inside, sharp as his queen's pain must have been. Now, seeing Narama, he saw how She must have looked like, and it was killing him. Narama's pain was his fault now, like Arkhalla's had been then. It was his weakness, his betrayal that had brought them to this.

On the third night he knew he could not take it anymore. It was just after dark and his troops were in the process of breaking camp to move on towards the capital. He had been sitting on the bed next to Narama. She had been writhing in a fever. Her eyes blinked, unseeing, and she was shivering. He soothed her brow with a wet compress and held her, and her eyes without a face opened, and he saw them looking at him, blue.

He jumped back and away from her as though she had been a snake.

Her eyes looked at him, blue.

Narama's were green.

He woke up with a start, with Narama asleep next to him, exhausted after hours of fighting the fever.

A dream. It had been nothing but a dream. And it had nearly stopped his heart.

Instead of staying by her side or wander a while about the camp to clear his head, he left Narama to the attention of his physicians and stormed out of the tent and onto his horse, leaving everyone behind him stunned.

The night was calm with the cold of an unloved season and the moon was full and bright. Only the howling of the desert wolves accompanied his mad ride across the dunes. He rode back the way they had come till he could see the far-off fires of the camp of his enemies to the west. His ride was desperate and fast, as though he was outrunning the past itself – or trying to and failing at it. Like Narama three dawns before, he pushed his horse almost to the point of death before he stopped and dismounted, alone in the great desert.

The wind rush that had dried the tears from his face during the hard ride was but a breeze now, and tears came flowing again, bidden by the despair crushing his heart. He cursed aloud, one harsh obscenity directed at the gods of fate. He wanted it to stop. He wanted everything to stop, he wanted the earth to stop turning and life, this long, long life to stop tormenting him. He dropped down to his knees on the hard, arid ground and smashed it with his fists.

"WHY?" he cried out. "WHY?"

All his pain, his regret, in one word, torn from his insides. A full mile away, only the crawling creatures of the desert heard his pained cry.

Why had she not loved him? Why had he loved her?

Why had he not been worthy? Why had he betrayed her?

He cried it out once more. Not once in all the times he did had he thought about Narama, and even as he did not he hated himself for it. It was Arkhalla he had loved with a fire that had destroyed him, and the Huntress with him. It was *her* that had ruined them all, even Narama, even Shamath. But it had been him who killed her and sealed their doom.

If a scorpion came and crawled onto his hand right then, he'd let it sting him. He wished for the moon to set and the sun to rise and burn him, burn it all away, because he lacked the strength to end it himself. Even at bringing about his own end he was a failure. All he had ever succeeded at was ruining everything.

There was nothing in his throat to form words now, even that single word of self-recrimination. All that was left was sobs swelling inside him and bursting out, the regret and the guilt and the shame wracking his great shoulders. He cried because of what he had done, and because he had done it to the only woman he could have ever loved.

Aisyah did not even have to try to keep herself busy over the next few days. An army is the most difficult thing on earth to move next to moving a mountain, and mountains come in one piece. Not only did the princess have to get these companies and battalions and squadrons and regiments of thousands of men to the city of Ur in the fastest, safest and most efficient way possible, but she had to see that they were nourished – which was easier said than done, as Bel had chosen to regroup his forces while retreating back towards the capital, which left only scorched earth, ravaged villages and poisoned wells in his wake. Shamath's way of dealing with that was to have scouts scan ahead of the main advance force, finding alternate wells not too far off their path and getting the nomad shepherd peoples of the desert to bring their cattle on and join their march. Every day, more and more flocks of sheep and goats arrived to feed their soldiers, and with proper rations, the water from the clean wells would suffice. Thanks to the shepherds, the march would not be stalled and they would press on against Bel, leaving him no time to marshal his retreat the way he would have planned. Once again, Aisyah had to marvel at the way the legend of Shamath and his Day of Reckoning was enough to get these folk to sacrifice their livelihoods without a single voice of disagreement. The stakes were high – the most impossible ever, and these simple shepherds knew it. She would see them come, these sun-baked, leather-skinned men and women and children, and like their flocks, they too would gather about Shamath as though he was their shepherd. Watching him with them, his simple farmer's bearing so similar to theirs and so unlike those of princes to the manner born, she could understand why they trusted him with nothing less than their lives. He was no haughty savior; just a man, with a man's courage and a man's task. That was what these people sensed in him. And it was no small thing.

The feeding of the men thus sorted left out a dozen other tasks for her and Shamath to fulfill and little time alone with him, for which Aisyah realized she was thankful. After Eridu, she found it hard to talk to Shamath, just as she found it hard to reconcile the man's quality – his strength, his vision, his compassion – with his ruthlessness and obsession. His drive for vengeance, the things he was prepared to do for it, these gave Aisyah pause. But Shamath's love for Arkhalla bothered and perplexed her. Was this dual, frightening nature of this admirable man a reflection of Her? Of what She was like and had wrought in that life that Aisyah now realized she knew nothing about other than horror stories? What had been the reality of that woman's life that had inspired love in a man as good as Shamath and treachery in one as monstrous as Bel? And what in that life, that love, had made this good and loving man that Aisyah had hooked her and her people's destiny with such a warrior to fear? Aisyah knew she was not aware of the whole story, and part of her dreaded that she might be wrong in things she had believed in all her life.

So Aisyah dreaded the moments the two of them would brush against each other during each day of moving an army of men to the battle that would judge the freedom of the world. She'd steal glances at Shamath as they gave the day's orders to their generals and lieutenants, and when they received the scouts and messengers that bore news of allies and enemies, and at the setting and breaking of camp and the apportioning of rations, and at the first hours of each morning given to sharpening the training of the men. By now the ragtag rebels and the Akkadians had merged into a formidable fighting unit. Unconventional tactics and strategy and might were enmeshed to a degree that would both daunt and surprise a foe used to fighting just in pure terms of raw strength, and each of the battles fought during the push into Ur had only honed this quality to its utmost. Aisyah had long since trained her men in all the ways mortals could take on the Undying – the feint and the subterfuge, the anticipating of the enemy's target rather than trying to match their inhuman speed, the avoidance of straight-on contests of brawn and reliance on evasion, the swift beheading stroke, and the splitting of the enemy's attention to multiple opponents at once – and that training the Akkadians had shared with their allies. Still, the sheer superiority of the Undying in single combat could never be underestimated, and every morning the men trained to their breaking point, with her and Shamath watching them, intent as peregrine falcons gauging prey. It was on such a training session that Aisyah caught Shamath's eye on her.

Her heart skipped a beat. Had he, too, been watching her all these days, when she wasn't looking?

Taking a deep breath, she cleared her head. Not for her was the pang of doubt, of indecision. She was one to the manner born, and she would deal with this head-on.

Everyone trained together in the approach to Ur. This was to be the final battle, the one with no second chance in the case of defeat, so defeat was not an option. Shamath and Aisyah were in the melee every moment with their men. She saw he was without an opponent at the moment and with a bold sidestroke of the broad side of her sickle-sword to her own sparring partner's feet, she threw him on the ground and assumed a challenging stance, bidding Shamath to her.

"I thought you had been giving me the cold shoulder," he said in that infuriating manner of his that never made her sure of whether he was jesting with her or not.

"We may be standing side by side in the fight," she threw back at him. "Cold shoulders are inadvisable."

She thrust. He parried.

Again.

And again.

"No," she said, exasperated. "Show me how you countered Narama."

He did. His swordsmanship was poetry. But she could not let him know.

"Again."

Again she attacked. He countered, masterfully.

"No," she said.

He saw the anger in her eyes. "Is this still training?"

"Shut up and fight."

She charged him, aping Narama's style as she had experienced it.

He held his ground.

"Your Highness—"

"I said fight."

She charged him, beating down on his defense.

He held his ground. For now.

"Do not make this about Eridu," he said, getting flustered.

"I am not."

He locked his sword's hilt to hers, bringing them to a standstill.

"What are you at, then?" He was panting.

She was breathing hard too, her face red. "You beat her with a trick."

He frowned. "I know you don't care for my methods."

"I don't care for them getting you killed, Shamath."

She dislodged her blade from his and they faced each other again.

"Trickery is like hate," she told him. "It is base and dirty and it works, but it will only get you so far."

"It worked so far," he retorted. "At the quicksand. At Eridu. With Narama." He breathed, trying to compose himself. "You know of another way to bring Bel to his knees?"

He wasn't calming down, he was getting angrier. That was his error. He was so angry, underneath, all the time. That was what was going to get him killed. And Aisyah knew all the way to the depths of her soul that she would not have that.

"Trickery is what you taught these men," Shamath went on. "It's what has kept them alive to fight this battle. Are you telling me you are wrong?"

"No. But they know, deep down, that trickery may fail." He circled her, looking for an opening. She gave him none.

"They know that when it comes to a straight, one-on-one, equal footing fight against an Undying, they can only run," she said. "But when we fight next, there will be no running."

"They know that. I know that."

"You may face Bel on that day."

He grinned. "I *want* to face Bel on that day."

Her charge was sudden, reckless, all-in. She threw all her weight behind it. Shamath was caught with no room to raise his sword without maiming himself. Her momentum brought them both down, her on top of him.

"This is Bel bearing down on you," she said.

Shamath roared in anger and thrust his head forward, his helm smashing into hers. She fell back and he swiped upwards with his blade to get her off him.

Aisyah lunged to the side and rolled her body, avoiding his stroke. The split second it took Shamath to snap to his feet was all it took for her to swipe her shield right onto his sword hand, dropping the blade from it.

"This is Bel's stroke full-on," she roared.

Shamath used his own shield to block her thrust and swerved round, bringing himself in close to Aisyah so that his elbow knocked the wind out of her. A lesser warrior disarmed would have tried to get away from a killing stroke rather than move in at even closer quarters, and would have gotten killed for it. Shamath's move brought him inside Aisyah's arms, and his blow loosened her grip on her weapon enough for him to grab it from her. This was the move of a master, and it could only be matched by another one.

It was too late when he realized that his ruse was what Aisyah had meant to happen. The tiny dagger lay pressed against his throat. One brisk move and his throat would be slit from side to side.

"And this," Aisyah said, panting, "is Bel's fangs on your throat."

The soldiers about them had ceased their sparring and stood watching them. From the look on their faces, it was as though they had seen a clash between two gods. Dumu, her blade in hand, stared at them aghast. Shamath could see in her eyes that the fight she had just witnessed was the real thing, and that she feared one of the two of them might have taken it too far. What he could not make out was whether she had feared it would have been him.

He eased Aisyah's hand off his throat, acceding her the fight. They faced each other, the gazes of their troops fixed on them.

"A one-on-one fight can be won, Shamath," the princess told him. "Against the Undying, against any foe, no matter their strength, and even when you're out of tricks. In the end, you'll have to be the better man. You have to be better. And you need to fight for something better."

Something in the way she said it pierced him. "Is that why you won just now, your highness? What better thing did you fight for?"

She did not hesitate. "You, Shamath. I fought for you."

And without another word, she turned and walked away. Shamath stood watching her, his cheeks aflame with sudden shame.

He had relied on tricks and playing dirty, and Aisyah was right. That luck would run out. And he could not beat Bel in a fair fight either. She was right about that, too. Not with the hate that poisoned his heart and the anger that dulled his skill. With them, against Bel, he was a dead man.

Aisyah had not just taught him he had to be better. She had bested him because, to her, he was. And she was telling him that he had to find it in his heart to be worthy of what she felt.

Or they would all be doomed.

CHAPTER 23

DAY OF RECKONING

It was the night that winter came to season when Shamath's advance squadrons, which had been marching day and night parallel to the main army's progress, moved into action as arranged. Coming up between the leading columns of Bel's retreating army and the city of Ur just visible along the horizon, they stopped the Undying warlord's troops on the high road that led to the capital. With his retreat curtailed, Bel had no option but to stand and fight. The irony of the situation was lost on him, but not on Shamath. This was the very place he had had his first glimpse of the black towering ziggurat of Ur and sensed that awe and enticement and foreboding that afterwards he realized had been the presence of Arkhalla. It would end where everything began.

The night was bitterly cold, and the first snowflakes began to fall as he and Aisyah oversaw the divisions and formations with which their men would march to battle. Sky gazers and priests studying the patterns of the weather often prophesied how one day the sun and desert gods would win the tug-of-war between them and their brethren in the sky, and snow would be a rarity in the lands of Ur in centuries to come. Bel did not really hope to live to see that time, but watching the snowfall across the plain from Shamath's army made him want to throw those priests butt-naked in the desert cold to test their own prophesies. Snow was another thing the humans would have in their favor. Tiredness and dejection after these long nights of retreat, as well as undernourishment and having to fight deprived of blood, with the effects of hunger dulling his men's edge, were the main other factors against the Undying. They still had their superior strength and numbers, but otherwise that was all they had. Bel watched the Black Guards and then the first and second squadrons of conscripts and his infantry battalions and cavalry line up and ready themselves, and his lieutenants ride to and fro coordinating their attack. It was either attacking first and forcing Shamath to fight now or waiting for the sun to come up and leave their fate to the rabble of conscripts who would scatter at the first opportunity. Shamath's advance squadrons had cut them off with surgical precision. The token contingent left to guard the capital was not enough to do much against them except bother them the way a horsefly bothers a steed's hind. All the fear of this moment which he had experienced in the nights leading up to it had come back, and all his inner struggle to conquer that fear, all his desire to prove himself true to his might of years past, had been wasted. Without even knowing what the cause of this fear was – and it was not of losing the battle, of that much he was sure – Bel spent this time of preparation in a depressed and wretched mood. A hundred times he almost turned to Narama to bolster up his nerve, only to be cruelly reminded of her not being at his side.

Shamath across the plain was his foe's opposite, channeling nerves into energy. The cold and the snow, rather than dull his reflexes, stirred up his blood, and he rode like a fiend out of the Lands Below along the front lines, the sight of him energizing his men. When he reached the spear point of the advance, where Aisyah stood waiting for him on her white steed, she hailed and stopped him.

"The men await your words," she leaned in and whispered to him.

Shamath shook his head. "You talk to them."

"I have, in all our battles, before and since we met. Tonight's the final battle, Shamath. They'll follow me, but they'll look up to you. They wish to."

Even after Eridu, she thought. But she did not say it.

"I am not a man of words, your highness. Deeds do the talking."

She frowned like clouds gathering on a sun-kissed sky. Not one man alive would wish to displease such humbling beauty. "These men live or die for you tonight, Shamath. Humanity lives or dies this hour. If such a sacrifice is offered to the Gods Below, the least you can do is find some words they'll take with them as they go into the dark."

Shamath thought he had grown used to the princess' ardor, so at odds with the darkness in his heart. But looking at her eyes fixed in his now, he knew he'd always be amazed by her.

With a nod, he turned to face the expectant faces of humanity, lit to display the gamut of all emotions in the torchlight. He saw fear and hatred and darkness, reflections of his own weaknesses. And there among those, he also saw hope, and loyalty, and a light so brilliant it made shambles of the sun.

"Ours is not a fine world," he began and stopped, startled by the volume and timbre of his own voice in the sudden quiet.

The faces of mankind were a captive audience, hung on what he was about to say.

"We all live our lives in bondage, waste them in fear and hate," he went on. "Above us rule the Undying, as they always have, since the days of your fathers and their fathers. And –"

Here he faltered, the truth drying the words in his mouth. "And you know in your hearts that this evil world is all that has been and ever will be. That even there were no Undying, and Arkhalla –"

Again his voice broke, the mention of her name a dagger stabbing him. "Even if She, the Undying Queen, did not bear and spread the curse of Asag like a pestilence onto the earth, our world still would not be fine, but far from it. For what was Arkhalla but a woman? And what are the Undying but men? Just men. It is not demons and curses that drive men to cruelty and bloodshed. We are not chariots of the dark gods' wrath. Our darkness lies within us. The curses, the demons, they are the ones driven, by our failures. By our weakness. Even Arkhalla's heart had once been pure before it was tainted by cruelty. And even the purest heart can be tainted so that it harbors demons. Had the Undying never existed, there would still be evil in the world, for man lives in it and evil lives in man. So you may ask yourselves, what good is fighting for a world like this? What good is anything except survival, except doing unto them before they do unto you? All else is fantasy; a pipe dream."

He saw surprise and shock and pain in the eyes of the men before him. And they now all were reflections of the pain that drove him, to hatred, to vengeance and cruelty, to all the things these men tried to denied and that Aisyah had told him would be his doom. He had spoken truth, and it hurt. But even so – and because of that – he had to go on.

"And yet we dream," he resumed. "My friend Yssur dreamed of peace, and he led you to make yourselves into an army to pledge your blood to, for that same peace. And he died for it. I told him I would share his dream, for it was not a lone one, but the dream of humanity. Some of you were there; too few, for so many of our comrades have died defending the same impossible dream. And here we are tonight. Friends, comrades, all in this together."

His eyes found Dumu's. She was on horseback, at the head of her command, hers the troops that would rush headfirst into the danger to break through the Undying defenses. Nimrod's great bow was slung across her back. Her face broke into a smile, of her trust, of her love. She nodded, and it filled his heart with gratitude. “Highborn and low caste, WE are all in this, together.”

Here his eyes sought Aisyah’s, who stood at his side. “In respect. In loyalty. In our love of each other. We are together.”

He saw the sheen of unshed tears in the princess’ eyes. He smiled at her, and she smiled back, and it filled his heart with hope against hope.

“Yes, friends, we are not free,” he resumed, turning back to the men lined before him on the plain, heedless of cold and snow. “We are here in the face of our slavery, chasing after an impossible dream, against a world that denies it to us, against the darkness of our own hearts, to which the monsters waiting on the plain are but a pale reflection. Well, now is the time to rise from that dark. Now is the time to lift ourselves to the light of a sun that shall destroy them. Now is the time to make the dream reality. Because despite all that the world has thrown to us, and all the ways we failed ourselves out of hatred and bitterness and the struggle to survive, I tell you we still dream.

“Tonight, my friends, we rise and live up to the meaning of the word ‘man’, or we let man die forever.

“Tonight the sons of slaves become free men, or we enslave even the memory of that dream of our fathers forever.

“Tonight we dare to dream there will be a tomorrow. That there will be a day to live and love and feel the sun of freedom warm our free men’s skins, or we live in night and nightmares forever.

“Tonight we dream that we shall live again. That we shall love again. For if we do not, then we truly are damned forever.

“This is our dream, friends. Our hope. That we go into the light of day with, or into darkness and death. And if we are to live and be free, tonight is when the dream comes true.

"So let the cry ring out like the crier's when a king or queen are dead. Let the death of the Undying tonight usher in the dawn of man. From this desert all the way to Ur, and to the edges of the world, let the cry ring out, and fight! Fight demons! Fight your hearts, your darkness! And be free, or die!"

Seated on his litter outside his tent, King Nimrod let the mighty cry wash over him, his heart forlorn with grim foreboding.

Bel heard the rising cry across the plain, and it filled his heart with a dull, crushing dread. The feeling of it was what rattled him worse than the sound. It was a lofty, beautiful feeling, almost as though the men uttering that cry would be happy to die – not in the way he was ready to cease his endless living, no, but to die before their leader's eyes, and for something they believed in. It was Shamath who had inspired that love, a love for life and hope and a future, even now in the moments that preceded the fight that would end them all. And it was that wretch who had inspired it, like he had woken the love in Arkhalla's breast. Bel's men had no such love for him. And neither had She.

About him the column-guides moved in and out among the troops, dividing them on the twin fronts that they'd have to fight, one between them and the city, the other back the way they had come. The smoke from the freshly-dug tar pits made the soldiers' eyes smart as they formed ranks. Bel and his commanders mounted, giving final instructions and orders. He left a five-man guard behind with Narama laid out on a litter and the commission to get to shelter in the hills along the swamp's edge. There was time for one last look at the unconscious, ravaged face before they carried her off. Then, with a grim frown, he gave the order to march.

The tramp of thousands of feet resounded on the plain, its dull rhythm that of a drum driving slaves or pacing the procession to a funeral. Their forces halved, Bel's troops marched to meet their foes.

"Have cavalry at our flanks to form a pincer," he said.

About them, the snowfall thickened. Up close the flakes were discernible and real; at distance they lost all shape, and in their dancing created a perception of fog so dense that even with the fires and torches they could not see thirty paces on any side, and the enemy in those four points in the horizon would be invisible. Weakened by starvation, the Undying's enhanced senses were little help immersed in this white hell.

"Quicken the pace," Bel ordered. "Run at them, hit them hard and fast." It was their one, best hope.

Shamath heard the sound of marching from inside the snow-fog, rapidly coming nearer, together with a roar of horses' hooves. He gave the signal and the human cavalry rushed across the plain into the snow cloud. There was the line of men up ahead, a company of black-garbed specters rising out of the nothingness.

"Charge!" shouted Shamath, urging his thoroughbred to full speed.

Dumu's brigade spearheaded the charge, intent to drive itself like unto a shaft within the center of the Undying's frontline, while Shamath's and Aisyah's main force of riders and shock infantry troops pounded its left and right before they had a chance to recover.

The masses of men came at one another from opposite sides like waves clashing together.

First the spearhead of the brigade tore into arms and flesh that crumbled before it as from a hurricane of fire. Its thrust was deep and true. Men fell trampled to pulp. Undying as great as mountain oak trees were felled, and even as they struggled to their feet and their comrades rushed to fill in the gap in the Urians' lines, the true wave led by Shamath and Aisyah hit them head-on.

The snow-fog turned red. Beyond that it was hard to make out what was happening. Flashes of blades streaked through the white and scarlet cloud, chasing each other, their gleam turning to bursts of sparks as they clashed. Only by those could one glimpse the moving masses of infantry and narrow lines of horsemen. There in the fog men charged about, and in front and behind lines of troops advanced and retreated in mere inches measured with scores of the felled.

Shamath charged deeper into the massacre. The bleeding were walking dead; the dead were carrion for their starved foes. Such was war against the Undying. With them feasting on the dead, they'd grow stronger as time passed. The fight would have to be won fast or be lost utterly. But still the humans persevered. The charge worked; they were hurting them.

He had not ridden fifty yards inside the mayhem when across the whole width of crimsoned fog to his left and right he saw the enormous mass of cavalry in coal-black uniforms highlighted with a sheen of red as they charged mounted on black horses out of the mist at them.

It was a pincer movement.

Like hands clapped together the Undying cavalry smashed against the humans' flanks. Had these being infantry – the standard of many a warlord's proven strategy – they would have been pulped and crushed before the onslaught. A Urian warhorse was a black mass sixteen hands high and hit with the weight of a brick wall. Shamath's and Aisyah's cavalry held – but only just.

That was the battle's first crucial moment. There were but three or four at most in any fight, and any single one could judge the winner.

"Hold!" Shamath cried. "Hold now!"

The Undying hit them like a great sea. The humans would be rocks, or they'd be washed away.

Dumu's brigade had almost disappeared in the fog. He heard the clash of swords and glimpsed them as they engaged deeper in the waves of enemy infantry. Without Shamath's and Aisyah's force behind them, the spearhead would be broken and that line of brave and fearsome riders would be chopped to bits.

"Aisyah!" he cried out to his left where he knew the princess was. "The brunt brigades! Now!"

Even before he uttered the words he knew they'd be drowned in the din of battle. It was his mind screaming, not his mouth. Only if Aisyah had thought of it as well – if she had *sensed* his cry and *felt* his mind – would she act and save them. Otherwise all was lost.

He heard it then – a rush and a roar of a mighty storm pounding the ground as they came running.

The brunt brigades were the regiments of foot guards, their infantry's main force held back until the charge of cavalry had slashed the deepest into the enemy lines. Aisyah had seen the danger; she'd signaled them forth before the enemy riders charged out of the fog, as soon as she had glimpsed no cavalry meeting them head-on.

That brilliant, beautiful girl! Shamath cried out in his head.

Now the humans were a cliff of wide and mighty rocks against the dark and giant sea. They held. They held! Shamath saw it about him.

"Fight, men! Push! Give it to them!"

And slowly, the cliff-side pushed against the sea, and pushed it back.

It was a miracle.

On nothing but guts and passion and sheer will backing Aisyah's bold play, the humans slowly pushed the Undying back.

If only the advance squadrons pushing against the Undying's rear fared just as well.

They had a chance. By all the lords of heaven and the light, they had a fighting chance.

That was the moment he caught sight of Bel.

Bel rode at the head of the wave breaking against their sides. Shamath saw him, a maniac splashed in red like rendered thus by a god painting the battle onto a wall as big as life. He swung great arcs with his great double-bitted axe and each was another stroke splashed onto the massive blood work. Shamath's eyes glimpsed a face mad and drunk with rage, screaming confused and garbled oaths that rose even above the clash and din of weapons. He looked like a man fighting not to live, but to die, taking as many of his enemies with him as he could fell.

His mouth a thin, bloodless line of lips pressed in determination, Shamath charged toward his foe, slaying enemies left and right. Asag himself would not stand in his way now.

Bel saw him coming, a lean, unstoppable ghost from his past. As soon as Shamath came thundering through the mist, he knew him. His body was a full-grown man's, not the young slave wretch's that Bel had brutalized so long ago, and there were lines of age and hardship on that once smooth and beardless face, but Bel knew him by that defiant fire in Shamath's eyes that he had never been able to snuff out no matter what cruelty and intimidation he had inflicted on the youth. In this man he almost preternaturally recognized was embodied the spirit of the men pushing and cutting through his starved, dejected army. He was the humans' unquenchable soul incarnate, grown far beyond what the warlord had kept crushed beneath his boot all these countless years. At once, the deep dread overcame Bel again, but now he knew it was not irrational. That was when he realized the war was already lost if he did not cut this warrior down.

With a great cry issuing from both their throats as though they were one man, they closed the space between them, their horses trampling over a trail of corpses. Fuelled by his passion fell Shamath's blade first upon Bel's axe, so swift and well-judged the stroke that Bel could not both parry it and secure his balance. It was the force of his foe's blow coupled with his own great weight that caused Bel's body to fall back, and when Shamath's charge brought their horses clashing with one another, Bel's steed reared on its hind legs, hooves slipping onto gore and snowed earth.

In retrospect, that was the battle's second crucial moment.

Unsteadied, his hold loose on the reins, Bel tipped all the way back and went tumbling down onto the carrion-covered ground.

The warlord's brain spun, already two moves ahead. What counted was not the fall, but how he landed and got back onto his feet. Instead of countering gravity and fighting to hold onto his horse, he pushed himself clear off and rolled with his fall, absorbing the force of it and turning it to movement. His action was timed well; the moment he rolled onto the ground, his panicked steed slipped and fell, twelve hundred pounds of mass that would have crushed down on him if he had not cleared it.

Up on one knee in a flash, Bel sensed fresh danger. His eyes went up just in time to glimpse Shamath as the young warrior leapt from his horse and clear over Bel's fallen steed straight at him, sickle-sword swinging. Bel raised his axe between his hands and blocked a blow that, strengthened by Shamath's speed and weight, could have split his skull in twain. He grunted with the strain as the blades locked together, and rather than gamble giving Shamath time for a second stroke while he was still knelt, he twisted and rolled away, causing Shamath to lose his balance as the young warrior fought to hold on to his blade. In that split second Bel was back on his feet. His counterstroke was swift and could have felled a tree if unstopped. But with a warrior born's reflexes Shamath managed to parry it.

They backed from each other on equal footing now, their eyes rehearsing the duel about to come. Bel, a lone bead of crimson sweat forming on his brow, had to admit to the young man's skill. Many a lesser warrior would have charged the fallen Bel on horseback and would have found the advantage cost them their lives. The seasoned warlord would have sliced at the steed's legs and felled it, then hacked his foolish foe to bits. Not Shamath. Not the sturdy man who faced him as an equal now, his breath coming out controlled and even in the cold winter air.

The fight around the two figures fell away, a far-off din of swords and screams as the world shrunk to just the two of them. Once more Bel had felt as cut off from the world as when he had faced Arkhalla in her throne room. He felt her presence with them again now in the air between them; her phantom joining the young cur to fight Bel one last time, avenging his betrayal. His eyes stung at the thought. He held back tears that would shame him before his foe.

Shamath assumed a fighting stance. Despite himself, Bel noted how his form was perfect. "Shamath," he offered the standard warrior's greeting with a nod.

"You remember me," Shamath replied. "I did not know you would." He returned the greeting. "Ill met again, Bel. One last time."

"You think you can face me and live?"

"It does not matter. Strike me dead and your war is still lost. All you have to do is look around you."

"Battles turn like the tide. But you shan't be there to see it."

"This tide has long turned. You face not wretches, but men."

Bel bristled with anger. "If you grew into a man, boy, it is because of me. Would you have been anything but a wretched worm if not for me? Your defiance that pumps the blood in your heart, your body built and strengthened with your hate. It was I who gave you these; who gave you your life as you lived it."

Shamath nodded. "Then it is only fitting that I give you death, Bel."

"Not tonight. Not by you. Tonight you die."

"You kill me not with words." Shamath fell silent, almost as though to let the din of battle begin to grow louder about them once again, to let Bel hear how the humans were winning.

At once he saw his act taking effect. Instead of lunging forth and fighting, Bel stood, washed over with the cacophony of clanging blades and piercing screams as all around him the Undying were overrun by a human tide. His eyes saw what Shamath had wrought onto his world, an unstoppable force of warriors who fell under his men's swords only for more to take their place and drive the Undying back, chipping away at their numbers. And at this berserk mob of men, *this* man, advancing towards him, this man who conquered the Undying before his very eyes.

Against himself, Bel took a step back. He did not even realize he cowered from the advancing Shamath. His feet took over from his mind, pumped by his frantically beating heart. Against everything he had stood for all his life, Bel took another step back. And then another.

Shamath rushed at him, his sickle-sword cutting a wide, deadly arc. Bel parried, taking another step back. Shamath pressed on, his eyes afire as though they caught the sparks thrown each time the two blades clashed. Thrust after thrust, he drove Bel back.

Bel parried and countered without rhyme or reason, his mind clouded by dread. He *feared* this battle, part of him realized without being able to do a thing about it. His limbs were heavy, his movements mired in sloth. It was though he *wished* to die.

No, that small part of him that still thought told him. *You deserve to die. And this wretch is Her hand.*

He backed away from Shamath as he would from the rising sun, and he knew why. He feared him as the Undying feared the light of day. The day brought with it reckoning for the long night of his life. And his dark deeds and his betrayals, made flesh in this relentless specter fighting him, they were the flames that'd burn him. Like the sun that burnt Narama. Like the flames that had destroyed Arkhalla.

Shamath hammered him left and right, each stroke a little closer to home. It'd be a matter of seconds now before one blow tore past his weakening defense. Soon, there'd be death. Perhaps even peace.

Or perhaps not.

Would that be all, or would She be waiting in the dark of hell?

Waiting to hound him for betraying her?

Arkhalla.

No, he thought. *No! Not that!*

He saw her in his mind's eye, a presence, pale and bloodless, emerging from the tendrils of the dark as though she was kin to it, to embrace him. To *punish* him. *Forever.*

No!

He parried, faster now.

No!

He countered; then, for the first time since that step backwards, he thrust.

Shamath sensed the change in Bel and put up his defense. Whatever had plagued his foe, whatever had overtaken him so much it had made Shamath press on almost to victory, it was not there now, but had been pushed back, deferred. Like a man waking from sleep, Bel shook the cobwebs of sloth off him and fought for real.

More than any foe he had ever faced up till now, Shamath stood his ground, but by the inch, he was starting to falter. Step by step, Bel regained the ground he'd lost. Now it was Bel's turn to hammer him, again, and again, the clang of blades so loud it sounded like a thunderclap across the field of battle.

"Not tonight!" Bel yelled, his face livid with rage. *"Not by you!"* he almost screamed, and this time he believed it.

If he died, if he still wished it, it would be by his own hand. Not by *hers*.

At last Shamath tired; his hand rose a split-second too late – and the blade of Bel's double-bitted axe swung across his face, its arc gashing a hot red trail after it.

Bel cried out in triumph as Shamath let out a gargle of pain and fell down his knees, his grip on his sickle-sword loosened. Now Bel loomed over him, the double-bitted axe raised high and then brought down to cleave him through the brain – before it stopped an inch short from his hair, halted by her blade.

For one long, terrible second, Bel thought She had come back from the grave, stopping his blade to help her lover. He glanced sideways at the armored woman that had halted his blow, the wild shock of dark hair across her face as she strained, keeping the two blades locked together. That second he thought Arkhalla had come back and it nearly stopped his heart.

And then Aisyah's head moved, and he saw her face.

It took him but an instant to snap back from his stupor but the damage had been done. With one expert twist of her blade, the Akkadian bitch severed the axe's hilt from Bel's hand. Still fresh stained with Shamath's blood, the mighty axe dropped onto the ground, adding its crimson sacrifice to scores of hecatombs poured for the Ones Below.

His wits his own again, Bel leapt back from Aisyah's swinging sickle-sword just as it slashed across his breastplate. Shamath rose to his feet still reeling from the blow but with his blade in hand. Bel saw him and his eyes widened. Even a gash more glancing than the deep cut sideways down his face would have had any other man blinded and doubled up in pain. What demon drove the wretch so?

Grabbing the swords from two of the bodies at his feet, Bel couldn't help feeling he knew the dreaded answer.

They came at him together now, Aisyah leading the attack as Shamath fought through the pain to join her. Bel wielded his two sickle-swords and braced himself. Their charge was as fierce as that of wolves charging a tiger, their moves fast-falling into a pattern coordinated to give him not an instant's breath. High swings combined with low, left with right. With whirlwind speed, they pivoted about him, switching positions, their dance driving Bel back and keeping him but one false move away from instant death. Bel parried and thrust and countered with his fangs on edge, gritted with strain as he fought back. Each of their blows erupted sparks from his blades and sent throbbing waves of pain up his arms. It was all he could do to stay alive.

From across the field of dead and dying Dumu saw them fight. Her heart aflutter with fear for Shamath and Aisyah, she charged forth on foot, readying her bow on the run. A breathless prayer to all the gods that listened left her lips, begging them not to let her be too late. She nocked an arrow against the bowstring and took aim without breaking her stride, but it was pointless; the three figures were at too close quarters to shoot without risking hitting one of her friends. She swore a heavy oath and ran twice as fast.

To truly counter his twin foes Bel had to hammer at their weakest link, and that was Shamath. The young warrior fought with a demon's will but still was handicapped by the blood he had to keep wiping from his eyes to see, and Bel attacked him as he defended himself from Aisyah's blows. His gamble was desperate, and balanced on a thread between success and the pit of failure, but it worked. Thrust after thrust Shamath began to struggle to keep his edge, and the Akkadian saw it.

Watching Shamath slow down out of the corner of her eye, Aisyah knew the danger he was in. More and more, each of her swings grew focused on aiding his defence rather than pressing her attack. It was a subtle shift, but Bel had been waiting for it.

With a blow as expert as hers had been, he disarmed her, sending her sickle-sword flying. A master's move.

Except it left him open to Shamath's attack.

The sickle-sword's blade came up slashing through Bel's extended lower arm. A howl of pain rocked him as the razor edge severed his hand at the wrist.

Running across the field towards them, Dumu saw it happen and her heart leapt with joy.

Bel dropped shaking on his knees as Shamath stood over him. Blood flowed from his wrist in thick spurting bursts. Aisyah looked on aghast.

The warlord looked up. "You whoreson of a wretch," he spat out. His face twitched with pain that was unbearable.

In Shamath's eyes, he saw Her. Arkhalla. From hell's own heart, she'd cut him down.

Panic raised itself within him again. *No,* his soul screamed. *NO.*

Shamath looked almost sad as he raised his sword. Whether it was because with Bel dead his own life, too, ceased to have meaning, or because his thought strayed to the woman he loved, perhaps not even he knew. What mattered was that it distracted him.

Shaking with pain, Bel's remaining hand inched towards the thin short blade tucked in his belt behind his back.

It was the coward's way, a trickster's sneaky move, and it stained his warrior's code with the brand of shame. But the panic in his heart was beyond measure. *Not like this. He would not be hers in hell.*

Aisyah, positioned next to him, saw his hand as it brought the dagger forward. The move was the fastest she had ever seen. Shamath would never bring his sword down before Bel's blade was plunged into his side.

She did not hesitate.

Shamath saw her throwing herself between them, as powerless to stop her as he was to halt Bel.

The dagger slid between her breastplate's joints, straight up her heart. Bel stared at her face in disbelief as Aisyah smiled at him.

NOOO!

It hadn't been one of the two men that uttered the soul-killing cry. That had come from Dumu, at last in range and with a clear shot, too late.

Nimrod's bow sang like it lamented for his daughter as it let loose its shaft.

Bel shivered and drew back, haunted by the stabbed girl's face. The move saved his life. Meant for his craven heart, Dumu's arrow pierced his shoulder, shattering the clavicle like the slimmest twig. Screaming pain shocked him to action. He sprinted back towards the mayhem in the snow-fog, dodging another shaft as though it were Asag's hounds snapping at his heels.

Aisyah collapsed in Shamath's arms. He caught her, stunned, a stab of pain coursing through his heart now. Even as he did, Bel vanished in the battle's din.

The princess' strength failed her. Her weight pulled them both down onto the blood and dirt. Shamath saw her blood through her fingers on the wound, rushing to join his and all the others', another offering to those gods that laughed from darkness.

"The coward ran off," she heard Dumu's anguished cry behind him as from a cave far away. He did not need to raise his tear-filled eyes at her to witness her despair, and even if he wanted to, he could not. His eyes were captive to Aisyah's gaze, to the life fading from her with every labored breath.

"I'm... sorry," she whispered.

A sob racked Shamath. He could not believe it. "Why?" was all he could say. "Why are *you* sorry?"

He had been the one who failed her. He had been the one who got her killed. What did this brave beautiful girl have to be sorry for?

"I... wish I knew... your heart's... desire," she tried to answer.

He held her in his arms. "Hush, Aisyah. Save your strength."

She smiled at how he said her name. She liked the way he said it.

Her eyelids fluttered. "Aisyah," he said, his heart breaking with his voice.

She tried to smile again, but couldn't. "I wish... I could have told you..."

"I know. It's all right."

She shook her head. "Wish... I... could... given you... what you... seek..."

Her head lulled and fell. She willed herself to life, a moment longer. To tell him. "The... way... to get her... back," she went on. "She must be...worth... going into...hell... for."

At last she found the strength to smile. "Think of me... sometimes."

"Always," Shamath said, and meant it.

And with that smile, she died, a gallant soul that loved him like no other.

CHAPTER 24

A KINGDOM FALLS

It was the end of Ur. Before the break of dawn the battle had been lost at all points. Of the Undying, more than two-thirds lay slain upon the field, while of the dreaded Black Guards none still breathed. It was as though Bel's cowardice and flight had spread among his troops like unto a plague, unstoppable. They had fought without a leader, without a cause except their own damned existence, whereas the humans had claim to both, and Aisyah's death had galvanized her troops to a passion they had hoped was worthy of her own.

The last defining moment of the battle had occurred when the conscripts laid down their arms. Without them, the columns of Undying were crippled of their limbs and sinews, and without Bel, their head, they fell back in confused masses of chaos. Crushed between the two-pronged front of humans, they fought until they perished or surrendered. The mortal prisoners were put in chains, bound for slavery. Of the Undying they left none to survive, but executed them right there on the spot or tied them onto posts along the way to the capital and left them to the mercy of the sunrise. The rows lining the two sides of the road stretched for a mile. The screams of the Undying as the grey dawn bled red on the horizon were heard for many more. And the glow of the flames from the two lines of pyres that lit up with the sunlight's kiss was a sight as terrible and awe-filled as to draw the eyes of the gods themselves.

The city had fallen long before that moment, its token garrison overtaken by the advancing human army. Its streets, whose oppressed silence under the rule of the Undying was only ever broken by the cries of their victims, now became haunted by the screams of the tormentors. Wounded and captured Undying were thrown on pyres and set alight, and all the manors, landmarks and possessions of those bloodthirsty tyrants were put to the torch. Thralls set free at last after the demise of their masters wandered lost among the flames, looking for loved ones and families they scarce remembered after lifetimes of slavery of their spirits, with most of those they sought long dead. The snowflakes falling on the hate-fuelled fires, too weak to put them out, were like a harbinger of the rain of ashes gathering in clouds of smoke that formed over the capital.

Thus on that night the Undying perished from the earth, almost to the last.

It was at sunrise, when the fighting and the massacre stopped, with burning corpses lined along the approach lighting his way, that Shamath rode through the gates of Ur into this hell. His beaten, tired figure holding onto the reins on sheer willpower alone, he urged his mare onward through the burning capital. His eyes looked up at the looming tower of the ziggurat, alive with yearning on a face so pale around the bloody gash traversing it that it seemed that of a dead man.

As he looked and the rays of the rising sun bathed the massive structure whence Arkhalla once ruled the world, there came a convulsion of the ground beneath his horses' hooves so massive that the earth itself was split asunder as by some giant blade. Shamath's horse reared in fear, and around him soldiers and survivors tumbled and fell on their knees. That same moment the sky rumbled with the sound of an unseen storm that did not come from the heavens but from the ziggurat itself, as the entire structure and the ground it stood on seemed to lift into the air and scatter in gigantic fragments, while a cloud of soot and sulfur shot out and upwards from it, its volume rapidly expanding to the point of dwarfing it. For one impossible second there was silence like unto that which comes between the lightning and the thunder, and then the breaking fragments of the structure came crashing down in a fierce cataclysm. Almost as though it was sucked back toward the earth, the massive smoke cloud sank in a flash back down and erupted through the streets, blowing through the whole town, just as the tower's collapse annihilated entire blocks that had stood about the structure.

Among the panicked people running from the smoke and past him towards the gates, Shamath tried to control his frightened mare. Coughing, his eyes smarting, he peered through the smoke as though he could still see the tower that no longer stood there, shock and revulsion filling him as he slowly realized what had happened.

The mirror chamber and everything above it, all the last vestiges of the Magi's knowledge that he sought. The means to cross over to the Lands Below, to see Arkhalla again. It was all gone.

Shamath screamed in despair, his cry rising even above those of the panicked crowd.

The nation of the Undying was no more. All that remained was ruins, scattered to the four corners of the earth as the fragments of the tower were scattered over the burning city. Of those of its once mighty council who still survived, no news surfaced, the word of Ur's destruction sending them scurrying even deeper into whatever faraway hole they had fled.

It was some nights after that when a small band of riders rode into a port town, carrying tied between two of their horses a litter with a frail sick woman in it. The six riders, all men that looked starved and beaten from their trek across the swamplands, sought neither sustenance nor shelter, but instead, they chartered a ship bound southwest and bearing a cargo of grain to those far desert lands travelers called The Sands Beyond the Sea. By their haggard appearance and shabby sackcloth garments and the fact that they bore no arms, they were surmised to be pilgrims, which the leader confirmed, saying they sought the holy men of the southern deserts hoping to find a cure for the disease that slowly claimed the life of his wife. Taking care of her seemed to be both his and his comrades' foremost task, and none of them emerged from the hold where they were put up for the night.

As the ship's crew prepared to sail, their passengers were forgotten. None of the seamen recognized Bel and the detail he had entrusted with Narama, nor could they have figured out who these pitiful pilgrims really were. Starvation and abandoning their arms and clothes in favor of the garments they had stripped off a small caravan of travelers were more than enough of a disguise against any that sought the once proud warlord of Ur. And neither would there be need for those once the ship was at sea and they emerged to feed on the crew and take their clothes and place once they reached their destination. As his men lay about him trying to while away their hunger with fitful snatches of sleep, Bel sat by Narama with her head resting on his lap. The phantom that had taken the place of his hand still tormented him with itch and pain, and many times he caught himself trying to run it through Narama's hair to soothe her. She rarely woke from a slumber that was part exhaustion and part the shadow of death still out to claim her. Her face and body showed signs of healing that were still too few and far between to harbor hope.

Bel sat looking at her in the darkness of the hold, as ruined inside as she was to the naked eye. Shame and regret had eaten up all that he was and filled the emptied carcass. The single thing that kept him going was Narama, she and the love she had for him – if she lived through this and if she still felt anything for him afterwards. All it had taken to bring them together was the end of their world. And perhaps even that had come too late.

The ziggurat had sunk into the earth and taken five blocks of the town with it, leaving in its wake nothing but a crater strewn with ash and rubble and vast as a field. No flame had touched the tower, nor had a human hand been laid upon the ziggurat to raze it. It was as though some god's hand had reached out from beneath the earth and brought it crashing back down into its bowels together with Shamath's last hope.

Days passed before the dead and wounded were retrieved from the ruins and Shamath found the courage to broach the edge of the crater. He stood and stared at the tons of rubble as though they were a grave. Beneath it was buried the chamber along with all of Erun's knowledge.

He knew not whether minutes or hours had gone by when he heard Dumu's voice behind him.

"I'm sorry, Shamath."

His eyes filled with tears, he turned and saw her. The sight of him made her face wince with sadness, and she drew a sharp intake of breath.

"I know how you craved to find your answers here," she went on. "And I hoped you would. Believe me."

Shamath nodded. "I do. But they're gone now. If ever they were here at all." He paused. "Sometimes it seems our whole lives are just echoes, Dumu. Moments reverberating across the void. Like me and you standing together in ash and ruins, mourning for Arkhalla. All those years ago, in Dilmun, and now."

"Some things change," she tried to comfort him. "The world has changed, given a chance for freedom, a new beginning." A faint smile creased her lips. "And neither you nor I are that boy and girl we were then. You have commanded armies and conquered realms."

He smiled back, nodding at her gentlewoman's attire. "Said the princess to the general," he added.

Dumu blushed. "Please don't jest with me. I'm still trying to get used to that."

Nimrod had held a twelve-day-long wake for Aisyah at his camp outside the gates of Ur, honoring his daughter with a hecatomb of sacrifices at the foot of the pyre that consumed the warrior princess' body. It was there, as he announced to his gathered allies and fellow mourners that on the morn of the thirteenth day he would depart for Akkad with his daughter's ashes, that he had called for Shamath and Dumu to join him at his tent and speak in private afterwards.

"I would not even burn her in this damned place but for the love and respect she and I had for the two of you," Nimrod had told them, reclined onto his camp bed. "But her ashes I take with me to Akkad, where she was born, where she belongs. Where I hope you shall join us."

Dumu and Shamath looked wide-eyed at him, then at each other.

"I am not long for this world," the king went on. "But my realm must live after me, and my daughter, the one I trusted to look after it when I am gone, is no more. After her, the only people I'd trust with it are the ones she fought with and gave her life for."

He then looked at Dumu, who blushed then even as she would days later at the edge of the giant pit.

"You were sister to her and fought with her like a warrior born," he had told her. "With my own bow you pierced her slayer. And you stood by me like a daughter, both when she lived and now

in our hours of grief. Be my daughter now, Dumu of Dilmun. Be Dumu of Akkad and rule it after my death with my blessing."

Dumu was dumbfounded. A gamut of emotions crossed her face at once, from shock to disbelief to tearful joy. "I don't know what to say, my lord."

"Say 'yes'," he said, his dread voice breaking. "And call me father."

She was in his arms and sobbing as soon as he finished. Together they cried, embraced. Shamath was moved, and looked at them for long seconds before the king turned to him.

"I always told Aisyah that even if she married, the realm would still be hers, not her husband's. But I knew her heart was drawn to you, Shamath, and that'd she'd give it to you if she'd lived. My realm needs a commander of its armies as worthy as you." He gave a soft chuckle through his tears. "I'd offer you my throne, but I'm partial to girls. Too used to it to have a son at my age. But be our general and the stewardship of Ur is yours for the taking." At this, he gave a sideways look at Dumu. "Maybe the throne, too, one day, if you two young people get some sense in your heads. Aisyah's spirit would bless it."

Both Dumu and Shamath lowered their heads, flushed with the king's intimation.

"You embarrass us, sire," said Dumu. "We're not –" "No,

not at all," added Shamath, just as uncomfortable.

"Ah," Nimrod exclaimed. "I am an old fool, children. And a better king than a matchmaker, as you can see. I spoke of a future that may never come. Now is the time for a more important decision. Will you accept Akkad's command, Shamath?" He held out his hand. "And the friendship of this fatherly old fool?"

Shamath grew even redder. "Sire, you honor me. Your trust –"

"Aisyah trusted you, too, son," the king cut him short. "She loved you."

The young warrior's embarrassment grew so pronounced now that it gave Nimrod pause. He looked at the face his daughter had been so fond of, fathoming the emotion that sizzled beneath it. "Ah," he said again, his changeable mood turned somber. "So you cannot."

"No, Sire," admitted Shamath. "I'm sorry."

Nimrod sighed. "Aisyah had hinted at some secret yearning in you. She would not break your trust by sharing it, but I could tell that it was a dark thing, and that it kept you apart from her. Is that what keeps you from Akkad now?"

"I mean no offence, sire. You honor me."

"None taken, my boy, none taken." Nimrod sighed, then, volcanic, he changed his mien. "His loss, eh, Dumu?"

The memory of the scene caused the two of them to smile with a mirth they both needed. "Gods bless that sweet old man," Dumu said, moved. "He took a girl with nothing and gave her everything."

"I'm happy for you, Dumu. You deserve it."

"And I am sad for you, you stubborn, headstrong man," she told him. "My work here's done. We've gotten the wounded care and shelter and the survivors settled temporarily while the plans for rebuilding and installing a stewardship are underway, so I leave for Akkad to join Nimrod there." She paused. "Take up his offer, Shamath. Rule Ur. Command Akkad's armies. You do not have to go through life alone."

A smile broke across her anxious face. "And I don't mean it like Nimrod did. You're not my type."

Shamath laughed. It felt good to laugh. There wasn't much space in his life left for it anymore.

"For what it's worth, Princess Dumu, you are a catch," he said. "I hope one day you find someone who deserves you. And that you love. As much as... well, as much you loved Eleesha."

She smiled, tearful. "And you," she said. "I do hope you find someone you'll love as much as you loved Arkhalla."

He did not tell Dumu that was not possible. She was his friend and she had spoken out of love at this last time they'd see each other in this life. Shamath did not want to break her heart any worse than he had already. So he smiled back.

"See? It's all echoes. Once more you ask me to live."

"So live."

And with smiles and tears in their faces, they held each other, like all those years ago before Arkhalla's ashes.

CHAPTER 25

ECHOES

He had joined the war for home and hearth and mankind. She'd have expected no less of him. The war lasted years, but at its end, the realm of the Undying was no more, and he came back to her.

It was a winter's morn, and snow was falling, covering the hillside and the grave. When he tried to light the hearth of his rundown house, the smoke that rose out of the stack was black like the carnage he had come back from. He felt older, and it was only in part because he'd aged. His beard was untrimmed and graying here and there, his huntsman's clothes that he wore the years he'd stayed in his small cabin replaced by blood-stained armor, and on his face he bore Bel's scar, not near as deep as the scars inside him. But he had done his part, and now he could be with her. With Arkhalla, his mistress, his queen. His forever love.

He stood before her grave a man divided. One part of him would stay here with her forever, would tend and till the earth until it was once more fruitful and flowers would come back in bloom over the hillside and the grave. And he would fix the house, as well as he could. He would finally be at peace with the world, so much that a butterfly could alight forever on his hand, and neither it nor he would mind each other. And this would be the peace she brought him. They had never been apart, not even in the years he was gone in the wars. He was with her, always, and would be. And his love would be with him every day. If it went on till the end of his days like that, it would have been an end any man should hope for.

But there was another part to him. A part that knew a man's life only ends as the gods see fit, and that if Shamath listened, very carefully, he might have heard the gods laughing. It was that part of him that could not rest with Arkhalla in his thoughts, in peace, because it glimpsed her in dreams of darkness haunting him. He could never live, not like Dumu had pleaded, not even how that other part of him wished, alone with her memories, not so long as the dreams told him she had no peace and was condemned to suffering in Asag's hell. It was the part of him that knew all this that spoke to her now.

"My love, my life," he said. "I'm sorry. I know you'd wish no more harm to come to me because of you. That you'd wish me to live. But without you, I cannot. I tried to for ten years living by your side on this lone hill. I tried it for ten more, fighting a war to purge the earth of the curse that damned you. And these twenty years were enough to tell me I cannot do it anymore."

He sighed, choking with emotion, but his heart felt light. It was the right decision.

"I'll find you, Arkhalla," he went on. "And I'll bring you back. I promise."

Deep beneath the ruins of Ur, in its chamber, the mirror glowed red, lighting up crumbled surroundings. Its light pulsated, the air above it crackling with bursts of black energy. Somewhere from inside its unimaginable depths, God laughed.

Like all things terrible, it began small. Out of the swirling tentacles of red glow and black power, a face formed upon the surface, so monstrous, so terrible, that if anyone saw it, their hair would turn white and they'd be driven mad. Words formed out of nothingness, twisted in chaos, their sound beautiful and misshapen at once, a melody played by a musician wracked with palsy.

HEED ME, MY ANGEL, the voice said.

Another one replied, blacker than night, yet soft and melodic; its sound was oddly wrong, almost as though the words were spoken backwards.

"You called, my dread lord?"

THEIR WORLD HAS CHANGED. I UNDERESTIMATED THE HUMAN BOY.

The voice paused, and the dark feared it.

BRING ME SHAMATH, MY ANGEL. I HAVE PLANS FOR HIM.

And in depths unimaginable, far in the Lands Below, God laughed again.

A moment passed as the command was fathomed.

"I go, my dread lord."

The dread Lord Asag sat back in his throne, rippling with satisfaction. To any observer, he – so long as any observer could even fathom Asag as a *He* before being rendered hopelessly insane – would appear still, so still as to think God a gigantic statue carved of nightmares and spread in dimensions that dwarfed the infinite. Asag was God, and God not merely ruled but *was* The Lands Below, the realm entire from the surface of the mirror down to the darkest depths of the true world to which the world of man is but a pale reflection. God was the throne and the world, and God knew everything. And the only mind that could grasp this concept and not be shattered by its magnitude was God's. Such was Asag's power and such was his curse.

Asag knew the wheels of worlds within worlds and of plans within plans were now in motion. His Angel of Darkness would perform her task. As would all Asag's daughters, for they, too, were part of God.

GALLIAH.

The Succubus replied at once, her voice a lyrical, wet dream.

"I'm here, my lord."

SARIAH.

War's voice was as seductive as her sisters', its melody that of the din of blades and the tender piercing of the flesh by a killer sword.

"Command me, Lord."

SHOW HER TO ME.

There was a sound that was no sound, like unto a million crystal shards breaking at once to part the curtain of the world. And once the last of these sang its oblivion, She was before them, on her knees, bound and chained and magnificent.

Tentacles rippled, dark with Asag's pleasure. How could this girl not be magnificent, blessed with the gifts of all God's daughters? Had not the Angel of Darkness gifted her command over her victims' souls? Had not the Succubus blessed her with her powers of seduction and the greatest beauty ever seen by all the generations of man? And had not Sariah, the Goddess of War, bestowed on her the Warrior's might?

Such promise.

Such a waste.

ARKHALLA.

Her eyes, changeable, then blue, fluttered. "Leave me be," the beautiful voice said.

I CANNOT.

"Then let me die the truest death, and cease to hear you."

YOU CANNOT, LITTLE SOUL. NOT EVEN IN DEATH. FOR YOU ARE MINE. AND SOON, SO WILL HE.

She shuddered. "Wh-who?"

YOU KNOW THE ANSWER. EVEN NOW, IT COURSES THROUGH YOUR HEART AND MIND, STRAIGHT TO YOUR LIPS.

"Shamath."

HE HAS DONE THE IMPOSSIBLE. HE HAS DEFIED MY WILL.

"No. Please."

THE UNDYING ARE NEAR GONE FROM THE WORLD, AND IT WAS AT HIS HANDS THIS CAME TO PASS. UR HAS FALLEN, ITS POWER SNUFFED OUT TOGETHER WITH THE LIVES OF THOSE YOU SIRED. HE HAS ERASED ASAG'S WRITING FROM THE EARTH, AND WHAT GOD WOULD I BE IF I LET THAT PASS?

"Please... Have your way with me, but let him be."

I ALREADY HAVE MY WAY WITH YOU, LITTLE SOUL. YOU ARE MINE. YOUR SHAMATH MUST MAKE UP TO ME FOR WHAT HE HAS DONE, OR REJOIN YOU IN THESE LANDS BELOW, FOREVER.

A great cry burst forth from Arkhalla's lips, so terrible and true it shook the depths of hell. It was a single scream of a prolonged *No*, but even in this land of darkness and death, it had, for but a moment, vibrated with *life*, and with something dreaded above all.

Love.

It troubled Asag greatly.

For love can bring down even God.

About the Author

ABRAHAM KAWA is a writer and critic of graphic novels and genre fiction. An author of fantasy, mystery and horror novels in his native Greece, including Pandora's Box, a cycle of tales about paranormal investigator and monster hunter Pandora Ormond, he has also written scripts for comics published both there and abroad. Other than The Arkhalla Trilogy and the script for the Queen of Vampires graphic novel that spawned it, his recent work includes Democracy, a historical graphic novel set in ancient Athens, and the werewolf story 'The Wolves Outside the Cage' in the anthology Mark of the Beast, while he's currently at work on a graphic novel inspired by the works of Bram Stoker and a prose mystery novel set in the late 1960s.

ARH
BOOKS

Made in the USA
Middletown, DE
26 November 2020

25261469R00189